Books by G.A. McKevett

Published by Kensington Publishing Corporation

G.A. McKevett

A Decadent WAY TO DIE

A SAVANNAH REID MYSTERY

KENSINGTON BOOKS
www.kensingtonbooks.com

KENSINGTON BOOKS are published by

Kensington Publishing Corp.
119 West 40th Street
New York, NY 10018

All Kensington titles, imprints and distributed lines are available at special quantity discounts for bulk purchases for sales promotion, premiums, fund-raising, educational or institutional use.

Special book excerpts or customized printings can also be created to fit specific needs. For details, write or phone the office of the Kensington Special Sales Manager: Kensington Publishing Corp., 119 West 40th Street, New York, NY, 10018. Attn. Special Sales Department. Phone: 1-800-221-2647.

ISBN-13: 978-0-7582-3811-5
ISBN-10: 0-7582-3811-8

First Hardcover Printing: February 2011
First Mass Market Printing: March 2012

10   9   8   7   6   5   4   3   2   1

Printed in the United States of America

Lovingly dedicated to Bruce,
who promised he would try his best to be
a good husband to me . . .
and has succeeded beyond my sweetest dreams.

I want to thank all the fans who write to me, sharing their thoughts and offering endless encouragement. Your stories touch my heart, and I enjoy your letters more than you know. I can be reached at:

sonja@sonjamassie.com
and
gamckevett.com

Chapter 1

"Land sakes, boy, my tailbone's done taken root to this floor," Savannah Reid said as she shifted from one side of her aching rear to the other. "Who'd have thought there wouldn't be a solitary decent chair in this joint?"

Beside her sat Dirk Coulter, an only slightly apologetic look on his face. "If there was one, you know I'd let you have it," he said.

"Yeah, sure. That's right up there with, 'If I win the lottery, I'll give you half.' Giving away something you ain't got is easy as falling off a wet log."

"Whatever happened to, 'It's the thought that counts'?"

"The thought counted two hours ago, when we still had snacks to eat and my butt didn't feel like a shark was gnawing on it."

With a sigh born of bone-deep weariness or moderate annoyance—with Dirk it was hard to tell the difference—he stood and walked to the other side of the small, dark pharmacy.

After bumping into a number of displays and

rummaging around a bit, he plucked some items off a shelf.

When he returned, he dumped a rich assortment of candy bars into her lap. "There ya go . . . snacks. Compliments of the house."

He peeled off his old leather bomber jacket, folded it twice, and slid the impromptu "cushion" between her back and the wall. "Lean on it or sit on it, whichever gives you the most relief."

"Aww, that's so sweet."

"Just keep your bellyaching to a minimum—"

"And you were doing so well . . ."

"Shh," he said. "I don't want those numbskulls out there to hear us arguing in here and pass on the break-in."

Savannah scowled up at him. "Maybe you should choose your words a mite more carefully. 'Bellyaching' is up there with 'nagging' and 'female moodiness.' They could get a guy smacked upside the head."

Savannah handed him one of the candy bars and unwrapped another for herself. "And speaking of burglars . . . excuse me for stating the obvious, but didn't you just steal these goodies off the shelf?"

Dirk shrugged as he bit into the bar. "I told the owner this moonlighting gig would cost him a couple hundred plus expenses. The candy's a necessary expense."

"And you get paid whether we catch the bad guys or not?"

"Yeah. Sweet, huh? Plus an expense account. Makes me feel like a private investigator, like you."

"Only you've got a badge."

Savannah tried not to sound bitter when she said those words. Most days she could convince herself that she was perfectly happy not to be a member of the San Carmelita Police Department anymore.

And some days she believed it.

She believed it on rainy days. Rainy days in July. Rainy days in July when the moon was in conjunction with the sun, Venus, and Jupiter . . . and she was struck by lightning twice before she got out of bed.

The rest of the time she experienced a small, nagging sadness that she was no longer a cop and Dirk's honest-to-goodness partner in crime detection and bad-guy nabbing.

Though tonight was almost as good, staking out a small, privately owned pharmacy that had been burglarized three times in the past month.

When the harried proprietor had informed the police that he intended to keep watch, night after night, with a shotgun in hand and dispatch the repeat thieves to the Promised Land, Dirk had volunteered his services . . . and Savannah's.

Dirk frequently volunteered her services. And, usually, she enjoyed it. When else did one get to play cops and robbers, eat pilfered candy, and manipulate a close friend into being deeply beholden all in the course of one evening?

"So, how much of that couple of hundred were you figuring to throw my way?" she asked, licking the chocolate off her thumb and forefinger.

His mood seemed to drop a few notches in spite of the recent sugar infusion. "Oh, I don't know. How much were you thinkin'?"

"A good backrub, and I'd probably call it even."

He brightened instantly. "Sure. I'd be glad to give you a backrub."

"Not *you*, sweet cheeks. A *professional* massage. One you actually pay money for."

"Oh."

She gave him a sideways glance and saw the slightly protruding lower lip. It looked ridiculous on a forty-plus, ruggedly handsome—with the emphasis on rugged—grown man. A cop who, for more than twenty years, had rubbed elbows with society's worst. Occasionally, fists and elbows, too.

Dirk didn't complain much when having to chase, tackle, and cuff the unbathed, undeodorized, alcohol-marinated, chemically altered, and ethically deficient. But ask him to part with a dollar and his mood plummeted.

And Savannah found the whole process quite entertaining.

"What's the matter?" she said, giving him a playful dig in the ribs with her elbow. "Don't you think I'm worth it?"

"Yeah, I guess. But those massages are expensive."

"Eh. About half of what you're getting for this gig should cover it, plus a pedicure and maybe—"

"Shhh."

"Don't you shush me, boy. I—"

"Shh! I hear something."

Then she heard it, too . . . the distinctive jiggling of a doorknob at the rear of the store.

She chuckled as a shot of adrenaline hit her bloodstream. "They think they're actually gonna come through the door like regular customers?" she whispered.

"Why break a window and climb through if you don't have to?" he replied as he stood and offered her a hand up.

"True." She rose and shook the stiffness out of her legs. "If you're gonna go to all that work, actually breaking in, a body might as well get a real job."

The doorknob rattling had stopped, and they could hear the scuffling of footsteps in gravel beside the building as the burglars made their way around to a window.

"That's how they got in last time, right?" Savannah said, her lips close to his ear.

"Yeah. And, more importantly, how they got out."

"Then, let's get over there."

They hurried to the other side of the store, being careful not to bump into any of the shelves or displays in the semidarkness.

For some reason, Savannah thought of the old pharmacy in the tiny, rural, Georgia town where she had been raised . . . so far, in so many ways, from San Carmelita, the posh seaside resort in Southern California.

As a child, Savannah had often imagined how fun it would be to spend the night locked in that store, which was a combination drugstore and five-and-dime. Having the place to herself—the ice cream counter, the comic book stand, the candy shelves, not to mention the paper dolls and coloring books—would have been pure heaven to a poor kid without a cent to spend on such luxuries.

But as she took a position on the right side of the window and squatted behind a stack of boxed baby diapers, she had to admit: This was far more fun than any childhood fantasy.

Listening to the youthful male voices muttering to each other outside the window, she felt a teeny bit sorry for them . . . for anyone who was so poverty-stricken, or drug-addicted, or lacking in moral upbringing that they resorted to stealing as a way of life.

But she felt a lot sorrier for the guy who owned the place, whose insurance rates had skyrocketed because his store and the other businesses in the area were being continually burglarized.

Looking over at Dirk, who was crouching behind a display of paper towels and toilet paper rolls, she could see the same light of excitement that she felt, shining in his eyes. Though neither of them would admit it, they were hardcore thrill junkies.

They lived for these moments.

He reached for his sidearm, a Smith & Wesson revolver, pulled it, and pointed the barrel toward the ceiling.

She pulled her 9mm Beretta from her shoulder holster and did the same.

"Get a rock," she heard one of the guys outside the window say.

"Here. This'll do," replied another.

She steeled herself for what was coming next. She turned her face away from the window, as did Dirk.

It didn't take long.

A moment later, something heavy crashed through the window, spraying glass for ten feet inside the store.

Some landed in her hair. She shook it out.

"Reach through there and unlock it," one of the burglars said.

"Window's nailed closed. Don't you remember last time?" replied his buddy.

"Oh, yeah. Give me a boost. I'll climb through."

Savannah heard a guy grunting as he lifted his companion.

Okay, she thought, *so there's a little bit of honest labor in thievery.*

A sneaker and a denim-covered leg poked through the broken window, followed by a butt, a torso, and then a head.

In the dim light, she could see the long, stringy, brown hair and the scraggly goatee. His black tank top revealed a large, distinctive tattoo of a vampire demon on his shoulder.

She knew him! It was Josh Murphy.

She and Dirk had busted Josh years ago, when she had still been on the job. He and his brother, Jesse, had robbed some high school kids on the beach on prom night. And Jesse had even gotten fresh with one of the girls, named Rosa Ortiz, adding sexual assault to his charges.

A few months ago, Savannah had run into Rosa in a grocery store. She'd told Savannah she still had nightmares about her prom night.

Suddenly, this assignment was a lot sweeter.

Sure enough . . . no sooner had Josh climbed through than Jesse followed. But as he was straddling the window pane with its jagged bits of remaining glass, he yelped with pain.

"Damn!" he said, grabbing his groin with his gloved hand. "I cut myself."

"Yeah, whatever," his brother replied. "Shoulda been more careful."

"Thanks for the sympathy, you no-good sonof-abitch."

Savannah wondered if it occurred to Jesse that he had just insulted his own mother. Or if he would care.

Probably not, she decided. Her past, brief associations with Jesse Murphy hadn't left her with an abiding faith in his intelligence or his respect for motherhood.

Remembering how Momma had jumped to her feet during her boys' trial and screamed obscenities at their victims, Savannah decided maybe Jesse was right about his brother's heritage.

"I'm not kidding," Jesse said, hopping around, clutching his crotch. "I'm seriously bleeding here."

Savannah cringed as Josh reached for one of the packages of toilet paper right by Dirk's head. She saw Dirk duck as Josh's hand nearly swiped him.

"Here," Josh said, pitching the pack at Jesse. "Do what you gotta do, and let's get on with this. We told Butch we'd have the oxycottons and percs to him tonight. You know how he gets when we stand him up."

Jesse ripped off his workman's gloves and tore open the package. He pulled out a roll of the toilet paper and jammed it against his wound. "Owww! Next time we're goin' in the door, or we ain't goin' in at all," he said. "I'm getting too old for this climbing-through-the-window crap."

But his brother was already in the back of the store.

Josh vaulted over the pharmacy counter, took a

flashlight from his jeans pocket, and trailed the beam up and down the shelves.

When he found what he wanted, he grabbed a couple of plastic bags from beneath the cash register and began filling them with bottles and boxes. "You gonna help me out here," he said, "or you gonna dance around, playin' with Big Jim and the twins?"

Jesse tossed away one roll of blood-soaked toilet paper, got out a fresh one, and pressed it to his privates. "Screw you and hurry up," he said. "When we get outta here, you gotta take me to the hospital. I mighta cut something off."

"Nothin' you'd ever need."

"It could be hangin' by a thread."

"Story of your life, dude." Josh crawled back over the counter, holding the bags filled with pharmaceutical booty.

"Let's get outta here, man. I gotta go get sewed up," Jesse said as he followed his brother back to the broken window, shuffling along with the roll of toilet paper clasped tightly between his thighs.

Savannah could hear her pulse pounding in her ears as they drew closer. Her hand tightened around the grip of the pistol.

"We ain't goin' to no hospital," Josh said. "They report stuff like that to the cops, you moron."

"*You're* the idiot. That's *gunshots* they report. Not cuts on your nuts."

"How're you gonna explain that? It's obvious you did it climbin' through a broke window."

"I'll tell 'em your pit bull bit me."

"I don't got no pit bull."

"Well, I ain't gonna tell 'em your stupid *cat* scratched me. How wussy would that sound?"

When Josh reached the window, he handed Jesse one of the bags and then started to bang on the windowsill with his flashlight, clearing the remaining shards of glass.

"Get it all," Jesse said. "I ain't climbin' back through there unless you've got it all outta there."

Savannah leaned her head out from behind the shelves, just enough to see Dirk. He saw her, gave her a nod, and they both jumped out of their hiding places.

"Police!" Dirk yelled. "Freeze!"

The brothers jumped and spun around to face them.

"I said 'freeze!' " Dirk repeated, stepping closer to them.

Savannah moved into the light, so they could see her . . . and more importantly, her Beretta pointed at them.

"What the hell?" Jesse dropped his bag and his roll of toilet paper and backed up against the wall, hands raised.

Josh lowered his bag, too, but he locked eyes with Savannah. And even in the dim light, she could see the hatred on his face and a rage that showed no sign of surrender.

He raised the flashlight in his other hand ever so slightly.

His eyes narrowed.

"No!" she shouted, sighting down the barrel of the raised gun that was aimed at his head. "Don't even think about it! Drop the flashlight!"

"Drop it!" Dirk said. "Now!"

Instead of lowering the torch, he raised it a bit higher.

"You're gonna die, Josh," Savannah said. "Drop

that weapon, or in about two seconds, we're gonna blow your brains all over your brother."

She took a step closer to him and her eyes went arctic cold. "Is that what you want?" she asked, her tone as icy as her eyes. "You wanna die today, Josh . . . like a whupped dog . . . right here in front of your little brother?"

Josh weighed his options, looking at the business end of Savannah's Beretta, then Dirk's Smith & Wesson.

"It ain't worth it, bro," Jesse said. "Give it up."

After what seemed like twelve or thirteen years to Savannah, Josh Murphy let the flashlight slip from his fingers. It clattered to the floor.

"Put your hands on your heads," Dirk said. "And turn around."

Instantly, Jesse did as he was told. Josh took a bit longer before he obeyed.

"Palms on the wall," Savannah told them, "feet apart. *Wide* apart."

Jesse yelped as he spread his feet. "I'm cut, you guys," he said. "I'm bleeding like a pig here. I'm about to die."

Revolver in his right hand, Dirk used his left to pass Savannah a pair of cuffs. "So, what do you expect us to do about it, Jesse?" Dirk asked. "Want us to tie a tourniquet around it? Cinch it up nice and tight? Cut off the blood flow?"

"Uh . . . no."

"I didn't think so."

Savannah holstered her weapon, pulled Josh's hand down, and clamped a cuff on one of his wrists, then the other.

As always, she felt a small sense of relief once the suspect was manacled. "It's the hands that'll hurt you," was the motto that had been drilled into her throughout her training.

And having the more aggressive of the two robbers under control, the worst part was done.

She compared it to eating your liver and onions so that you could enjoy your chocolate cake dessert.

As she cuffed Jesse, Savannah could see the blood dripping onto the floor from his crotch. Dark red blood stained the whole seat of his jeans.

The guy wasn't kidding; he really was badly cut. They were going to have to make an unscheduled pit stop at the hospital.

Dirk grabbed Josh and headed toward the back door.

Savannah followed, with the leaking brother in tow.

As Dirk used the pharmacy owner's keys to open the back door, Savannah waited patiently with her prisoner.

"Jesse," she told him, "you make a piss-poor burglar. You oughta take up some other line of work. Wasn't there something worthwhile you wanted to be when you grew up, other than a low-life scumbag who's always getting busted? Didn't you have a dream, boy?"

Jesse shrugged, thought about it, then gave her a sheepish little grin. "Yeah, I wanted to grow up and be Superman . . . or the Incredible Hulk . . . or maybe Spider-Man."

"And you were how old when you decided on 'super hero' as a life vocation?"

"Oh, I don't know. When I was about seventeen or eighteen. I dropped outta school in the tenth grade . . . got held back a few years."

"And what was the big appeal, other than being able to leap tall buildings in a single bound, stuff like that?"

"You get to wear cool outfits, and they put your picture in the paper."

Savannah looked into his eyes.

Jesse was dead serious.

"Okay," she said, leading him through the open door. "Never mind. I reckon you made the right career choice after all."

Chapter 2

"Um . . . is that what you're wearing?" Tammy asked when Savannah came downstairs the next morning in her Minnie Mouse pajamas, pink chenille robe, and furry slippers.

Even though Savannah had just rolled out of bed and her mind was as fuzzy as her house shoes, she caught the gentle criticism underlying the question. Tammy wasn't asking for information, she was making a statement.

Perky Miss Tammy Hart sat at the rolled-top desk in the corner of the living room—Savannah's official "office"—working on the computer, a slightly disapproving frown on her pretty face. Though she normally wore yoga workout garb, jeans, or shorts to work, Tammy was decked out in a joyously bright, aqua pantsuit with a ruffled, floral-print, girlie blouse.

Savannah swallowed her own fashion review as her tired brain tried to process this change of scenery. And while she was at it, she made a mental note to redefine her assistant's job description.

It would not include fashion critique.

She walked over to the windowsill to pet the cats, who were curled up on their perch. They looked like miniature black leopards, soaking in the morning sunlight. "So, what's up?" she asked, "You don't approve of my sleeping attire?"

"I love your Minnie Mouse jammies . . . for sleeping in. Not so great for interviewing a client, though."

"A client? What cli—? Oh, shoot! I forgot!"

She turned and raced up the stairs, furry slippers pounding the steps as she ran.

"Don't worry," Tammy called after her. "I'll entertain her when she gets here. I dressed up special, just in case."

"In case you need to deliver a weather report today?" Savannah mumbled as she hurried into her bedroom to find something to wear to greet her 9:00 A.M. client.

Something other than cartoon-spangled pajamas . . . or a suit the color of a Southern California swimming pool.

Savannah sat in her comfy, wing-backed chair with Cleopatra—a purring, glossy black ball of feline contentment—in her lap. As she scratched behind the cat's ear, she watched the young woman on her sofa and listened to her sad story.

Clients always had sad stories.

Nobody hired a private detective because their relationships were happy, their lives carefree, their loved ones all safe and accounted for.

And Emma Strauss, as she had introduced herself, had big green eyes, short red hair, high-end clothes, plenty of tastefully decadent jewelry . . . and a serious problem with her grandmother.

"You have to help me, Savannah," she was saying. "My grandmother's losing her mind! She keeps trying to kill herself, and this last time she almost did it!"

Emma's eyes filled with tears as she stared down at her hands, which were folded demurely in her lap. But Savannah could see how tightly her fingers were clenched. And her heart went out to any granddaughter who loved her grandmother so dearly.

Savannah had a granny of her own who meant the world to her. She couldn't imagine how distraught she'd be if Gran were in danger of harming herself. And yet . . .

"I'm so sorry for your predicament, Emma," she said, offering the woman a tissue from a box on the end table between them. "It must be just awful, what you're going through. But if your grandmother has a problem with her mental faculties, I'm not sure a private investigator is what you need. Maybe a psychologist or even your family physician?"

"Our doctor said there's nothing physically wrong with her. She's in amazing shape for a woman in her eighties. And if you were to suggest that she needs a shrink, you'd better be ready to duck and cover. She'd probably smack you in the head with a brick."

Savannah couldn't help chuckling. "That sounds like my Granny Reid. Only she'd brain you with a skillet. She's always been a big believer in skillet-smackin'."

Emma wiped her tears and blew her nose. She tucked the used tissue into her designer handbag . . . a purse that, Savannah was fairly certain, cost more than her entire wardrobe. Then she ran her fingers through her hair and sat up straighter. "Actually," she said, "your grandmother is part of the reason why I came to you for help."

"My grandmother?" Savannah's mind tried to process that tidbit of information but couldn't make sense of it. "What would my granny in Georgia have to do with this?"

"Oma Helene and I were watching television one night, not too long ago, when we saw you and your . . . uh . . . granny on a news show. You solved a case, a homicide, and she helped you. I think they said she was visiting you here in California. It was just a short news clip, but we could see how close the two of you were, how much love and respect you have for each other."

Savannah nodded. "That's true. I adore Gran. She raised me, my brothers and sisters . . . all nine of us. I figure if that doesn't earn a body sainthood, nothin' does."

Emma smiled. "I agree. Oma Helene and I talked about you, and how close we are, too. She liked you and your grandma. I could tell. And she's not a person who likes very many people."

"I'm honored."

"You should be. My grandmother is an excellent judge of character."

"Which is probably the reason she doesn't like very many people."

"Exactly."

Savannah scooped the sleeping cat off her lap and set her gently on the floor. Cleo woke instantly, gave Savannah a dirty look, and walked away with an indignant twitch of her tail.

Reaching for a plate of pecan brownies on the coffee table, Savannah said, "Tell me more about your grandmother's suicide attempts." She offered the goodies to Emma, who shook her head, then relented and took one.

"First she drove her scooter over a cliff."

"Her scooter? Your grandma rides a motorbike?"

"Oh, yeah. She used to ride a Harley till Ada took her keys away from her."

"Who's Ada?"

"Oma Helene's niece. She runs the family business . . . and everything else now. She tries to run Oma's life. She and Oma hate each other."

"Okay. So, how did your grandmother drive off a cliff and live to tell about it?"

"Fortunately, her leather jacket caught on a bush. The gardener found her dangling there . . . kicking and screaming."

"Wow!"

"Yeah. And then, last week, she dumped a bunch of her sleep aid medication into a cup of hot chocolate and drank it. We found her unconscious on the floor and rushed her to the hospital. She was out cold for twenty-four hours. The doctor said a less hearty soul would have died."

Savannah took a brownie for herself and nibbled at the chocolate frosting as she considered what she'd just heard. "Has your grandmother been depressed lately?"

"No. Oma loves life. She hates people, but she's thankful for every day she's given."

"Has she shown any signs of senility?"

"You mean, other than intolerance of her fellow man?"

Savannah grinned. "That isn't senility. That's wisdom born of longevity."

Emma shook her head. "My grandmother has every brain cell she came into the world with. Nothing gets past her."

"What does she say about these 'suicide attempts'?"

"She says she accidentally lost control of the scooter, and that she didn't put anything in the hot chocolate but milk, sugar, cocoa, and a dash of vanilla."

"So, why don't you believe her?"

Emma's big green eyes filled with tears again. She bit her lower lip. "Because . . ." she said, ". . . the scooter spill might have been an accident. It could have happened to anyone. But somebody, somehow, deliberately put an overdose of medication in that hot chocolate. And if it wasn't my grandmother, then that means somebody is trying to . . . I can't stand to even think that."

Savannah reached over and rested her hand on the young woman's forearm. "You were right to come to me," she said. "You do need a private investigator. Take me to Grandma Helene. I have a feeling I'm going to like her."

"Okay, I'd like her a lot better if she wasn't totin' a gun," Savannah told Emma as they watched Helene Strauss charge out her front door and rush down the driveway toward them, a rifle in her hands.

Three minutes before, Emma had turned off

the main highway and driven down a winding road through an enchanting forest. With its thick, shady trees and patches of sunlit meadows all colorfully sprinkled with bright wildflowers, the property looked like something from a fairy tale.

Savannah could easily imagine the wee folk peeking at them from behind the mossy rocks that bordered the creek flowing parallel to the road.

And when they arrived at the Strauss mansion, Savannah was sure she'd been transported to a land of fantasy. The Bavarian-style, timber-framed beauty was straight from the pages of a storybook, with its graceful lines and steeply pitched red roof, its chocolate brown crisscrossing over cream stucco. Flower boxes decorated each balcony, overflowing with rose-colored geraniums, snowy alyssum, and royal blue lobelia.

But the fairy tale ended the moment Savannah put one foot outside of Emma's BMW and caught sight of an armed and apparently dangerous, eighty-something-year-old woman charging out of the house.

Without hesitation, Savannah slid back into the passenger's seat and locked the door.

Emma chuckled and reached for her purse. "Pay no attention to the gun. She's had it for years, but, as far as we know, she hasn't actually shot anybody with it yet."

"Gee. How comforting."

Savannah's brain whirred, trying to remember anything her former police training might have taught her about what to do in a situation like this.

If the person rushing toward her had been a twenty-something gangbanger, or a yahoo like Josh or Jesse Murphy, she would have already pulled

her Beretta from its holster, taken a position behind the car door, and demanded he drop his
weapon or die.

She didn't recall anybody at the academy saying
anything about how to deal with a raging granny.

Tossing her keys into her purse, Emma got out
of the car. "Oma, it's me, Emma," she called out.
"Put down the gun, and come give me a hug."

Helene stopped at the front of the car and
peered across the hood at Savannah. "Who's that
you've got with you?"

Savannah realized the sun was in the woman's
eyes.

"A friend of mine," Emma replied.

"Not that weird boyfriend of yours with the
black nail polish and the earrings sticking out of
his face."

"No, it isn't Kyd."

"Good. I can't stand the look of him. He's ugly
enough without all that stuff he does to himself."

Savannah felt a rush of relief as Emma gently
took the rifle from her grandmother's hands. The
vision of her own funeral, where the boys in blue
were both grieving and giggling over her casket,
hadn't been a pleasant one. After all the truly
tough guys she'd taken down over the years, she
didn't want her autopsy report to list the cause of
death as "Shot by a Disgruntled Octogenarian."

Slowly, she reopened her door and got out of
the car.

Helene Strauss looked her up and down, then
squinted, studying her face. "Do I know you?" she
asked.

"You've seen her, Oma," Emma said. "It's Savannah Reid, that private detective who was on the news with her Southern granny. You remember . . . ?"

"Of course I remember. I remember World War II, for Pete's sake." She walked around the car and offered Savannah her hand. "I like you. I like a woman who catches a cold-blooded murderer and then takes her grandmother to Disneyland."

"Hey, Gran's a big fan of the Mouse. I didn't have much choice."

Helene smiled, and Savannah couldn't help thinking she must have been a beauty in her day. For that matter, she still was. Her pale green eyes sparkled with wit and wisdom. Her smile was warm and inviting. Her blond hair had more silver than gold but framed her face in soft, thick curls. She was wearing a smoky pink, silk caftan with tiny pearls embroidered around the neckline. Though petite, she looked strong for her age. Not at all frail or fragile.

Minus the expensive garment and the diamond and pearl earrings, Helene Strauss reminded Savannah a lot of her own grandmother. They were both glowing examples of graceful aging, and Savannah wanted to be exactly like them when she "grew up someday."

"Your grandmother is very lucky to have a granddaughter like you," Helene said. She looked at Emma, and her green eyes went even softer. "And so am I." Then she cleared her throat and assumed a businesslike tone. "You two want to come inside and have a cup of coffee and some apple strudel? I just took it out of the oven."

Savannah's face lit up. "If apple strudel is even a kissin' cousin to apple pie, I'd be delighted."

"But we just had brownies . . ." Emma said, ". . . for *breakfast.*"

"We live in Southern California," Savannah replied. "We could have the 'Big One' any minute. And wouldn't you feel stupid if you died right after you turned down a piece of warm strudel?"

Emma thought for a moment. "Well, if I were dead, I wouldn't be thinking about anything. I'd be—"

"Girl, your rationalization skills need serious honing." Savannah wrapped her arm around Emma's shoulder as they followed Helene to the house. "Just stick with me, observe, and learn from a master."

It wasn't the intricately carved, hand-painted furniture, the delicate, lace curtains, or the brightly polished, teak floors that caught Savannah's attention when she entered the Strauss mansion. The spacious rooms with their vaulted ceilings and mullioned windows were impressive, and the bookcases filled with antique books and fine porcelain vases were lovely. The nine-foot concert grand piano in the great room was breathtaking.

But Savannah only saw the dolls.

On either side of a giant, floor-to-ceiling, stone fireplace stood large wooden cabinets with glass doors. And displayed inside the lit cupboards were over one hundred of the most exquisite dolls Savannah had ever seen.

"What in the world . . . ?" she said as she stared, spellbound.

Delicate lady dolls with bouffant hairdos, wearing silk and lace dresses, sat next to lifelike babies in flowing christening gowns. Boys in ragamuffin costumes stood beside princes in satin pantaloons. But most of the dolls were little girls . . . girls with a distinctive beauty: big, soulful eyes, rosy cheeks, glowing skin, and shimmering locks of long hair flowing over their shoulders.

Savannah caught her breath as she realized whose house she was standing in. She turned to her hostess. "Oh, my goodness," she said. "You're *the* Helene! Helene the doll maker!"

Helene Strauss simply nodded.

Emma's eyes sparkled with pride as she said, "You know my grandmother's dolls?"

"*Know* them? I *have* one of them! My granny gave her to me when I was twelve years old. She's always been my most prized possession!"

Helene smiled. She seemed genuinely touched. "That's lovely, dear. Which one do you have?"

"*The* Helene, of course, modeled after you, I believe."

Walking over to one of the cabinets, Helene said, "Yes, she was one of our prettiest, if I do say so myself, designed after a painting that was done of me as a child."

She opened the glass door, reached in, and took out one of the dolls. Offering it to Savannah, she said, "Is your doll like this one?"

Reverently, Savannah took the beautiful toy into her hands and, for a moment, just looked and enjoyed the plaything that was a work of art. The cherublike face, the golden waves of hair, the bright green eyes that matched its jade satin dress. "Yes, this is just like mine, except my doll has black hair and blue eyes and a blue dress. Granny Reid said she chose her because her coloring was the same as mine."

"And you still have her?

"She's in my cedar chest, along with my other most precious treasures. If the house ever catches on fire, that chest is the first thing going out . . . after the cats, that is."

"You should take her out of the chest," Helene said. "I can't imagine she's happy in there."

Savannah chuckled and looked into the older woman's eyes, expecting to see a teasing smile on her face. But Helene was completely serious.

"Yes," Savannah said, "I suppose you're right. I should take her out and display her."

"What did you name your doll?" Emma asked.

"Valdosta."

Emma made a face. "*Valdosta?*"

"I call her Val for short. I wanted to name her after a town in Georgia. My momma named all her younguns after Georgia cities, and she had a passel of 'em . . . didn't leave me a lot of choices."

"How many of you were there?" Helene asked.

"Nine, including me."

Helene nodded somberly. "I'm not sure what a passel is, but that sounds like a passel, all right."

She looked deeply into Savannah's eyes, then added, "I guess a special doll would be precious to a little girl with eight siblings. I don't suppose toys were very plentiful."

"Nothing was plentiful, but love. Granny Reid raised us. She made sure we didn't want for affection and attention. Even with nine of us."

"Bless her."

"I do every day."

"I feel the same way about my grandmother," Emma said, resting her hand lightly on Helene's shoulder. "She raised me, too."

Helene cleared her throat and abruptly took the doll from Savannah. Gently, she smoothed its hair. "You girls don't have to be all that grateful," she said with a touch of gruffness. "I'm sure your Granny Reid feels the same way I do; it isn't work if you enjoy it."

She set the doll back in the cupboard, fluffing its skirt and posing its arms just so. Closing the cabinet door, she said, "Let's go have some of that strudel before it gets cold."

Helene led them through the great room, down a hallway, and into a large, but cozy and quaint kitchen. As Savannah looked around at the cobalt blue and white tiles and the cabinets with their fanciful scrollwork and folk painting accents, she asked Emma, "Did you grow up in this house?"

"Yes, I did."

With a wave of her hand, Helene invited them to sit in a breakfast nook in the corner.

Savannah slid into the booth and looked around the crisp, white curtains with their navy blue polka dots. Outside the window was an herb and vegetable garden brimming with savory goodies.

For a moment, Savannah imagined Gran in her own garden back home in Georgia, a hoe in her hand, a sunbonnet shading her skin from the hot summer sun.

"What a joy that must have been, being a child in a place like this," Savannah said, as Emma sat in the booth across from her. "You must have felt like a fairy princess every day."

Emma glanced over at Helene, who was busy pouring coffee and arranging the pastry on a plate. She leaned across the table and lowered her voice so only Savannah could hear. "Actually, it was rather sad at first. My mother died in a car accident when I was five. That's when I came here to live with Oma."

"I'm sorry," Savannah said softly. "That must have been very difficult . . . for everyone."

"How about you? Why did your grandmother raise you? Did your mother die, too?"

"No, she's still living." Savannah mentally shoved aside the image of her mother sitting on a bar stool, under an eight-by-ten, glossy, black-and-white picture of Elvis . . . a cigarette in one hand, a beer in the other. "She was just better at making babies than taking care of them."

"I'm sorry," Emma said. "That must have been difficult, too."

"It had its moments." Savannah shrugged. "But that was then, and this is now. And no matter how rough you had it, somebody in the world had it worse, so . . ."

Helene walked over to the table and set some exquisite china plates in front of them, rimmed with gold and hand painted with beautiful, pink cabbage roses.

"Those dishes are too pretty to eat off of," Savannah said.

Helene sniffed. "When you get to be my age, you start using all your good stuff for every day. What's the point in waiting for special occasions? Every day is special."

She set matching saucers and delicate cups brimming with fragrant coffee next to the plates.

"You girls should learn that *now*. Don't waste a single day of your lives complaining about anything that happened yesterday or worrying about what'll happen tomorrow. Life's meant to be lived one day, one moment, at a time."

"And when did you figure that out?" Savannah asked.

"Last week," Helene replied with a half grin. "So, if you get it straight now, you'll have a big jump on me."

She placed the platter with the strudel in the center of the table and paused, obviously awaiting a positive critique from her guests.

"Gorgeous!" Savannah said, admiring the flaky crust, lightly sprinkled with a bit of powdered sugar. Through the slits in the pastry, she could see the golden apples and raisins shining through. The smell of cinnamon filled the air, mingling with the aroma of the coffee.

Helene slid into the booth next to her granddaughter. "My mother and grandmother used to serve their strudels cooled, with vanilla sauce," she said, her voice tinged with nostalgia and a touch of sadness. "But I've always liked them right from the oven."

"Everything's best straight from the stove," Savannah said as her hostess cut the pastry and laid a generous piece on the plate in front of her.

"So, you're a good cook yourself, Savannah?" Helene gave Emma a slice, as well.

"Yes, ma'am, I am. I have to admit it," Savannah replied. "I'm humble about some things, but my cookin' ain't one of 'em."

"A woman should have an honest evaluation of herself, her gifts, her abilities." Helene nodded toward Emma. "Now my granddaughter here, she's a fine artist. She paints the most beautiful water-colors you ever saw, and she sculpts, too. She's even designed some dolls for us, some exception-ally pretty ones."

A look of sorrow passed over the older woman's face. "Unfortunately, they're the *only* pretty ones we've done for a long time, thanks to that stupid niece of mine." She shook her head. "Oh well, as I was saying . . . Emma is a great artist. Not a great judge of men, but . . ."

"Don't start, Oma." Emma reached for the sugar bowl and added a liberal helping to her cof-fee. To Savannah, she said, "In case you haven't surmised, she isn't fond of my boyfriend."

Savannah chuckled. "Yes, I picked up on that earlier, when I was staring down the barrel of her rifle. I'm not a private detective for nothing, you know."

"He's a punk, who's only after my money . . . and whatever else he can get out of her along the way," Helene added with an eye roll.

"I didn't bring Savannah here to listen to your list of complaints about Kyd," Emma said.

"Then why *did* you bring her?" Helene asked. "Not that I'm not happy to meet her, but . . ."

When Emma didn't answer right away, Helene gave her a suspicious look.

"This isn't about that hot chocolate mess, is it? Or the scooter incident?" Helene nudged her granddaughter. "Is it? You hired a private detective for me without even asking me whether I wanted one or not? Is that what this is all about?"

Savannah leaned forward, started to put her hand on the older woman's arm, then thought better of it. A dangerous glint in those bright green eyes told her that Helene Strauss wasn't someone she wanted as an enemy.

"Mrs. Strauss," she said gently. "Emma loves you dearly, and she can't help but be a little concerned about your welfare, considering . . ."

"I do not need a professional babysitter!"

"No, ma'am. I'm sure you don't. I'd never presume—"

"I've taken care of myself for over eighty years, and I've got the process down pat by now."

"I'm sure you have. But please . . . Mrs. Strauss . . ."

"My name is Helene. My mother-in-law was Mrs. Strauss, and I didn't like her one bit."

"I'm sure you had your reasons, Helene, and—"

"You're damned right I did. And . . . well . . . we don't want to ruin today by thinking about yesterday. Otherwise I'd give you an earful about that one."

"I'm sure you could at that," Savannah said. She drew a deep breath. "But we really should talk about the business with the scooter accident and the hot chocolate."

Helene jumped up from her seat, bumping the table and nearly spilling their coffee. "I will not talk about that! Hanging from a bush on the side of a cliff, screaming my lungs out for help . . . that was the most humiliating half hour of my life. Can you even imagine?"

Savannah stood, too. "Yes, ma'am, I can. When I was a kid, I got my backside stuck in an outhouse seat hole most of an afternoon, and nobody even came looking for me. If my sister, Vidalia, hadn't eaten too many prunes the day before, heaven knows when they would have found me! I'd probably be sitting there still, crying and looking through the Sears and Roebuck catalogue."

Helene stared at her, stunned. "Oh, dear. That *is* worse."

"You're darned tootin' it's worse. So, if you'd be so kind, please sit back down, and let's talk about the scooter and the hot chocolate business, too. I don't want to embarrass you, Mrs. . . . Helene. I just want to make mighty sure that nobody around here is trying to do you harm."

When Helene didn't reply, but just continued to stare at her, Savannah added, "You can't imagine how bad I'd feel if I heard that something terrible happened to you. I simply couldn't bear it. So, please, for my sake and your granddaughter's . . ."

Reluctantly, Helene sat back down, so Savannah did, too.

The older woman sighed, and for a moment, she looked her age. "Someone *is* trying to do me harm," she said. "I have no doubt about that. But I'll catch them myself, and when I do, *I'll* deal with them . . . in my own way."

The evil gleam that lit her green eyes sent a chill through Savannah. She'd seen that look many times before . . . being from the South, where sweet revenge was more popular and more frequently served than sweet tea.

"Let me catch them for you," Savannah said with an equally wicked tone in her voice. "It's what I do for a living, and—as a woman who knows her own talents—I can say, I'm very good at it. Once I've got them, I'll hand them over to you. What you do with them . . . that's up to you."

Helene thought about it, then a smile crossed

her face. It wasn't a pleasant smile, sweet and warm, like her apple strudel. It was a cold, nasty smile, and for a heartbeat, Savannah felt half sorry for whoever was behind this skullduggery.

But only *half* sorry.

And only for one heartbeat.

Chapter 3

"Thank you for being willing to bring me here," Savannah said as she, Emma, and Helene stood at the edge of the cliff, staring down at the scene of Helene's humiliation. "I know it isn't easy for you."

"You have no idea," Helene replied as she gingerly peeped over the precipice. "Just seeing this place again brings it all back. Me hanging there, my jacket caught on that branch."

She pointed to a half-broken tree limb jutting out of the rocky cliff covered with sage scrub brush.

"I dangled there like an idiot, screaming bloody murder, waiting for that branch to crack any minute and send me straight into the hereafter."

Emma shuddered. "Just thinking about it scares me to death."

As Savannah studied the cliff, she saw numerous areas below the protruding limb where the sage bushes had been broken and the rocks dislodged.

"Your motor scooter went down the cliff with you?" she asked.

"Sure," Helene replied. "I was still sitting on it when I headed over the edge. The limb caught me, and the bike kept going . . . landed there on the beach by those big rocks."

"Where is it now?"

"The junkyard," Emma said. "Waldo and Tiago drove down the beach and got it, brought it back for Oma."

"Brought it back in pieces, you mean," Helene said, shaking her head sadly. "I really liked that bike, too. It wasn't nearly as much fun as the Harley, but . . ."

"Who are Waldo and Tiago?" Savannah asked.

"Waldo is my great-nephew," Helene told her. "My good-for-nothing niece's boy. He lives here on the estate and helps me out. He's a nice young man."

Savannah couldn't help but notice Emma's eye roll. Apparently, Emma's estimation of Waldo's worth wasn't quite so lofty as Helene's.

"And Tiago Medina is my gardener," Helene continued. "Thank goodness for Tiago. He's the one who heard me hollering. He risked his life climbing down the cliff to pull me off that branch."

This time Emma agreed, nodding vigorously. "Tiago's a gem. He's the one who's priceless around here, not that nitwit Waldo."

"Did I hear my name mentioned . . ." said a male voice behind them, ". . . and not in a very nice way?"

They turned around to see a man in his early thirties, wearing stylishly tattered shorts and a faded surfer tee-shirt. His long blond hair hung in his eyes, sun-fried and frizzled. His darkly tanned face was already creased with deep wrinkles. He had the same startlingly green eyes as Helene. But they lacked her sparkle of wit and intelligence.

Briefly, Savannah felt a pang of sympathy for him. It wouldn't be easy being born into a highly successful family of attractive, brilliant people, having less than your share of looks, brain, and charm. Not to mention being stuck with the name Waldo.

Maybe he was kind. And as Granny Reid always said, "Kind's more important than pretty'll ever be."

"I heard you call me a nitwit," he told Emma. "That's pretty funny, coming from a girl so ugly that she has to *pay* guys to go out with her."

Okay, Savannah thought, *so much for the "kind" theory.*

"Stop it!" Helene snapped. "We're family, for heaven's sake! You two be nice to each other, or I'll slap you down . . . both of you!"

Savannah stifled a giggle, thinking that was exactly the sort of threat and logic that Granny Reid was famous for.

"My name is Savannah," she said, extending her hand to Waldo. She started to add that she was a friend of Emma's but thought better of it. "I'm visiting your aunt today. She was just telling me what a fright she had, going off this cliff."

"Yeah, that was a bummer," Waldo said, shaking his mop head. "I hate to say it, Oma, but Mom told you to stop riding bikes. You aren't as young as you used to be and—"

"And you won't go adding insult to injury if you

know what's good for you," Helene said, cutting him off sharply. "My age had nothing whatsoever to do with the accident. Anybody could have gone off that cliff . . . even you."

"Especially you," Emma mumbled, "drunk or stoned all the time like you are. . . ."

Waldo shot her a dark look.

"Where were you when your aunt had her accident?" Savannah asked.

"What do you mean? Like do I have an alibi or something?" Waldo's green eyes squinted. "Do I need an alibi?"

"Who said anything about an alibi?" Savannah shrugged. "I was just making small talk. Like, 'Where were you when you heard Elvis died . . . ?'"

"I think I was a baby."

"Oh, yeah." She sighed. "They keep making the younger generation younger and younger." She drew a deep breath and turned to Helene. "What time of day was your accident?"

"About ten fifteen in the morning. I always ride my bike to the main road to get the mail from the mailbox."

Savannah turned to Emma. "Where were you at ten fifteen the morning of your grandmother's mishap?"

"I was at home with my boyfriend, Kyd. He lives with me now. We were probably still in bed. He had a gig the night before, so we were sleeping in. He's a musician. "

"Oh, please!" Helene put her hands over her ears. "You're going to give me a headache, just thinking about it!"

Savannah turned back to Waldo. Try, try, try

again. "And where were *you* at ten fifteen that morning?" she asked slowly, deliberately, as though talking to a three-year-old.

"Sleeping," Emma piped up. "That's all he ever does—sleep and smoke pot and drink beer and look at porn on his computer and play video games. And that's what he's going to be doing until he's sixty-five. The big question is: What's he going to do when he retires? What'll he do with all his spare time, when he's stopped doing absolutely *nothing?*"

Suddenly, Savannah felt exhausted, empty. As though somebody had pulled a plug from the bottom of her right foot and all her energy had flowed out and swirled down some cosmic drain hole.

Donning her most patient look—the one she usually wore while trying to resist the urge to do someone bodily harm—she laced her arm through Waldo's and led him a few steps away from the two women.

"Waldo, my man," she said, "you've got some mighty critical womenfolk in your inner family circle."

"No kidding." He bobbed his blond head vigorously. "And Emma's not nearly as bad as my mom. Man, she's ragging on me day and night about getting a job or going to school or making something of myself."

"She hasn't figured out how pointless that is, huh?"

"Nope. I keep waiting for her to get it through her thick head, but . . ."

"Moms." Savannah gave him a sympathetic tsk-

tsk and shook her head. "Always pushing their kids to succeed. Don't they know the damage they do?"

"Yeah."

Savannah guided him a few feet farther down the path and patted his arm companionably. He responded to the female attention with the shy grin of a guy who didn't get much.

"Do you normally sleep in," she asked him, "like Emma said? Not that there's anything wrong with that. Who wouldn't if they could?"

He nodded. "Yeah. But I stay up late at night. It's not like I'm not doin' nothin' with my life."

"Of course not. And the morning your aunt had her accident, do you think you slept in then, too, or . . ."

"I guess so. I don't remember doing anything different."

"How did you find out about her mishap?"

"The siren woke me up. I looked out the window of my house over there"—he pointed through the trees, and Savannah could just see the top of the roof of a tiny cottage that reminded her of a *Goldilocks and the Three Bears* book her granny had read to them—"and I saw the ambulance coming down the road. They stopped there by the cliff and then I saw her laying on the ground, with Tiago kneeling next to her. I knew it wasn't good."

"That must have been a shock to the system, seeing that," Savannah said, studying his face closely.

"Oh, it was! I thought for sure she was a goner!"

"You and your aunt pretty close, are you?"

"She's the only person in the world who loves me," he said with a candor that took Savannah by surprise. "My mother hates me. Emma does, too. And I've sorta run out of friends the last few years."

"I'm sorry to hear that." Savannah looked into his green eyes and saw a lot of pain. "Any particular reason why your friends flew the coop?"

"I only had two to start with. One of 'em got married and his new wife doesn't want him hanging out with me anymore . . . says I'm a loser. The other friend OD'd."

"Waldo, that's a hard-luck tale if ever I heard one," Savannah said. But her tone lacked the ring of sincerity, because she was distracted.

Looking down at the path, about three feet from where they stood, she had noticed something strange.

Wanting to investigate without an audience, she took Waldo by the arm and led him back toward his aunt and Emma. "Thank you for that information," she told him as she pulled a small notebook and pen from her purse. "If I have any other questions and need to call you, where can I reach you?"

He gave her his email address and, at her prompting, supplied a phone number, as well. She jotted them down.

Turning to Helene and Emma, she said, "I won't keep y'all out here any longer. I reckon you've got things to do and places to be."

"I certainly do," Helene said. She turned to Waldo, "I have to go see that mother of yours and give her a piece of my mind about that ridiculous new doll she's planning. Go take a shower. I want you to drive me to the office."

He mumbled something that sounded like a halfhearted objection, then moped down the path toward the cottage among the trees.

Helene extended her hand to Savannah. "I'm sorry I wasn't very hospitable when you first got here. Next time we'll skip the gun and go straight to the strudel."

Savannah gave the woman's hand an affectionate squeeze and smiled. "That sounds like an excellent plan. And one of these days, you'll have to come to my house and sample my apple pie and homemade ice cream."

Helene's green eyes twinkled. "I've worked eighty years on my strudel recipe. Do you really think you can top it?"

"Granny Reid's older than you, and it's her recipe. So, maybe . . ."

"We shall see. We shall see."

"I get to judge that contest." Emma nodded toward the main house. "So, Savannah, are you ready for me to take you home?"

Savannah thought of what she'd seen on the path and shook her head. "Actually, I think I can arrange my own ride back home," she told Emma. "And, if you don't mind, Helene, I'd like to spend a little time here on your property, just looking around a bit. Would that be okay?"

"Poking around is more like it," Helene replied.

Savannah grinned. "Looking, poking, nosing around . . . pretty much the same thing in my neck of the woods."

"Okay. Stay as long as you like."

Savannah decided to press her luck. "And is there any way that I could get back into the house . . . if you're gone and there was something I really wanted to look at . . . say . . . in your kitchen."

Helene raised one eyebrow. "If you're thinking of snooping around for my strudel recipe, don't waste your time. The only copy of it is in my head."

"Actually," Savannah replied, "I'm more interested in your cocoa tin . . . and sugar canister . . . and . . ."

"I suppose. If you want to go into the house after I'm gone, ask Tiago, the gardener, to let you in. Tell him I said you are family now. His cottage is down the road, past Waldo's." Helene gave her a sly little grin. "I put vanilla in my hot chocolate, too," she said. "And a pinch of salt."

"I'll keep that in mind. And milk and . . ."

"Milk?" Helene sniffed. "Milk is for wimps. Half-and-half."

"Ahhh . . . a woman after my own heart."

Once Helene and Emma were gone, and Savannah was certain she was alone, she walked back down the path and knelt on one knee next to the suspicious area she had noticed before.

She poked at the traffic-hardened dirt with one finger, then tested the section next to it.

Slowly, she stood and dusted off her hand.

She looked at the path . . . the cliff where Helene Strauss had nearly met her death.

Savannah's eyes went cold, her face hard, as she took her cell phone from her purse and called Dirk.

"Hi," she said. "I need you."

"And how many times a day do women tell me that?"

He must be finished doing the paperwork on the Murphy brothers, she thought. Dirk never flirted—or even cracked a grin, for that matter—when he was at his desk.

"I mean it," she said. "I'm at a beachfront property about five miles north of town. It's just past the Vista del Sol restaurant where I took you for your birthday. First drive on the left. I'll meet you at the main house."

"Ooo-kaay," he said. "You gonna tell me why?"

"I'll fill you in when you get here. Bring evidence bags, your camera, and a stiff ruler."

No sooner had she said it than she knew it was coming. He was, after all, male.

"You might not need a stiff ruler if *I'm* there. Whatcha gonna measure?"

"Something longer than three and a half inches, so bring the friggin' ruler."

He chuckled.

That was one thing she loved about Dirk—his tough hide. He took insults better than most.

"You gonna buy me dinner again?" he asked.

"Sure."

"Really? Wow! I'll be right out."

She clicked the phone closed. "Sure, I'll buy you a dee-luxe cheeseburger, fries, and a beer . . . your very next birthday."

Chapter 4

Half an hour later, Dirk was standing over Savannah, watching as she shoved the wooden yardstick into a strip of soft dirt that crossed the path, from one side to the other.

"See how the straightedge slides right down, nice and easy like?" she said. "This section's been dug out recently, then filled back in."

He kicked at the path with the toe of his sneaker. "Yeah. I see that. It's hard as a rock here. You'd break that ruler if you tried to push it in here." He moved to the other side of her and tested that soil, too. "And it's just as hard over here."

He looked up and down the path. "This road's old . . . beaten down over the years. I'll bet there's not another spot like that anywhere on it."

"Me, too."

She pushed the yardstick easily through the dirt until it met resistance. "Fourteen inches," she said. "That'd be deep enough to do the trick for sure."

"What trick?" he asked.

She pulled the ruler out and continued to poke around. "And about six inches across."

"What's this all about?" he said.

"But how would they know she wouldn't see it and stop or go around it?" she muttered to herself as she stood, then walked several feet down the path, back toward the main road.

"She, who?" Dirk wanted to know.

"Helene Strauss, the wonderful elderly lady who owns this property. She reminds me of Gran. She was riding her motorbike from the main house to the mailbox out on the highway, like she did every morning. She hit that hole and went over the cliff right there."

"Your granny doesn't ride a motorbike."

"She would if she had one. Hush up, boy... you're interferin' with my concentration."

"God forbid."

"So, why dig the hole *there?*" she said. "The path runs close to the cliff for quite a stretch here."

Dirk walked over to Savannah and surveyed the area, up and down. After a few moments, he said matter-of-factly, "The view."

She looked up at him and couldn't help noticing the moderately smug look on his face. "What?"

"The view. It's the best here. Back there and up ahead there's more bushes and trees, blocking the view of the ocean."

"That's true." Savannah nodded, looking through the break in the foliage that afforded a breathtaking vista of sea, sand, and sky. "Even if I rode through here every day, I'd turn my head and soak in that gorgeous scenery every time. Look at how pretty it is."

She turned to Dirk. "Boy, I take back what I've

said about you behind your back over the years. You *do* have the sense God gave a goose."

"Gee. Thanks. How often does a guy get a compliment like that?"

"I want a house like that," Savannah said as she and Dirk rounded a curve in the path and saw the first cottage.

She had already fallen in love, having glimpsed bits of the roof and upper story through the trees. The mullioned windows with their dark red shutters, the steeply pitched roof, and lacy gingerbread woodwork seemed fit for a fairy-tale princess.

Though the tie-dyed tee-shirt and tattered beach towel draped over the upstairs balcony railing, and the dried-up vines that trailed from the flower boxes suggested that someone other than Snow White or Cinderella lived there.

"Call it a hunch," she told Dirk, "that's Waldo's place."

"Who's Waldo?"

"Helene's rare-do-well great-nephew, who lives here on the property."

"And sponges off the old biddy?"

"I wouldn't say that."

"That he's a sponge?"

"That she's old or a biddy. First time I saw her, she was toting a rifle, and I'll betcha dollars to donuts she knows exactly how to use it."

"She'd shoot me for calling her a 'biddy'?"

"She's a mite sensitive right now, and I don't blame her one bit. Thinking that somebody's been trying to kill you will do that to a gal."

They passed the house, with its unattractive

laundry hanging out to dry, and walked on down the path toward another, slightly smaller, but equally charming cottage.

This one, a miniature version of the mansion, had flower boxes brimming with healthy plants, immaculately trimmed shrubs, and a thriving herbal garden besides.

The windows were open, and white, ruffled curtains danced lightly in the breeze.

A pretty young Latino woman, wearing a simple white shirt and jeans, her flowing black hair tied back in a ponytail, had some garden shears in one hand and a cell phone in the other.

She was speaking Spanish, and although Savannah's Español was limited at best, she thought she heard her say something like, "*Tener cuidado con lo que dices.*" And she was pretty sure that meant, "Be careful what you say."

That alone would have been enough to pique Savannah's extremely piqueable curiosity. But when the woman saw them, she jumped, snapped the phone closed, and shoved it into her jeans pocket.

With a tense and guilty look on her face, she began to frantically harvest cilantro from among the herbs.

"*Hola,*" Savannah said. "*Buenas dias.*"

Yes, no doubt about it, Savannah thought. The young lady appeared nervous, upset that she had been overheard. And by a Spanish-speaking person at that.

"*Bue*nos *dias,*" Dirk whispered. "*Bue*nos, not *bue*nas."

Okay, Savannah admitted to herself, *a semi-Spanish-speaking person.*

"Hello," the woman responded, not quite meeting Savannah's eyes.

Savannah walked closer to her and stood, deliberately, a bit inside her personal space. From her worried expression and the way she kept shifting from one foot to the other, Savannah knew she had succeeded in making her even more uncomfortable.

Savannah liked it when people were uncomfortable . . . at least when she was on the job. Whether they intended to or not, nervous people revealed more of themselves than relaxed folks ever would.

"I'm Savannah Reid," she said, putting out her hand to the woman. "And you are . . . ?"

She fumbled with her herbs and her shears for a moment, before freeing her right hand. Shaking Savannah's, she mumbled, "I'm Blanca."

"I'm happy to meet you, Blanca. And this is my friend, Detective Sergeant Dirk Coulter."

Dirk gave the young woman his most intimidating "cowboy gunfighter" scowl . . . the one that made Savannah feel the need to bop him and tell him to be nice.

The look worked well on tough gangbangers, but when used on less hardcore citizens, it scared the daylights out of them and frequently caused them to withdraw.

Blanca looked like a turtle pulling into her shell as she took a step backward, ducked her head, and crossed her arms over her chest.

"Detective?" she whispered. "You are police?"

"I'm not the police," Savannah told her. "And he's just my friend. We're here to make sure that everything's okay for Mrs. Strauss."

"Miss Helene," Blanca corrected her. "You call her Mrs. Strauss, she gets very mad. She did not like her mother-in-law."

"Oh, right." Savannah smiled. "I forgot. Miss Helene. We're just checking a few things to make sure that she's okay. You heard what happened to her . . . the accidents?"

"Yes!" She nodded vigorously, her beautiful, dark brown eyes wide. "I heard! She fell off the mountain! My husband saved her."

"Then your husband is the gardener?" Savannah asked.

"Yes. She was going to fall. He pulled her back."

"Were you there when it happened? Did you see it?"

Blanca glanced right and left, then down at her sneakers. "No. I was not there."

"Where were you?" the still-scowling Dirk wanted to know.

"In *el castillo*. I was cleaning. I clean for Miss Helene."

"*El castillo*? Oh, the castle . . . the big house?"

"Yes. I clean the house and my husband is the gardener. And he takes care of the cars."

Savannah looked deep into the mahogany-colored eyes that seemed so reluctant to meet hers. "Blanca, do you know anyone who would want to hurt Miss Helene?"

The young woman dropped her shears. She bent over and took her time picking them up. When she did, Savannah noticed that the handful of cilantro she was holding was shaking like a willow tree in a Georgia wind storm.

"No," Blanca said. "Miss Helene is like an angel.

She gets mad sometimes, and she screams at people sometimes. But she isn't bad. She's good."

"Who does she scream at?" Dirk asked.

Blanca shrugged. "Everyone, when they don't do things right. She wants everyone to do their work right. But she's good."

"And you can't think of anyone who would want to hurt her?" Savannah asked again.

Blanca hesitated just a bit too long, then shook her head. "No. I can think of no one."

Savannah lowered her voice to a soft whisper. "If you think of someone, would you tell me? You know . . . to help Miss Helene?"

Blanca looked up at Savannah with eyes filled with painful secrets. After several long, tense seconds, she finally nodded.

"Thank you," Savannah told her, reaching into her purse and pulling out a business card. She held it out to the woman. "My phone number is on there. You can call me any time at all, day or night. Okay?"

Blanca mumbled a halfhearted, "Okay," and shoved the card into her jeans pocket.

Savannah glanced around. "Where is your husband, Blanca? We need to speak to him, too."

A look of fresh fear crossed the housekeeper's face.

"Just for a moment," Savannah added. "There's no problem. We just need to ask him about how he saved her. He's a real hero, your husband."

Blanca gave her a weak smile and a slight nod. "Yes. A hero." She pointed toward the back of the cottage. "He's working on the chicken house."

Savannah heard Dirk groan, and she couldn't help smiling just a little.

Dirk liked cats and dogs, but he was no fan of livestock . . . beyond eating them.

"Thank you, *señora*," Savannah told Blanca. "Please call if me you think of anything."

"I will."

No, you won't, Savannah thought.

Her internal lie detector was pretty reliable, and even though she had sensed that Blanca harbored a certain degree of affection for her employer, she wasn't expecting the phone to jingle any time soon with a call from the housekeeper.

Savannah reached for Dirk's arm and gave him a little tug. "Let's get going, big boy," she whispered to him.

"Chickens," he said, resisting.

She pulled harder. "I don't see you turning your nose up at the fried chicken I serve on my granny's blue china platter every Sunday afternoon."

He acquiesced and fell into step beside her. "Southern fried drumsticks don't bite."

"Neither do nice little hens. They just lay eggs and—"

"Roosters bite . . . and claw . . . and scratch . . . and jump up on your shoulder and flap their wings all over your head and scare the crap outta you!"

She gave him a quick, sideways glance and saw the unadulterated terror in his eyes. "Wow," she said. "That sort of heartfelt conviction comes from personal experience, I'd say."

"Damn right, it does, and I don't want to talk about it."

"When did it happen? Were you a little kid? Wow . . . that must have been traumatic for a youngster to—"

"I said, I don't wanna talk about it."

"That kind of thing can be so awful for a young 'un. Did you have nightmares about it for years?"

"Still do."

"That's plum awful. I'm so sorry. I feel so bad when things like that happen to helpless, little, impressionable children."

"Yeah, well . . . whatever." He shuddered. "How was I supposed to know that perp would have a rooster the size of a school bus for a guard dog when I chased him into the backyard?"

"Perp?"

He shot her a wary look. "I told you, I don't wanna talk about it. Just drop it, okay?"

"You were on the job? You were a grown up?"

"It was a really, really big frickin' chicken! Just shut up about it."

She swallowed a snicker. "Okay."

They walked along in silence a little way.

Finally, he said, "That's part of why I really like to eat your Southern fried chicken legs on Sunday afternoons."

"Every bite is a kind of revenge?"

"Exactly."

"And here I thought it was my granny's blue-ribbon recipe."

"That, too."

They had entered a garden filled with wild flowers, artistically placed rockery, and a pond brimming with water lilies.

The smell of lavender and star jasmine scented the air, and Savannah had to pause and savor the experience.

"Ah," she said, breathing deeply, taking it all in, "it just makes life worth living, a moment like this."

"Yeah, I guess," he replied. "I'd probably get more out of it if I wasn't going to a henhouse."

"And speaking of . . . there it is."

She pointed ahead, through some trees, to a tiny structure that looked like a playhouse for children. Like the main house and the cottages, it was festooned with decorative gingerbread and even had shutters and window boxes.

But having been raised in a rural area, Savannah recognized the telltale signs that identified it as a bonafide chicken coop: the miniature gangplank leading up to a small door, the yard surrounded by wire fencing and covered with protective netting.

Not to mention the four red hens and three white ones pecking and scratching contentedly among the scattered straw in the yard.

"I don't see a rooster," Dirk said with so much relief in his voice that Savannah couldn't help giggling.

They did, however, see a young Latino, walking toward the henhouse, carrying a fresh bale of hay.

He was an attractive man with a strong jaw, pronounced cheekbones, thick hair, and a physique that appeared to be naturally muscular, the result of hard work rather than hours spent at a gym.

When he saw them, it occurred to Savannah that he didn't appear particularly pleased or at all surprised.

Since the advent of cell phones, she had found it harder and harder to sneak up on people.

"*Hola,*" Dirk greeted him.

He tossed the bale onto the ground next to the coop's wire fence and dusted his palms on his jeans. "*Hola,*" he replied warily.

"I'm Detective Sergeant Dirk Coulter." Dirk took his badge from inside his jacket pocket, flipped it open, and showed him. "This is my friend, Savannah Reid. Are you the gardener here?"

He hesitated, as though having to decide whether or not to admit it. "Yes," he said finally. "I am."

"And your name is Tiago?" Savannah asked.

"Tiago Medina." Again, he couldn't appear less enthused about their presence.

"I hear you are *el héroe*, Tiago," she told him with a dimpled smile and a slight fluttering of eyelashes.

He looked confused for a moment, then shook his head and glanced down at his worn work boots. "No. I'm not a hero."

Savannah was slightly surprised that the dimple/eyelash business hadn't worked. Even if the guy was at least ten years her junior, males from eight to eighty usually succumbed to the Southern Belle Double Whammy.

Maybe the old girl's losing her touch? she thought. *Naw, it couldn't be that.*

"But you saved Mrs. Strauss's life when she fell down the cliff," Dirk said, picking up where she had left off. "That makes a guy a hero in my book."

Tiago shoved his hands into his jeans pockets. "Miss Helene has been good to me. She gave me a job, a house, for years. And my wife, too." A momentary look of sadness crossed his face. "Miss Helene was in trouble. I helped."

"I've seen that cliff," Savannah said. "It's very high, very steep. You risked your life saving her."

He shrugged and smiled. "She would have done the same for me, if it had been me hanging there."

Savannah thought it over for a moment and laughed. "Yes, I've only known Helene Strauss for a few minutes, and I agree. She'd probably climbed right down that cliff to get you."

Tiago's eyes twinkled. "She is like my grandmother in Ecuador. She is ... what you say ... a *pistola.*"

"Yes," Savannah agreed. "A pistol. Your grandma, mine, and Helene, too."

"And the apple doesn't fall far from the tree," Dirk mumbled, giving Savannah a nudge.

"Speaking of apples," Savannah said. "Miss Helene baked some strudel for me earlier today, and I'd like to go back into her kitchen and look for something. She's gone to her office, but she said you could let me back into the house. Would you mind, Tiago?"

"Miss Helene told you to ask me to let you into the house?"

"Yes. She said the gardener would open the door for me."

"What did she say, exactly?"

"She told me, 'You are family now.'"

He nodded, obviously satisfied. "Come with me. I'll let you inside." He headed down the path, back toward the main house.

Savannah and Dirk fell into step beside him.

"I suppose that's some sort of code," Savannah prompted him. "The business about me being 'family'?"

"Yes," Tiago said. "Miss Helene has lots of codes. Codes for everything. She trusts no one."

"Why do you think that is?" Savannah asked, recalling the vision of Helene Strauss charging out of her mansion, gun in hand.

"She was a little girl in Bavaria during the war," Tiago said. "The big war."

"World War II?" Dirk asked.

"Yes."

As they walked along, a sadness seemed to sweep over Tiago. His shoulders slumped, and he stared blankly ahead, down the path, as though seeing nothing.

Savannah suspected his change in mood had to do with his previous comment, so she decided to pursue it. "That must have been very hard for Helene," she said, "a child, living through the horrors of that war."

"It was very hard for her," Tiago said. "She told me some things. Very bad things that happened to her family."

"Was her family Jewish?"

"Some of them were."

Savannah thought of the pain she had seen in Helene's green eyes, the guarded wariness, even when the woman had been acting the perfect hostess, serving apple strudel at the kitchen table.

She thought of how those eyes had looked, sighting down the barrel of a gun.

She thought of that little girl growing up in such turbulent, horrible times with family members who were Jewish.

Shaking her head, Savannah said, "Who knows what that woman has experienced in her day? No wonder she has trust issues."

Chapter 5

Sitting in the passenger's seat of Dirk's decrepit, old Buick Skylark, Savannah had to suppress a chuckle. It never failed to amaze her how much trouble he would go to just to avoid having to face Eileen Bradley alone.

A tough cookie—and an all-around great gal, in Savannah's estimation—Eileen ruled the county forensics lab with a fist of steel, usually covered by a surgical glove. Few people, other than Savannah, genuinely liked her. But most folks respected her and everybody was afraid of her.

And that was exactly the way Eileen liked it.

"Pathological people-pleasing" was nowhere to be found on her list of character flaws.

Eileen had a number of personality types she disliked. Anyone with a lazy streak, even a very small one, offended her. She had no use for people who wasted her precious time. And she hated anyone who pushed her for speedy lab results.

Dirk wasted copious amounts of her time by

calling constantly, trying to get his evidence processed before anyone else's. So, she loathed him.

As Savannah rode along, savoring the warmth of the California sun on her face, listening to the breeze rustling the palm trees that lined the street, and seeing the light glimmer on the dancing fronds . . . she just couldn't resist annoying him. He was such an easy target. And she firmly believed you had to take your pleasures in life wherever you found them.

"You really could have just dropped this stuff off at the lab yourself," she said, giving him a sly, sideways glance. "You didn't need me to tag along."

He grunted and reached for a plastic bag on the dash. Some time back, he'd given up cigarettes and substituted cinnamon sticks. He smelled so nice—a bit like apple pie—that she had decided not to tell him how silly he looked, sucking on them.

Far be it from her to interfere with personal growth. Silly looking or not, she was enormously proud of him. Him giving up cigarettes was as monumental as her giving up chocolate. And she knew that was never going to happen.

Popping a stick in his mouth, he said, "Eileen's not gonna be all that jazzed about running tests on a cocoa tin and a sugar canister, especially when we don't even have a crime yet."

"We have a crime! Attempted murder of a dear old lady. That's a felony in my law book!"

"You have nothing, Van, and you know it," he said. "You've got a woman who took a tumble off a bike and nearly killed herself, then accidentally took too much of one of her medications with her hot chocolate. There's nothing felonious about that."

"What about that dug-up dirt on the trail?"

"You've got a soft spot on a path. Maybe a dog buried a bone there or whatever."

"Helene Strauss didn't accidentally take that many extra pills. That woman's got her act together more than you or I'll ever have. I'd venture to say she never did anything accidental in her whole life."

"She's old, Savannah. Sometimes older people—"

"Hold it right there, buddy! If Granny Reid's taught me anything, it's that old folks aren't any different from anybody else, except that they've been around longer! And if anything, that makes them smarter, not dumber!"

"Whoa!" He held up one hand. "I know your granny, and I totally agree with you. I'm just making the point that sometimes, the older you get, the harder it is to remember stuff. You know, senility and all that."

She snorted. "'Senility' is a word a lot of people throw at an older person when they don't agree with what they're saying. Somebody who's getting along in years speaks their mind and if someone else finds what they're saying to be inconvenient, they label them 'senile.' And that's just downright disrespectful and cruel."

Dirk reached over and gently patted her knee. "I'm sure that happens sometimes, and I agree, it's very wrong. I'm just saying that these . . . mishaps . . . could have been accidents."

"Helene Strauss is a hundred miles from senile."

She took a deep breath. "True, the bike business might have been an accident. And there may be some other explanation for the soft area in the path. But there's no way on God's green earth that Helene mistakenly swallowed a bunch of pills instead of one. It didn't happen. I know it, sure as I'm sittin' here with my teeth in my mouth."

"Okay. I believe you."

She gave him a searching look. "You do?"

"I do."

"Because . . . ?"

"Because I trust your judgment." He gave her a warm grin. "And because I can clearly see you've got your teeth in your mouth."

"Good."

They drove along several more blocks in silence.

Finally, he said, "I never did understand that teeth-in-the mouth thing you always say."

Savannah smiled and shrugged. "In the town where I'm from, people don't have a lot of money to spend on preventive dentistry. They do well to put food on the table and have a roof over their heads. Teeth in, teeth out . . . for a lot of folks, it's optional."

"Oh, okay. Gotcha."

"I hate this stupid place," Savannah said as she and Dirk walked across the parking lot and up to the nondescript gray door of a nondescript gray building that was part of the massive gray, nondescript complex known as the San Carmelita Industrial Park.

"Ambiance" hadn't been high on the list of priorities when the so-called park had been erected on the edge of town ten years ago.

Savannah and her fellow, environmentally conscious San Carmelitans had carried signs and protested loudly as the orange groves had been hacked down and strawberry fields uprooted so that this cement and asphalt wonder could be erected. But progress could not be halted, and in spite of their best efforts to prevent it, Los Angeles had "sprawled" across this end of their picturesque community.

Savannah had never gotten over it, and she seldom passed or entered this area without muttering unladylike comments under her breath.

"Dammit, there used to be strawberry fields here," she said as they approached the door with its official county seal.

"I know," Dirk said. "You tell me that every time we come here."

"And orange groves. You know how sweet an orange grove smells, the fruit and the blossoms all warm in the sunshine?"

"You've mentioned that a time or two."

"Asphalt in the sunshine smells like a wet dog's butt."

"Well, I haven't smelled a lot of wet dogs' butts, but—"

"Let me do the talking here."

They walked up to the door, and he pushed the buzzer button.

"You said that before," he grumbled. "I have every intention of letting you do the talking. Why do you think I brought you along?"

They both looked up at the camera mounted above the door and plastered too-broad smiles on their faces.

Grinning ear-to-ear, teeth gritted, she whispered, "Try hard not to piss her off this time."

"Who me?" he mumbled back. "Who do you think I am?"

"I know exactly who you are. That's why I'm saying watch it."

A sharp, brusque female voice crackled through the speaker mounted beside the camera. "What the hell do you two want?"

"What do you mean, 'what do you want?'" Dirk snapped back. "We gotta have an engraved invitation to come here? Huh?" He took out his badge and held it up to the camera. "There ya go. That's a gold shield, sister. That's our frickin' invitation."

He held the badge high for a moment, then glanced down at Savannah.

Her blue eyes were glacial as she glared up at him.

Slowly, he lowered the badge and tucked it back into his jacket, cleared his throat, and shifted from one foot to the other.

Savannah took a deep breath and shook her head.

The door buzzed and swung open. She elbowed him aside and walked through. "In case I forget later on," she said over her shoulder, "remind me to slap you."

Just inside the door stood a large, sixty-something woman with long silver hair that curled softly around her face. But her hair was the only soft thing about Eileen.

Eileen had been head honcho of the county

forensic lab since before Savannah had joined the police force. And she ruled her kingdom with an air of authority born of experience, knowledge, and supreme confidence.

Eileen had strong opinions on everything, and Savannah had never known her to be wrong.

Except today.

"So," Eileen said, sticking her nose a bit too close to Dirk's, "you're here to lean on me to process something for you ASAP—as in, push it to the front of the line, ahead of everybody else's."

Savannah tapped her gently on the shoulder. "Uh, actually, he just came along with me today. I'm the one asking for a favor."

Instantly, Eileen melted and turned a smiling face toward Savannah. "Oh, well . . . in that case . . ."

Dirk bristled. "Look how nice you are to her! When it's me, you just assume the worst and—"

"And the worst is what I always get from you," Eileen tossed back at him. "When are you *ever* not a pain in the ass?"

Dirk opened his mouth to speak, then closed it.

Savannah cleared her throat. "He's usually pretty agreeable when he's eating my cooking."

"Yeah, well"—Eileen sniffed—"who isn't? Stick one of your chocolate chip pecan cookies in my mouth, and I'll perk right up, too."

Savannah opened her purse and pulled out a plastic zipper bag. "How about cherry oatmeal?"

"That'll do." Eileen snatched the bag out of her hand, opened it, and smelled the contents. "Oh, my God . . . I can feel my mood rising already."

At a nearby computer, a young red-haired woman watched and listened, eyeing the bag. "Enough in there to share?"

"Yes," Savannah said, "but whether she will or not . . . ?"

"You work here over forty years, like I have," Eileen told her, "you can accept bribes, too. Till then, get back to those prints."

The redhead sighed and turned back to her computer screen, where a pair of latent prints were being analyzed and compared.

To the right, a young man sat at a lab bench, staring through a microscope. On the wall to the left, another guy was examining a bed sheet with an ultraviolet light.

Savannah cringed to think what he was seeing through his goggles. Years before, she had made the mistake of looking at a hotel bedspread with a UV light. And ever since, when she'd spent the night somewhere other than her own bed, she had packed her sleeping bag along with her pajamas and toothbrush.

Too much knowledge could ruin almost anything.

"So," Eileen said around a bite of cookie, "what have you got for me?"

Savannah reached into her purse and pulled out four small, brown evidence bags. Handing them to Eileen, she said, "I have a client, a wonderful lady, eighty-plus years old, who thinks somebody's been trying to kill her. And I think she's right."

"That bites."

"Darned right, it does. I've got a granny that age."

"My mom's eighty-five. If somebody tried to hurt her, I'd take them out in a heartbeat . . . in the most painful way possible."

Dirk perked up. "And what way would that be?"

"Like I'm going to tell *you*." Eileen shot him a look, then turned back to Savannah. "What's in these bags?"

"Food from her kitchen. She drank her nightly hot chocolate and passed out cold. They took her to the hospital, where she slept for hours."

"And you think somebody put sleeping pills, or whatever, in her drink?"

Savannah nodded. "We took samples from her cocoa tin, sugar canister, and her half-and-half carton, and a bottle of vanilla."

Eileen opened one of the envelopes and peered inside. "Any idea what we're looking for?"

"She had a prescription for a sleep medication called Zolpedone," Dirk said. "But when we counted the pills and compared them to what's left, it didn't look like any were missing."

"Okey dokey." Eileen popped the rest of the cookie into her mouth. "We'll get on it."

"You'll get on it right away?" Dirk asked.

Savannah nudged him in the ribs with her elbow. She gave Eileen a bright smile. "It would probably take me a few hours to go home, bake up a batch of those chocolate chip pecan cookies you're so fond of, and get back here."

Eileen returned the smile. "The universe is just filled with coincidences. That's exactly how long it'll take us to run these samples."

Chapter 6

Savannah took bribery very seriously. And as soon as she got home, she hauled her bowls, measuring cups, and mixer out of the cupboards and got busy making chocolate chip pecan cookies.

Dirk and Tammy kept her company, sitting at her kitchen table, watching, waiting, and offering advice.

When Savannah dumped in a cup full of brown sugar, Tammy grimaced and took a swig from a glass filled with her favorite beverage—filtered, organic, pure, mountain spring water.

Until Savannah met Tammy, she wasn't aware there was such a thing as "organic" water. And she was pretty sure that, in spite of the high price and fancy labeling, the sparkling, crystalline stuff was coming from somebody's backyard garden hose in Oxnard.

"You know," Tammy said, "you could put honey and whole wheat flour in those cookies, and they'd be a lot healthier."

"Or . . ." Dirk added for good measure, ". . . you could triple the recipe and give me a care package to take home with me."

"Or I could ignore the two of you and do things the way I want to."

Tammy nodded. "That's always an option. Not the best one, but . . ."

"Hush up and drink your water, Nature Girl." Savannah tossed twice the amount of chocolate chips into the dough. She'd learned long ago not to scrimp on the goodies when concocting a bribe.

"How long till those things will be ready?" Dirk asked for the fourth time since he had sat down at her table.

"Fifteen minutes," she replied, "unless you ask me again, and then it'll be five days."

"Five days?" His face fell. "How come five days?"

" 'Cause it'll probably be five days before I'm in the mood to do more baking."

"Oh."

"Get a chicken leg out of the ice box and gnaw on that while you're waiting."

"Okay!" He jumped up from the table and nearly knocked her over as he passed her on his way to the refrigerator.

Tammy shook her head. "When it comes to food, Dirko, you have no dignity at all."

"What's dignity got to do with anything?" he asked, pulling out a cellophane-wrapped plate of fried chicken.

"He's getting revenge," Savannah said with a snicker.

"What?" Tammy watched him bite into a drumstick with gusto.

"Long story," he mumbled. "And a private one, Savannah. Keep it to yourself."

"Do you really think someone's trying to kill our client's grandmother?" Tammy asked, watching Savannah drop the spoonfuls of batter onto a cookie sheet.

Savannah smiled, thinking how sweet it was that Tammy referred to every person who walked through Savannah's front door as "our" client. Poor girl. She got precious little payment for her labors on behalf of the Moonlight Magnolia Detective Agency. Whatever modicum of self-satisfaction she received from her mundane duties of answering the phone, doing paperwork, and computer research was well deserved.

"I think it's highly likely," Savannah said. "And what really burns my biscuits is that they're not only trying to do her harm, but trying to make her look like a doddering old fool in the process. I don't cotton to that sort of mistreatment of the elderly."

Tammy grinned. "Granny Reid wouldn't have anything to do with that, would she?"

Savannah shoved the cookies into the oven with far more vigor than necessary. "I'm sure she's a bit of a factor. When you've got somebody in your life, someone you love, who's older, but full of life and vital, it makes you realize how disrespectfully our senior citizens are treated."

"Yeah," Dirk said, "and the older you get, the more you realize you're gonna be in the same boat someday. It makes you think."

Tammy nodded in solemn agreement. "That's

so true. And speaking of Granny Reid, when is she coming to see us again? I miss her."

Savannah wiped her hands on a dish towel and walked to the refrigerator. She reached inside and took out a pitcher of tea. "Not for a while. She started taking a class on art appreciation at the community college over in Halderville, and that's filled up all her spare time."

Tammy sighed. "I hope I'm like her when I'm her age."

"Heck," Savannah said, "I'd be happy to be like her at *my* age."

Savannah poured herself a large glass of tea and tossed in some ice cubes. Then she joined Dirk and Tammy at the table.

"You know," Dirk said, "even if the lab finds something in those samples, we're not going to be able to nail anybody with just that and some loose dirt on a path."

"I know." Savannah traced the top of the frosty glass with her fingertip. "But it's a start."

"What did the gardener have to say about that soft spot on the road?" Tammy asked, glancing at her watch.

"We showed it to him when he was taking us to the house," Savannah said. "He acted like it was the first time he'd seen it or heard anything about it."

"Did you believe him?"

Savannah shrugged. "I guess. I swear people are better at lying than they used to be. It's getting harder and harder to tell."

"But if the gardener rescued her off the cliff," Tammy reasoned, "and the trench was the cause of her accident, it would have still been there. It seems like he would have seen it."

"She says she hung there on the cliff for half an hour, yelling for somebody to help her before he came along," Dirk said. "Whoever dug it in the first place would have had enough time to fill it back in."

Savannah nodded. "If I'd set up an accident like that, I wouldn't be able to resist hanging around in the bushes somewhere, waiting to see if it worked."

Dirk walked over to the waste can and disposed of his drumstick bone. Pulling some paper towels off the roll, he said, "It wouldn't take more than two minutes to shovel that dirt back in place and stomp it down."

He wiped his fingers and his face, then pitched the towels into the garbage. "He could have had everything looking normal before the gardener even heard her cries for help."

"Or the gardener himself could have done it all," Tammy said. "He may have set her up, and then changed his mind when he heard her yelling and pulled her off the cliff."

Savannah shook her head. "I doubt it. Why go to all that trouble and risk your own life to save her if you're just going to poison her later?"

"I didn't like his wife," Dirk said. "She acted hinky when she first saw us."

"Yeah." Savannah took a sip of tea. "And I heard her say something on the phone in Spanish. It sounded like, 'be careful what you say.' "

"A lot of people are paranoid. It doesn't necessarily mean they've broken the law," Tammy said, glancing up at Savannah's cat clock with its swinging tail and rolling eyes.

"You got someplace you gotta be, sugar?" Savannah asked her.

Tammy grinned. "Actually, someone's dropping by in a few minutes to get me."

Savannah was all ears. "Oh? Someone special? Like maybe that new boyfriend we keep hearing about?"

Blushing, Tammy nodded. "Yeah . . . but you have to be nice to him."

"Nice?" Dirk said. "We have to be nice? To heck with 'nice.' How much fun would *that* be?"

"We'll be absolutely adorable to your new honey-bunny," Savannah said, kicking Dirk under the table. "I'll give him cookies and milk, and Dirk can ask him if he's on parole or—"

"Oh, God . . . I'm doomed." Tammy put her hands over her face.

The oven timer went off and the phone rang simultaneously. Savannah jumped up and ran to the stove. Tammy hurried to the counter and grabbed the phone.

"Moonlight Magnolia Detective Agency," she said in her breathiest, most sultry tone.

Once Savannah had suggested that she sounded more like she was answering the phone on a Talk-Dirty-to-Me-Because-I'm-A-Loser-with-No-Love-Life line. Tammy had taken the gentle criticism to heart . . . for one day. Then it was back to her usual, wannabe Marilyn Monroe.

As Savannah pulled the cookie sheet from the oven, she heard Tammy say, "Oh, hi, Eileen. Yes, she's just taking your cookies out right now. Let me get her for you."

Savannah glanced over at Dirk and saw her own anxious anticipation on his face.

She took the phone from Tammy. "Hey, girl. What's shakin' over there?"

"You were right."

Savannah had to admit, as a general rule, those words were sweet to hear—even when spoken by Eileen in that gravelly, deep voice. But this time, Savannah would have preferred to hear that she was mistaken.

It wasn't always a blessing . . . being right.

"What did you find?" she asked, nodding to Dirk.

He sat up straight in his chair.

"We found," Eileen said, "Zolpedone in the cocoa, just like you suspected."

"How much?"

"Well, let me explain it like this: If you were to use the entire container of cocoa to make one cup of hot chocolate—impossible, obviously—you'd consume enough to kill a horse. But the amount you'd use for one nightly mug full . . . it would be the equivalent of a triple dose. Certainly not a healthy amount, but probably not fatal."

"Which would explain why it didn't kill her, just knocked her out for hours," Savannah mused. "Anything else?"

"That's all we found. The sugar, vanilla, and half-and-half were uncontaminated."

"Thank you, Eileen. I owe you." She looked over at the golden brown cookies cooling on the baking sheet. "In fact, your bribery payment just came out of the oven."

"Don't worry about it," Eileen replied. "I love your cookies, but, considering our results, I'm sure you have more important things to do. Like saving that lady's life."

"You're a gem, Eileen."

"Good luck."

"Thank you."

Savannah hung up the phone and turned to Dirk and Tammy. "The sleep-aid medication was in the cocoa."

"I gathered," Dirk said. "And that makes it official—attempted murder."

"Who would want to kill an elderly woman who makes dolls?" Tammy said. "That's sorta like trying to murder Mrs. Claus."

Savannah nodded. "And they're not only mean, but a bit on the stupid side. At the very least, we know our would-be killer isn't much of a cook. They had no clue how much cocoa it takes to make a cup of hot chocolate. And that's probably what saved Helene Strauss's life."

The doorbell rang, and Tammy jumped like someone had touched her backside with a live wire.

"Oh! I'll bet that's him!" she said, racing out of the kitchen and through the living room to the front door.

"Wow," Savannah said to Dirk. "He must be something pretty special to get a rise like that out of her."

Dirk grunted. "Men. We're scum buckets—every last one of us. And nobody knows that better than us guys. If you women knew half of what we're up to, you'd kill us all in our sleep."

Savannah stared at him a moment, then slowly nodded. "Ooookay. Good to know."

A couple of moments later, Tammy walked into the kitchen holding the hand of an extremely tall, blond stud muffin with a blinding white smile, bright blue eyes, and muscles that rippled inside his snug, designer polo shirt when he reached out to shake Savannah's hand.

"Hi," he said, teeth flashing, eyes sparkling. "I'm Chad."

He squeezed Savannah's hand so hard that she winced.

"Most pleased to make your acquaintance," she said through gritted teeth. She pulled her fingers out of his grasp and waved toward Dirk. "Chad, I'd like you to meet my friend, Detective Sergeant Dirk Coulter."

Dirk received a smile from Chad, too, though Savannah noted it wasn't as bright as the one he had given her.

The handshake was just as firm; she could tell by the way Dirk flinched and scowled.

"It's an honor to meet you, sir," Chad told him. "Tammy's told me so much about you. I'm a great supporter of law enforcement."

"*Are* you, now . . . ?" Dirk's eyes bored into Chad's, and Savannah could see the younger man grimace as Dirk returned the crushing grip—plus a bit more for good measure.

Tammy looked alarmed and whispered to Dirk, "Nice . . . nice . . ."

Savannah jumped to the rescue. "How about some cookies, Chad? Chocolate chip . . . still warm and gooey."

She decided against offering him a glass of milk to go with it. Now that she had seen him in all of his six-feet, three-inch, two-hundred-twenty-pound frame, a kindergartner's snack seemed inappropriate.

"I can make a fresh pot of coffee to go with the

cookies, if you've got time to sit a spell," she said instead.

"No, thanks," Chad said, rubbing the fingers of his right hand, which no doubt ached after Dirk's revenge shake. "We have to get going, or we'll be late for the auto show. I want to be there when they open the doors. I don't like being late."

He glanced up and down Tammy's turquoise suit with an obvious look of disdain on his handsome face.

Savannah decided it was a face that was getting less handsome by the moment, sparkling teeth or not.

"I'm going to have to take you home first," he told Tammy, "so you can change. You aren't going anywhere with me wearing that outfit. Where did you buy that? The local thrift store?"

When Savannah saw the hurt and embarrassment on Tammy's face, her temper flared. For a moment, she imagined what it would be like to lop off Chad's head with a sword and watch it roll across the floor.

Would it still be smiling ear-to-ear, white teeth flashing?

"We had a special client appointment this morning," Savannah told him, keeping her voice low and even. "I asked Tammy to dress up a bit for the occasion."

"I guess I'll have to teach you how to dress," he told Tammy. "Anybody with a smokin' hot body like yours shouldn't wear something out of an old lady's closet."

Savannah couldn't hold back any longer. "Whoa, Chad, you really need to watch your—"

"It's okay," Tammy said, grabbing Savannah's

arm. "Really. I do need to change before we go out. I don't know what I was thinking wearing this. I just . . ."

Tammy gazed up at her date with a mixture of adoration, nervousness, and fear that made Savannah's stomach churn.

"We have to go," Tammy said, releasing Savannah and scurrying to pick up her purse from the table. "Chad is a very punctual person, and, well . . . I'll see you tomorrow, okay?"

"Yeah, okay." Savannah watched as the two of them turned and walked toward the back door.

"Nice meeting you," Chad called back over his shoulder.

He didn't wait for a reply before he walked out the door, leaving Tammy to follow dutifully in his wake.

Savannah barely waited for the door to close before she said, "Oh . . . oh, how I hate him."

She turned to Dirk, and one look at his face told her he was feeling the same as she was. Sick and furious.

"What I just told you about all men being scum . . . ?" he said.

"Yeah?"

"That's just us regular guys. That one there . . . he's in another category all together."

Chapter 7

Savannah wasn't sure what she was expecting when she arrived at Strauss Doll Works, Inc. But whatever image her imagination might have conjured up as the birthplace of all those beautiful dolls, it hadn't been this.

She hadn't thought she would find a Bavarian, storybook structure like the Strauss mansion in downtown Los Angeles. She had visited the neighborhood too many times to be that naïve. Nor had she believed it would look like a Santa's workshop.

But somehow, she hadn't anticipated a suite of offices on the thirty-second floor of a steel, glass, and concrete high-rise.

And as she stepped off the elevator and onto the plush, dove gray carpeting and walked toward the giant glass door with its gracefully etched "SDW" logo, it also occurred to her that doll making was a lucrative business. At least, for the Strauss family.

On the other side of the door was a posh reception area with white leather chairs and sleek chrome tables. On the walls hung beautiful black-and-white photos of children playing with some of the better-known Strauss dolls . . . including the famous "Helene" doll, like the one Savannah owned.

She walked up to the receptionist, a sharply dressed young man in his twenties with a business-like, barely civil half smile.

"Good afternoon," he said with a sigh, glancing down at his watch. "May I help you?"

"I'm Savannah Reid, here to see Mrs. Strauss."

"By 'Mrs. Strauss,' I assume you mean Helene?" he asked with a slightly elevated nose.

"Sorry. I keep forgetting. I'm just not accustomed to referring to my elders by their first names. Where I'm from, a youngun can get switched for that."

"I see."

She could tell he didn't see. Had zero interest in seeing. But it didn't bother her much.

"Will you please inform Helene that I'm here?"

He glanced down at an open, leather-bound scheduling book on the counter in front of him. "You have an appointment?"

"I spoke to her earlier on the phone. She said I should come here to talk to her in person."

Once again, he glanced at his watch.

Her last thread of patience unraveled. "Look. I know it's seven minutes to five and you're, no doubt, poised to bolt through that door in six minutes. But I just drove like a bat outta hell all the way from San Carmelita, through LA traffic and smog, to get here before five, so that I could talk to Mrs. . . . . Miss Helene. And unless you want me to start a big ruckus that'll last at least an hour and a half, you'd better tell her I'm here. Make it snappy."

Rolling his eyes like a petulant adolescent, he reached for the phone. He punched in a number and waited, tapping his fingers on the desk. "Yes, I'm sorry to bother you," he said into the phone. "I know you're getting ready to leave for the day"—He gave Savannah an annoyed look, which she returned with dividends—"there's a Savannah Leed to see you."

"Reid."

"Excuse me. *Reid*." He listened for a moment. Then he gave Savannah another quick look—one that held a smidgen of respect. "Yes, ma'am. I'll bring her right back."

He hung up. "This way, please, Ms. Reid. She's in Ms. Fischer's office. I'd be glad to take you there."

As he escorted her down a long corridor, past what seemed like endless offices, he seemed nervous. All cockiness gone.

"Apparently, you're a . . . um . . . friend of Helene's," he said.

"Apparently so," she replied, wondering at this change in his behavior.

"She doesn't come to the offices very often. In fact, I've been here three months, and today was the first time I've ever seen her."

Savannah decided not to mention that, before today, she had never seen the lady either.

"She seems to be in a bad mood," he continued. "I mean, not 'bad,' just, well, she got kind of mad that I said your name wrong."

Savannah stopped in the middle of the hallway and laid one hand lightly on his arm. "Young man, I'm not going to make a big deal out of you getting my name wrong. In the overall scope of human events, that's not a biggie."

"Thank you," he said.

"And I'm not going to mention to your boss that you acted like a jackass when you 'greeted' me at the desk. But you've got a job, and these days, a lot of folks don't. You need to be a wee bit more grateful . . . and a sight better at it."

He nodded sheepishly.

Ahead, at the end of the hall, was a doorway with silver lettering that said, ADA FISCHER, PRESIDENT. Savannah pointed to it. "I think I can find my own way from here."

As the receptionist trailed away, Savannah approached the office door and paused, ready to knock. But inside she could hear two women arguing, and she couldn't resist hesitating just a moment to eavesdrop.

"If you keep this up, Aunt Helene, I'm going to have to put you away somewhere," one woman said, "where people can keep an eye on you. We can't have you running around delusional like this. You could hurt yourself."

"I have no intention of hurting myself," answered a strong, distinctive voice that Savannah instantly recognized as Helene's. "If I hurt anybody around here, it's going to be *you*! I came down here to warn you . . . do not mess with me!"

Savannah thought she'd better intervene, so she knocked softly on the door.

"Are you threatening me?" asked the first woman. "You better not be, because that sounds like a threat to me!"

Savannah knocked louder, and there was an instant hush inside the room.

"That's her," Helene said. "The woman I was telling you about. I've got somebody on my side now, missy. Somebody who believes me when I tell her I'm perfectly fine and not imagining anything!"

The door swung open, and Savannah found herself face-to-face with a very red-faced Helene. The quaint, Southern phrase, "she's so mad, she's spittin' fire," came to mind as she stared at her new friend.

"Helene," she said, walking into the office and putting her hands on the woman's shoulders, "you've gotta calm down there. Your blood pressure's gotta be through the roof."

"Don't you worry about my blood pressure." Helene brushed her hands away. "I've got entirely too many people worrying about things that aren't any of their business!"

Savannah held up her hands in surrender. "Okay, okay. I understand. I don't like it when people tell me what I should, or shouldn't, be thinking or feeling. And I reckon you're just the same."

"Thank you. Now get *her* to understand that, and we'll all be better off!"

Helene pointed to a woman standing behind an enormous desk, arms crossed over her chest, an ugly frown on her heavily made-up and obviously surgically enhanced face.

Without being told, Savannah was pretty darned

sure this was the infamous and much-despised niece.

From her frosted and permed, big, blond hair to her hot pink lipstick, Cleopatra eyeliner, and aqua eye shadow, it was pretty obvious that Ada was stuck on a look that had worked for her twenty-plus years ago . . . and never would again. And the plastic surgeon's efforts to erase every line, raise sagging eyebrows, and plump naturally thinning lips had stolen any hope of graceful aging without recapturing the bloom of youth.

As Savannah glanced over the woman's expensive, designer suit, heels, and jewelry, she did a quick calculation and decided that Ada's outfit cost more than most people's cars.

But the elegance of the linen tweed ensemble and Rodeo Drive jewels was ruined by the too-tight fit of the suit and the plunging neckline of the sheer lace blouse she wore beneath it.

For a woman in her fifties, Ada had a nice figure—including a suspiciously perky bustline—but she just seemed to be trying too hard.

Savannah thought of something her grandmother had always told her: "You don't have to remind the world who you used to be. Just celebrate who you've become!"

Extending her hand, Savannah walked over to Ada. "I'm Savannah Reid. Glad to meet you."

Ada glanced down at the outstretched hand but kept her arms crossed over her chest. She gave Savannah a look of such pure contempt that, for a moment, Savannah wondered if she had dirt on her hands or chocolate smeared across her face.

Either way, she felt a bit stupid, standing there

with her hand out. So, she smiled . . . reached up and rubbed her nose with her extended middle finger.

She heard a chuckle and glanced at Helene, who was standing beside her—green eyes sparkling with mischief.

"My feelings exactly," Helene said.

"What?" Ada looked from Savannah to her aunt, a look of total annoyance and confusion on her face.

"Nothing, my dear niece," Helene said without a trace of familial affection. "Let's just say, I invited Savannah here for a reason . . . which should be apparent to her right now."

"Oh, I was perfectly prepared to take your word for it," Savannah said, "but seeing is believing, for sure."

Ada stepped behind her desk and pulled her purse from the bottom drawer. "If you two," she said, "want to have this private little conversation, I suggest you take it out of my office. *I'm* leaving for the day. Unlike *you*, Aunt Helene, I have a life. I have something to do and someone to do it with."

Helene snickered. "If you call that harebrained, pinhead gigolo 'someone' . . ."

"I don't keep Vern around for his wit," Ada said with a toss of her head and massive hair.

Savannah was sure Ada thought the movement sexy. Savannah wondered if she had a good chiropractor. If she did that frequently, she would need one.

"Nobody's sure why you keep Vern around," Helene told her niece. "But it's obvious why he stays."

"Vern *loves* me."

"Vern loves anything in a skirt with a checkbook."

"You're just jealous!"

Helene's green eyes flashed. "Of your little boy toy? In case you've forgotten, I could have had Vern. I didn't want him. I don't need a piece of fluff like that to convince myself that I'm still twenty-five."

Ada rushed around the desk and, for a moment, Savannah thought she was going to have to get between the two women to protect her friend. But Ada stopped short, a few feet from Helene. "Get out of my office! Now!"

"We were just leaving." Helene walked over to a display shelf, where a number of dolls stood. She snatched one of them and headed for the door.

"Hey!" Ada headed after her. "Put that back!"

"I will not!" Helene hugged the doll to her chest. "This monstrosity is *not* going into our line!"

"I've spent a fortune developing that doll, and it's debuting at IDEX, no matter what you do!"

"We'll see about that." Helene grabbed Savannah by the elbow and shoved her toward the door. "Come on, Savannah. We're out of here."

As Helene shoved her out of the office, Savannah collided head-on with an Armani suit.

For a moment, she was nose-to-nose and chest-to-chest with a fellow she could only describe as "handsome in a local-channel-weatherman sort of way."

From his too-orange fake-bake tan to his recently installed hair plugs, he seemed the perfect male counterpart to Ada Fischer . . . other than the fact that he was about twenty years her junior.

Like her, no expense had been spared in the pursuit of personal enhancement, but the investment had paid disappointing dividends.

"Excuse me," she said, as she backed away, removing her ample bosom from the vicinity of his suit lapels.

"No problem," he replied, looking her up and down with thinly veiled lechery. "And who are you?"

"Nobody you'd be interested in, Vern," Helene said, pulling Savannah on down the hall. "She doesn't have a Fortune 500 company or a fat trust fund."

Instantly, Ada appeared in the office doorway. She grabbed Vern by the arm, yanked him inside, and slammed the door.

"That was Vern, the cheap gigolo," Helene said as she and Savannah walked away.

"Yes, I gathered," Savannah replied. "But judging from the suit, gold watch, and diamond pinky ring, I don't know if I'd call him 'cheap.' He looks like an expensive pastime to me."

"Cheap as in tasteless, flashy, raunchy, and trashy. He's an overdressed pig. A waste of a beautiful suit."

Savannah grinned down at the feisty lady at her side . . . so much like her own grandmother. "Why don't you tell me how you really feel about him, Helene?"

"I've hated Vern Oldham since the moment I first laid eyes on him. And he's hated me since the moment I gave him a fat lip and flattened his balls."

"You flattened his—"

"Yes, and if he ever tried to climb into bed with me again, I'd do it a second time . . . and he'd need more than an ice pack to set things right."

Visions swirled, unbidden, through Savannah's head. Strange, awful images: Vern crawling into bed with a woman old enough to be his grandmother, Helene delivering a crushing blow to his nether regions, Vern clutching an ice pack to his—

She shook her head, trying to clear her brain. After watching Jesse Murphy dance around with a roll of toilet paper between his legs, she'd seen, and imagined, enough male groin injuries to last her for a while. She didn't need Vern and his ice bag in her brain, too.

"So, are you disappointed in me?" Helene grinned, her eyes twinkling. "Kneeing a guy in the crotch like that . . . maybe I'm not the great lady you thought I was."

Savannah returned the smile. "Quite the contrary. You've risen a few notches in my estimation. I'd have done the very same, and so would anybody I'm related to."

"Sounds like you come from a family of great ladies yourself."

"Well, feisty females, to be sure." She laced her arm through Helene's. "You see," she said, "I'm from south of the Mason-Dixon Line. And down there, we handle things a mite different when a guy messes with one of our womenfolk."

"Oh?"

"Yes, ma'am. We don't abide such nonsense. If that polecat Vern ever tries anything ungentlemanly like that again with you, you just let me

know, and I'll shoot him between the eyes . . . or
any other place of your choosing."

"Can I watch?"

"You can hold him down while I do it."

"That's a deal."

Chapter 8

Helene led Savannah to the opposite end of the suite and a door that bore gold letters, identifying it as the office of "Helene Strauss, CEO."

When they went inside, Savannah's spirit took a deep breath and her imagination took flight.

This was what a doll maker's studio should look like . . . at least in her estimation.

Unlike Ada's cold, sterile space with its bare, stark white walls and glass and steel furniture, this room had warm, creamy tones that complemented the wood furnishings. A large desk with ornately carved, filigree scrollwork dominated the center of the room. And, like the great room of the Strauss mansion, wooden shelves lined the walls, filled with beautiful dolls.

To the right, floor-to-ceiling windows provided a sweeping view of the City of Angels. But it wasn't the panorama of Los Angeles that caught Savannah's eye. It was the large picture on the back wall, behind the desk.

Unlike the black-and-white photos hanging in

the reception area, this one had, obviously, not been taken by a professional. The others had been crisp, artistically shot pictures of children in contemporary clothing in modern settings. But the photograph that dominated the wall in Helene's office was an enlargement of what must have been a very old snapshot, taken many, many years ago.

In the faded, grainy picture, a young girl, maybe six or seven years old, stood on the sidewalk of a quaint, European town. With its half-timbered buildings and steeply pitched roofs, the village reminded Savannah of the Strauss mansion. The child was dressed in a simple, plain dress that seemed a couple of sizes too big for her. A large hair ribbon did little to hold her long ringlets back. They spilled around her sweet, baby face, making her look like a cherub in a Victorian painting.

In her arms, she clutched a doll that bore a striking resemblance to Savannah's Helene doll.

"Is that you?" Savannah asked Helene.

Helene glanced up at the picture for a moment. And in that instant, Savannah saw a look of deep pain and sadness cross her face.

"No," she said simply.

Helene walked over to the desk and, as she sat down, tossed the doll she had brought from Ada's office into a nearby waste can.

"That piece of garbage," she mumbled. "I'd rather be dead than have my company supply something like that to children." She grinned perversely. "Better yet, I'd rather see Ada dead."

"Now, now . . ." Savannah shook her head. "Don't go saying things you don't mean."

When Helene didn't reply, but gave her an even,

unblinking stare, Savannah added, "And if you *do* mean it, that's all the more reason to keep it to yourself. I don't want you confessing to any murders that haven't been committed yet."

"Speaking as a former police officer?" Helene said.

"Yes, but I'll tell you a little secret: There's no such thing as a *former* police officer. Once a cop, always a cop."

Curious, Savannah walked over to the waste can and looked down at the doll inside. "May I?" she asked.

Helene shrugged. "Go ahead . . . as long as you put it back where you found it."

Savannah leaned down and picked the doll out of the can and looked her over.

She was a fashion doll, about fourteen inches tall, with long blond hair, big brown eyes, and a mini-dress and strappy stilettos. While Savannah recognized the outfit as the sort that a lot of hookers wore on Sunset Boulevard, the doll wasn't really any more objectionable than a lot of dolls she had seen recently on toy-store shelves. And even though she usually chose more innocent-looking baby dolls for her nieces, she didn't quite understand Helene's strong reaction to this prototype.

"It's a disgusting piece of trash," Helene said as she sat at her desk, thumbing through a stack of mail. "Ada knew I'd hate it; that's why she didn't show it to me until the last minute . . . thought I couldn't stop it once she had it in production. Well, she's in for a big surprise."

Savannah turned the doll over and over in her hand. Other than the fact that its figure was unrealistically tall and thin, it was a pretty doll with a sweeter than usual face.

"If you don't mind me asking," she said, "why do you hate it so much? I mean, I know the thing about not setting an artificial standard for little girls, but . . ."

"Take off its clothes," Helene told her.

Savannah sat in a side chair next to the desk and removed the doll's dress. On the doll's back, she saw two small buttons . . . one at its waist, another just above it.

"The doll's name," Helene said, "is Spa Helene. Instead of a house or a condo, she comes with a 'spa,' where a male doll, a plastic surgeon, can fix all her so-called imperfections."

"Oh, dear."

"Exactly." Helene shook her head. "Push the top button on her back."

"I'm afraid to."

"You should be afraid. Do it."

Savannah pushed the top button and felt a creepy movement inside the doll. A second later, the doll's bust pushed forward, going from what might have been a B cup to proportions those hookers on Sunset Boulevard would have envied.

"Oh, my goodness," she said.

"Push the bottom one."

Reluctantly, Savannah did, and there was a similar vibration, which resulted in the doll's somewhat flat buttocks transforming into a remarkably rounded rear.

"This is a joke, right?" Savannah said. "A toy to sell in an adult porn store, or—"

"I only wish it were. And that's not all." Helene left her desk and walked over to a carved wooden cupboard. She opened the door, revealing a small refrigerator filled with bottles of water, juices, and fresh fruit. She took out a water bottle and took it back to her desk.

"Give me that thing," she said, pointing to the doll.

Savannah handed it to her.

Helene opened a desk drawer, rummaged around, and brought out a cotton swab.

"It comes with something Ada calls a beauty wand, made to look like some sort of surgical tool. The child wets the end of the tool"—she opened the bottle and dipped the cotton swab inside—"and swipes it across the doll's face like this."

Savannah bent over the desk and watched closely.

As Helene wetted first one eye, then the other, the brown irises turned bright blue. She dampened the pink lips, and they instantly became bright red and at least twice as thick. The cheeks looked like someone had just applied a handful of blush with a trowel.

The transformation was complete. "Spa Helene" had gone from the girl next door to full-fledged tramp. What more could a child want?

"Does Ada really think a toy like this will sell?" Savannah asked. "What mother would buy such a thing for her daughter?"

"Oh, you'd be surprised. The kid throws a fit for it in the aisle of the toy store, and mommy caves. Happens every day."

Helene tossed the doll back into the garbage can, along with the cotton swab. "My niece has some serious body-image issues, and it's clouding— no, destroying—her business judgment. I made a terrible mistake, appointing her president of this company. She's just so different from the person she used to be."

"What changed her?" Savannah asked, settling back into her chair.

"Five years ago, out of the blue, her husband of twenty years ran off with a much younger woman. She loved him dearly. It was such a blow to her self-esteem, I don't think she'll ever get over it."

"That's why all the hair and makeup and clothes that aren't—"

"Age appropriate?"

"Something like that."

"Yes. When he left her, she lost weight, started working out compulsively at the gym, bleached her hair, and had a ton of plastic surgery to enhance this and take away that." Helene sighed and shook her head. "Don't get me wrong. I'm all for self-improvement, making the best of what you've got, all that. But Ada was a beautiful woman before . . . and now, I don't even recognize the person she's become, inside or out. She was truly dear to me. I miss her."

In the heavy silence that followed, Savannah thought long and hard about what she was going to say. She didn't want to alarm the woman, but . . .

"Helene," she said, as gently as she could, "I know there's been bad blood between you and Ada. I have to ask you: Do you think your niece could do you harm?"

"If you'd asked me that question five years ago, I would have thought you were crazy. I never believed that little girl I watched grow up, who loved me and I loved her, would ever be a threat to me. I'd have told you that I would die for her and her for me."

Helene stood and walked over to the picture of the child with the doll on the wall. She looked up at it a long time.

Finally, she turned to Savannah with tears in her eyes. "Everything changes, Savannah," she said. "People, places, circumstances . . . everything changes with time. Often in ways you can't even imagine."

She walked back to the desk and slumped into her chair, suddenly looking her age . . . and maybe a few years more.

She added, "I think the hardest thing in life is to acknowledge those changes and not become bitter when they happen."

Savannah sensed Helene was speaking of more than a niece's betrayal, but she decided not to pry.

"You ask me if my niece could do me harm, but what you mean is, do I think she's capable of murdering me. Right?"

Savannah nodded.

Helene took a tissue from inside her desk, dabbed at her eyes, then tossed it in the trash with the discarded doll. "That's another of life's hard lessons I've learned, Savannah. Human beings are capable of anything."

By the time Savannah had driven through the Los Angeles late-rush-hour traffic and arrived back in quiet, seaside San Carmelita, it was past dinner time, and her presupper dropsies were in full control. There was nothing quite like low blood sugar and drivers cutting you off, and then flipping you off, to make a girl want to draw her weapon and shoot out a few tires.

She debated about swinging into a fast-food joint, getting something from the window, and eating off her lap. But after a hard day, she had a yen for her own good home cooking.

Other than the problems in the Strauss family, there was nothing wrong with her world that some chicken and dumplings couldn't fix.

If only she'd thought to poke a few of those chocolate chip cookies in her purse before setting out for the big city.

Another reason to head home and cook a meal was the prospect of luring Dirk to her house for the evening. Not that Dirk required "luring" by any stretch of the imagination. She was convinced he could smell her cooking anywhere in town, because he invariably showed up just as she was setting the table.

The first few years of their friendship, she had complained about that. But along the way, she had admitted—at least to herself—that she would much prefer to sit down to a table with him than to eat in front of the TV with her two cats.

Diamante and Cleopatra were better conversationalists, but . . . being cats . . . they were finicky. And it was much more fun to cook for someone like Dirk, who was wildly in love with everything you put on his plate.

As she sat, waiting for a particularly slow light to cycle, she reached into her purse and pulled out her cell phone. She punched in his number and put it on speaker.

"Hey, you," he said, sounding a bit more chipper than usual . . . or, at least, less grumpy.

"Hey, yourself. Wanna come over for dinner tonight?"

"Yeah, sure. But I'm hungry now."

"So, come over now. I'm five minutes from the house."

Click.

He was on his way.

She grinned and hung up. That's what she liked . . . a guy who played hard to get.

Savannah sat in her cozy chair, holding an equally cozy dish of Ben & Jerry's Chunky Monkey ice cream with a hearty helping of hot fudge on top.

Her cats sat on either sides of her house slippers on the footstool, covetously eyeing every bite she took.

Sprawled on her sofa, his feet propped on her coffee table, Dirk had his own bowl. But his was Cherry Garcia—also with hot fudge. They could never agree on a single flavor, and that was a good thing, because neither was likely to share a pint without significant bloodshed.

"I appreciate you running those checks for me," she said, digging out a particularly large chocolate chunk with her spoon.

"No problem." He scooped up a ridiculously big spoonful, and she gave him the same sort of disapproving look as when he was eating ribs and got barbecue sauce on the backs of his fists.

He took a smaller portion and said, "Are you going to tell Waldo's grandma on him?"

"She's not his grandmother. She's his great-aunt. And I have a feeling she already knows he has a record. I wouldn't be surprised if she was the one who bailed him out and paid for his lawyers."

"I've known women like that. They overlook all sorts of things they shouldn't when it comes to the men in their lives."

"Like putting their feet on their coffee tables?"

"I took my shoes off first."

"And leaving the toilet lid up?"

"I'm getting better at that."

"After me yelling at you a hundred times."

"It's a long, slow learning curve."

Savannah dipped her pinky into the melted ice cream and let Cleo lick it off her fingertip. She had to do the same with her ring finger immediately for Diamante or risk a fur-flying cat fight.

"Speaking of women who tolerate more than they should, can you believe Tammy and that new guy of hers?" she said.

"I didn't like the way he was putting her down."

"I didn't like the way she was tolerating him putting her down."

He shrugged. "Tammy's a gentler soul than you are. You would have ripped his head off and handed it to him."

"Actually, I had a fantasy along those lines, only involving a sword."

"We'll have to keep an eye on her."

Savannah thought of the glow she'd seen in Tammy's eyes as she'd gazed up at her new beau. She thought of other women—her friends, her sisters, herself—who had made bad purchases at the registers of the romance department.

"It won't do any good," she told him. "I know the look. No matter what we do or say, she's a goner."

"Guys aren't the only ones with a long, slow learning curve?"

"Nope. Women, too. We all have to love one or two bad guys sometime during our lives so that we can appreciate that good one when he comes along."

He gave her a quick, sideways glance, then concentrated on his ice cream. "And you're still waiting, I guess? For that good one, I mean. . . ."

"The one who looks like Tom Selleck, sings like Elvis, cooks like Emeril, and who can do body work on my Mustang and build an addition onto the back of my house?"

His smile sagged. "Yeah. That dude."

"Naw. I'm not waiting for him. I'd settle for a guy who puts the toilet seat down and keeps his feet off my coffee table."

He sighed, rolled his eyes, and lowered his feet to the floor. "Happy?"

"Ecstatic."

Chapter 9

The next morning, Savannah decided to have a visit with Emma. The granddaughter was, after all, her client, not Helene. And Savannah believed a good private investigator kept her employer well-informed. Well-informed, satisfied clients were more likely to write checks. Checks could be cashed. Electric bills could be paid.

It was a nice system.

So, when Tammy phoned and asked if she could take the morning off, Savannah did the daily paperwork herself and made a few calls, including one to Emma, asking if she could drop by for an investigator-to-client chat.

With any luck, she could pick up that all-important retainer check while she was at it.

Emma's tiny beach cottage was three houses from the ocean on one of the many narrow streets in the area of San Carmelita called The Lanes.

Years ago, The Lanes had been plagued by criminal activity, mostly drug related, and as a cop, Savannah had chased many a fleet-footed perp between these tiny houses that sat only a few feet apart.

But now, the beach-front area had become gentrified. And the town's miscreants could no longer afford to live in the tiny cracker-box houses with their nautical-themed decorations of boat oars, ships' wheels, fishermen's nets, and the occasional dinghy in the postage stamp–sized front yard.

Emma's house was nicer than her neighbors'. Recently painted a cheerful, pale yellow with white trim, the place appeared well-loved. On either side of the door, container gardens bloomed with orange and red nasturtiums, reminding Savannah of Helene's estate.

Emma's sporty little BMW was parked out front on a thin strip of sand between the street and the cottage. Next to the car sat an enormous black van that dwarfed the car and the bungalow. Without a doubt, it was the focal point of the entire block.

Its sides were painted with a giant logo of a skull with red, glowing eyes and nails protruding from it like the bristles of a highly annoyed porcupine. And above the skull, in ornate letters, dripping with blood, were the words, "Poison Nails."

"Lovely," Savannah muttered as she tried to squeeze her Mustang into a spot between the BMW and the van. "You must be the hit of the neighborhood with a monstrosity like that."

As Savannah got out of her car and walked up to the cottage, she heard some frenetic, metallic screeching that, at first, she thought was some sort of machinery in its death throes.

The last time she had heard something like that, her Mustang's engine had just thrown a rod on the Ventura Highway.

The racket seemed to be coming from a small shed beside the house.

Then she heard a man's voice shrieking something that sounded like, "Death and blood! Thrash and die!" And she realized it was music. Sort of.

"Great," she mumbled, walking up to the front door. "A catchy little tune like that . . . It'll be stuck in my head all day long."

She knocked on the door and, a moment later, it was opened by a far more casual version of Emma than Savannah had seen the day before.

Wearing a tank top, a pair of baggy men's boxer shorts, and hot pink flip-flops, Emma looked like most of the other residents of The Lanes—relaxed and ready for a day of doing absolutely nothing.

Savannah decided she wanted to be a Lanes resident when she grew up someday.

"Good morning, Savannah," Emma said, throwing the door wide open. "Come on in."

"And a good morning to you, too."

Savannah walked inside the tiny house with a living room that was approximately the size of her own bathroom.

One glance around told her that the place had once been decorated with careful consideration and good taste. Like the exterior, yellow and white were the principal tones on the walls and country cottage furniture. The sofa was upholstered in a cheerful lemon and cream French toile, accented by sapphire throw pillows.

A collection of antique cobalt blue bottles sat on shelves in the windows, sparkling in the morning light.

And several bright, colorful, abstract watercolors hung on the walls. Savannah recalled what

Helene had said about Emma being a talented artist, and she suspected they were hers.

But like the space in front of Emma's house, this area had also been invaded by an alien presence.

When Emma invited Savannah to take a seat on the sofa, she could hardly walk across the floor without tripping over the jumble of musical equipment. Black electronic boxes—small, large, and enormous—connected by what seemed like miles of tangled cords occupied nearly every inch of spare space in the small room.

"Sorry about the mess," Emma said as Savannah nearly sat on a microphone shaped like a penis with pointed studs protruding from the top.

Gingerly holding it with two fingers, Savannah moved the mic to a nearby chair. "A girl wouldn't wanna park herself on something like that," she said. "She'd wind up sitting on a heating pad for the rest of the day."

"Like I told you at Oma's, my boyfriend, Kyd, is in a band," Emma said, plopping down on the other end of the sofa. "You probably heard him practicing when you walked up."

Savannah listened for a moment to the screeching and shouting, which could still be heard all too clearly. "Uh . . . yes. And I'm still enjoying it, even in here," she said. "I saw his van outside. Poison Nails, huh? Creative name. Did he think of that himself?"

"Yes." She shrugged and looked a little embarrassed. "It's not everybody's cup of tea, but . . ."

"Hey, art comes in all forms. Expression of the human spirit and all that."

A particularly loud screech set Savannah's teeth

on edge and made her think of the time Dirk had accidentally stepped on Cleopatra's tail, hard enough to warrant a visit to the vet.

She wondered what aspect of Kyd's spirit that particular riff expressed. Would it qualify as pure demon possession or just a case of bad taste?

"I came to talk to you about your grandmother," Savannah said. "And to tell you what I've uncovered so far."

"Actually, Oma Helene called me this morning, right after you did. She told me that you found sleeping medication in her cocoa."

"Yes, the police lab processed it yesterday and confirmed my worst suspicions."

"The police are involved now?"

Savannah nodded. "I invited a friend of mine to your grandmother's property to have a look and give me his impressions. He's a detective in the San Carmelita Police Department. I was his partner for a long time, back when I was a cop. He's a little rough around the edges, but he's a gifted investigator."

"And he thinks there's foul play, too?"

"Absolutely. We also found an area of the road that had been dug out, right by where your grandmother lost control of her motorbike. We figure that's at least two serious attempts on her life."

Emma bit her lower lip and blinked her eyes several times. "Then it's true. Someone's trying to kill Oma. I can't believe it. I knew it, but to hear you say it makes it so real, so horrible."

"I'm sorry, Emma. It must be very upsetting. But at least you got help for your grandmother, and that's what's important right now. We have to do everything we can to keep her safe."

Emma thought for a moment. "I'll move out there with her, at least for now. If I'm there at the house, I can keep an eye on her, make sure no one gets to her . . . hurts her."

"If you can do that, I think it's a great idea. And I have an even better one, if you'd be willing to entertain it."

"Sure. Anything for Oma."

"I talked to her about this yesterday, when I saw her there at her offices in Los Angeles. But she pitched a fit—wouldn't hear of it. Maybe you could persuade her. . . ."

"If you think it's a good idea, I'll give it a try. What is it?"

"I know these two men—dear, dear friends of mine for years—who are professional bodyguards. They're the best of the best . . . former FBI agents who've provided security for some of the—"

"No, no. Oma would *never*—"

"I know. She nearly threw me out of her office on my ear when I mentioned them to her. But if she could only meet them. They've got more charm than the law should allow. I promise you, she'd want to marry John and adopt Ryan on the spot."

"I can't imagine her agreeing to have bodyguards. My grandmother really values her privacy. That's why she insists on having her staff live in separate quarters from the main house."

"I understand. But for right now, until we can figure out what's going on and who's trying to hurt her . . ."

"I agree. It's a good idea. I'll see what I can do."

"Thank you."

Hearing another particularly loud and unpleasant blast of noise from the shed, Savannah glanced over at the studded microphone and thought of the unpleasant men she had encountered in the past twenty-four hours.

"By the way," she said, "I had the misfortune of literally bumping into Vern yesterday at your grandmother's offices. What can you tell me about him?"

Emma's big green eyes went cold at the mention of his name. She crossed her arms over the front of her tank top. "Vern is a slimy rat, pure vermin, who should have been exterminated long ago."

"That was pretty much my take on him, too."

"He should have been arrested for what he tried to do to my grandmother."

"What she told me was true, then? He tried to seduce her?"

"*Seduce* her? *Rape* her is more like it. He snuck into her house at night and tried to climb into bed with her while she was sleeping."

Emma smiled a nasty little smirk and nodded. "She hurt him really bad. It's a wonder she didn't shoot him. He's lucky to have escaped with his life."

Savannah chuckled. "I like your grandmother. I'm sure mine would have reacted the same way. We come from feisty stock, you and I."

Emma laughed. "It's true. We do."

"And does Ada know about all this?"

"She does. Oma told her right away, but she refused to believe it. Called my grandmother a liar."

"I'm sure that went over well with Helene."

"I think Ada believed her more than she let on. Right after it happened, Ada took away Vern's new

Ferrari and his president's Rolex. I'm sure there was some sort of connection."

"Poor Vern."

"Yeah. Life was hardly worth living for him without his new Ferrari and Rolex. He had to go back to his old Rolex and last year's Ferrari."

"Not to mention his flat, bruised equipment."

At that moment, the back door opened and a guy with spiked black hair, heavy eye makeup, and at least half a dozen studs protruding from his face walked in. He carried a guitar decorated with a skull and crossbones. His bare chest bore the tattoo of a giant grim reaper.

Just the sort of guy you wanted to bring home to Mom.

Or maybe not, Savannah decided.

Instantly, she could see that Kyd was as appealing as his music. And she could also understand why matriarch Helene wasn't enamored with him.

"Hi," he said when he saw her. "Who are you?"

"Savannah," Emma said, "this is my boyfriend, Kyd. Baby, this is Savannah Reid, the lady I told you about. The one I hired to help Oma."

"Oh, yeah. The private investigator." He walked to Savannah and held out his hand. "That's pretty cool, what you do. You find lost people and catch cheating husbands and cool stuff like that, right?"

"We pretty much leave the cheating husbands to their wives to catch, but we've found some lost people, yes."

He pulled a large speaker monitor off a chair and onto the floor and took a seat.

Savannah noticed he had skulls and crossbones on his flannel pajama bottoms, too. *Definitely a case of fashion stagnation and death fixation,* she told herself.

As though reading her thoughts, he said, "You ever find dead people or catch murderers, cool stuff like that?"

She thought if he used the word "cool" one more time, she might smack him with his dickshaped microphone.

"I've found a few dead people in my time," she said in her most patient, long-suffering voice—the one she reserved for fools who deeply annoyed her. "It wasn't cool at all. I've also brought some killers to justice. Now, *that* was cool. Extremely cool, in fact."

He gave her a long, appraising look. "I guess you'd have to be pretty smart to do that."

She shrugged. "Everybody's smart in one way or another, about one thing or the other. I guess I'm smart in that way."

"Kyd's an amazing musician," Emma piped up. "People don't realize how hard it is to play death metal. It's like jazz in a way . . . harder than you might think if you aren't into it."

"You like death metal?" Kyd asked Savannah with a sarcastic little grin, as though defying her to say she didn't.

"Not really," she said. "I guess the lyrics turn me off."

He dropped the grin. "They aren't meant to be taken literally. Everybody knows that. Everybody who's *knowledgeable* about the art form, that is."

"No," she said. "Of course not. No one in their right mind would take subjects like rape, torture, murder, and dismemberment seriously."

Kyd stood and ran his fingers through his spiked hair, re-encouraging it to stand on end. He adjusted his sagging pajama bottoms that were about to fall off. "I gotta go practice some more," he told Savannah. "We got a gig tonight at Hell's Inferno in the valley. If you've got nothing else to do, no killers to catch, drop by, and I'll buy you a drink." He extended his hand for a parting shake.

"I think my social calendar's full," she said, shaking his hand and feeling the hair gel slickness on his palm, "but thank you for the invitation. Maybe some other time."

Sometime when I can bring ear plugs, a blindfold, and gloves, she silently added. She also made a mental note to squirt some hand sanitizer on her palms when she got back into her car to leave.

As Kyd picked up his guitar, then retreated through the back door, stopping at the refrigerator for a breakfast beer, Savannah glanced over at Emma. She saw the same lovesick, puppy-dog look on her face that Tammy had been wearing yesterday. And it made Savannah feel the need to swallow an entire bottle of antacid tablets right away.

"I think I'll get going, too," Savannah said, rising and stepping over an amplifier and guitar case. "Please speak to your grandmother about the bodyguards."

"I will, for all the good it'll do. And I'll pack a bag and go out there. She's always complaining that I don't visit her enough since Kyd moved in."

"That's an excellent idea," Savannah told her. "You know, Emma . . . guys come and go, but you don't get that many grandmothers per lifetime."

Emma's eyes softened. She nodded. "That's

true. I'll go out there today and spend the evening and night with her. I'll stay for as long as you think I should."

"Actually," Savannah said, "today and tonight will be fine. If I have anything to do with it, your grandmother's going to be busy this evening."

Chapter 10

When Savannah left her dinner guests in her backyard and rushed inside to answer the phone, she had a sense of foreboding. All wasn't right in her world, and more specifically, with everyone she loved.

She could feel it.

Besides, she knew Tammy's habits. And Tammy Hart was never late for anything.

She picked up the phone and didn't recognize the caller ID: Laura Hendricks.

"Hello," she said.

"Hi, Savannah." It was an apologetic Tammy on the other end. "I'm so sorry I didn't call you earlier."

"I was wondering where you were." Savannah glanced over at the raspberry-fudge cake on the counter with its birthday candles. "The chicken and pork chops are on the grill, but I've got a tofu burger for you."

"Oh, no. I'm really sorry," Tammy replied. "I should have called you sooner. I thought we'd make it over, but . . . well . . . Chad isn't feeling well, and he wants me to stay here at his place with him tonight and keep him company."

Savannah got that sick feeling in the pit of her stomach again. "Well, okay. We're sure going to miss you."

"I'll miss you, too." Tammy sounded like she was about to cry. "Please tell Ryan 'happy birthday' for me."

"He's out in the backyard. Do you want me to get him on the phone so you can tell him yourself?"

"Um, sure, I—"

Savannah heard a male voice in the background, and she was pretty sure it was Chad.

"Wrap that up over there," he was saying. "We've gotta get going. You're going to make me late."

"Sorry, Savannah. Gotta go," Tammy said. "Bye."

Click.

Savannah stared at the dead phone in her hand, and the uneasy feeling in her stomach spread through her body, making her knees weak.

"Oh, Tammy," she whispered.

She heard a knock at the front door and went to answer it.

Dirk was standing there, a six-pack of beer in one hand and a large grocery bag stuffed with several types of chips in the other.

Chips and beer were Dirk's standby contributions to any potluck affair. He wasn't much for slaving over a hot stove all day.

"What's the matter?" he asked the moment he saw her face.

"Oh, nothing," she said, opening the door and motioning him inside.

He walked through the door and followed her to the kitchen. "I know you. And I know that look. Spill it."

"It's Tammy," she said, opening one of the bags of chips. "She just called me, and she's not coming."

"To Ryan's birthday party? Are you kidding? She's nuts about Ryan!"

"Tell me about it."

Savannah looked out her kitchen window at the breathtaking, classically tall, dark, and handsome hunk, who was sipping a glass of wine and watching the grill for her.

Dressed in cream-colored linen slacks and a matching silk shirt, Ryan Stone was the stuff female dreams were made of.

Unfortunately, male, too. Ryan had been with his partner, John Gibson, for years, but that wasn't enough to squelch the romantic aspirations of all women who laid eyes on them.

Long ago, Savannah had accepted the futility of her fantasies. But being younger and more optimistic about life in general, Tammy clung to her hopes of someday changing Ryan's orientation.

Dirk took a beer from the pack and stuck the others in the refrigerator. "Tammy's pretty transparent about her Ryan crush," he said. "It's obvious she wants to marry him."

"She wants to marry him and John, too." Savannah dumped the chips into a large bowl. "She's still a kid. Life hasn't kicked all of the Pollyanna out of her yet."

She thought of the guy she had overheard on the phone and his nasty, controlling tone of voice. "And I hope she never does get kicked that hard. I like my Tammy just the way she is—sweet, naïve, and eternally hopeful."

"Me, too. I mean, she's a total bimbo, but you can't help but love 'er." Dirk took a swig of his beer and glanced out the window. "Hey, speaking of John . . . look who he's dancing with."

Savannah smiled when she saw the suave British fox glide across her lawn with Helene Strauss in his arms. His gray dress shirt and charcoal slacks complemented his thick mane of silver hair and matching mustache. John Gibson was the epitome of delicious, old-fashioned debonair.

And in her flowing, white party dress, Helene was his worthy complement.

"They make a nice couple . . . even if she *is* old enough to be his mother," Savannah said. "I put some big-band music on the boom box. I figured it might lead to a bit of high stepping. And look at them . . . they're really good!"

Dirk watched with her as John swirled and dipped his partner. Helene threw back her head and laughed heartily as she clung to him.

"Does she know this is a setup?" Dirk asked.

"Naw." Savannah started toward the door, chips and a bowl of homemade salsa in hand. "I'm pretty good at this sort of thing. I'm sure she doesn't have a clue."

"Young lady, I'll have you know, the last time I was invited to dinner and realized I was on a blind date," Helene told Savannah," Richard Nixon was still in office."

Savannah flipped a couple of chicken breasts, then brushed them with more barbecue sauce.

She smiled at Helene, who had stopped by the grill as John took her empty wineglass to the beverage table for a refill.

Helene's tone was stern, but the twinkle in her green eyes told Savannah she was anything but angry about her present circumstances.

"It's not exactly a date," Savannah said. "I mean, Ryan's here and—"

"Oh, I know." She twisted a strand of her hair behind the rose bud that John had tucked behind her right ear. "I could tell they're a couple right away, but that doesn't mean this whole thing isn't a stacked deck."

"Well, not the *whole* thing. It *is* Ryan's birthday."

"And you decided to invite me, someone you just met yesterday, to a small, private party for one of your dearest friends?"

Savannah grinned at her. "Hey, what can I say? You and I bonded instantly . . . or at least, as soon as you put the gun down."

Helene looked around her, at John pouring her a fresh glass of chardonnay, at Ryan who was chatting with Dirk.

"I can see why you wanted me to spend time with them," she said. "They *are* charming, and they certainly inspire confidence."

"Those two have provided protection for some of biggest celebrities in Hollywood. Their client roster is confidential, but you'd be impressed, I assure you."

"And I'm equally sure they charge an arm and a leg for their elite services."

"You can afford them. They'll give you the family rate."

Helene gave a sniff. "With a family like mine, the rate would be fifty percent more."

Savannah laughed. "Mine, too. At the very least."

Moving some of the chicken pieces and pork chops onto a rose-spangled platter that Granny Reid had given her years ago, Savannah dropped her smile and gave Helene a far more serious, searching look.

"I didn't see you drive up tonight," she said. "Did Waldo chauffeur you?"

"Yes, he did," Helene replied, a bit defiantly. "Why do you ask?"

"I just wondered."

"I know you did a background check on him. I'm not surprised. I suppose you have to, as part of your investigation. But I want you to know that I'm fully aware of my grandnephew's run-ins with the law. And it makes no difference to me at all."

"Then you know he's been arrested numerous times for drug possession and even dealing?"

"He has an addiction. It's an illness."

"I know. I'm sorry."

"It's been a source of heartbreak for us all."

"I'm sure it has."

Savannah looked into the woman's eyes and saw her sadness. She wanted to drop the subject and spare her any more pain. But she had to know. . . .

"Are you aware that he's been arrested for breaking and entering, and in two instances, for assault?"

"Yes, I do. Both of those charges were also drug related. Again, he has an addiction. And it's caused him to do things he wouldn't ordinarily have done."

"Of course."

"But whatever Waldo's done in the past, whatever crimes he's committed, he would never, ever, harm me or anyone else in his family. I know him as well as I would my own son. It simply isn't possible."

"Okay."

"So, I don't want to hear any more about him. You can stop wasting your time. Move on. Investigate someone else."

"Yes, ma'am. We are. We're checking out everyone."

"Good."

Savannah was happy to see John approaching, full wineglass in hand.

He glanced at Helene, then Savannah. He seemed to sense he had arrived at a tense moment. "And how are my lovely ladies?" he asked with his delightfully polished, crisp, British accent.

"Hungry," Savannah said, handing him the platter laden with steaming, fragrant meat. "Let's eat!"

Several hours later, after Waldo had collected Helene from the party, Ryan and John were in Savannah's foyer, saying good-bye to her and Dirk.

Savannah stood on tiptoe to give Ryan a kiss on the cheek. "I hope you had a nice birthday, sweetie," she told him. "You don't look an hour older, let alone a year."

"You keep me young, Savannah," he told her, wrapping her in a hearty hug.

"I did notice a new gray hair on your temple during dinner," John said, "but being a gentleman, I didn't mention it."

"I've got a long way to go to catch up with you," Ryan returned, slapping him on the back.

"We should be going." John shook Dirk's hand. "We promised that dear lady we'd arrive at her house before she goes to bed. And she looked pretty tired when she left."

"It was all that fancy footwork you two were doing there on the lawn," Ryan told him. "Savannah's grass will never be the same."

Dirk grunted. "The last time I saw that many divots was when you two took me golfing."

"I'm just glad you got the gig," Savannah told them. "I'll rest easier now, knowing she's in good hands. I'd feel awful if anything happened to that remarkable lady."

"We all would," John said. "And we'll keep our eyes open for anything that might help in your investigation."

Both Savannah and Dirk wished Ryan another "happy birthday" and sent them on their way with two large slices of chocolate cake in a Savannah-style doggy bag—complete with napkins and forks. "Just in case you get an attack of the ugly hungries on the way home," Savannah told them.

No one suffered a hunger pang in Savannah's presence. It simply wasn't allowed.

Once Ryan and John were on their way, Savannah said good night to Dirk, too. And he left with a cake goodie bag of his own.

"You can never be too safe when it comes to staving off starvation," was her motto, handed down to her through the generations of amply-padded Reid womenfolk.

But once the guys were all gone, and it was just her and the cats, Savannah hurried to the telephone. With a quickening pulse rate she punched in Tammy's number.

One, two, three, four, five rings.

Her machine answered. "Hi! This is Tammy!" said the bright, perky voice. "I'm sorry I missed your call. I'm probably out sleuthing or on a run. Leave a message."

Savannah felt a tightening in her throat. Tammy was the only detective—private, professional, or amateur—Savannah knew who used the term "sleuthing." And Savannah found it infinitely endearing.

"Hi, sugar," she said. "I just wanted you to know that I saved you a piece of Ryan's birthday cake. I know you don't usually eat cake, but . . . well . . . We missed you, and I'm thinking of you, sweetie. You take care of yourself, you hear?"

As the water ran into her bathtub, Savannah walked to the guest bedroom and over to a large cedar chest at the foot of the bed. She knelt in front of the chest and removed the handmade quilt that lay folded across it. Meticulously handsewn of colorful scraps of blue and green, the quilt had been a gift from her grandmother to mark the occasion of Savannah's fortieth birthday.

Savannah remembered thinking that the quilt was the only thing good about turning forty. Though now, a few years later, she had decided it was a good thing—turning the calendar to a new year, even a new decade.

She figured she looked almost as good as she had ten years before, and was a heck of a lot smarter. So, it was a fair trade-off.

She laid the quilt on the foot of the bed, as always, smoothing her hand over it and feeling her grandmother's loving aura, forever infused into those tiny, even stitches.

Long ago, she had heard that some Native Americans believed that a bit of a craftsman's soul entered into the weapons he made or the tools he created.

She liked to believe it was true. When she missed Granny a little too much, felt sad or particularly tired, or had the sniffles, she wrapped herself in the quilt and imagined she was being hugged by her beloved grandmother. And it helped.

Lifting the top of the old chest that her grandfather had built for Gran as a wedding present, so many years ago, Savannah breathed in the rich, earthy scent of the cedar.

That smell had always represented love, safety, and stability to Savannah, and had the ability to transport her back to a sweeter, more innocent time in her life. A time long before forensic reports, autopsy results, homicide investigations, and murderers' grisly confessions. Before she knew what human beings were capable of doing to one another.

She reached inside the chest and, beneath some of Gran's doilies and a set of her own hand-embroidered pillowcases, she found Valdosta. She was wrapped in a square of green velvet cloth cut from an old Christmas decoration. Nothing had been wasted in Granny Reid's house.

Lovingly, Savannah unwrapped her and looked down into the doll's beautiful, lifelike eyes. Her long, curling locks of black hair, the lace-trimmed satin dress that was the same blue as her eyes, her creamy skin and perfectly shaped mouth . . . she was a work of art. Helene Strauss's art.

"Hello, little sweetie," Savannah whispered. "It's been too long since I took you out of there."

She kissed the doll's face and felt its smooth cool cheek against her lips.

"I met the woman who made you today," she told her, "and a lot of your sisters and even some brothers. Her name is Helene, and she's a great lady. You come from a fine family."

Savannah stood and walked to the side of the bed.

"Helene says you aren't happy, living in that dark old trunk. She told me to take you out and display you. What do you think about that? You want to be on display?"

Although Valdosta didn't reply, Savannah could swear that her smile widened a tad.

"I don't have a Bavarian-style mansion for you to live in, like your relatives, or even a glass display case, but you can lie here on my guest bed, if you like. How would that be?"

Gently, she placed the doll, just so, in the middle of the bed, her head on the pillows, her full skirt spread out around her.

"And at least once a day, I'll come in here, give you a kiss and ask how you're doing. What do you think of that?"

Yes, she could definitely see the pink mouth curving upward, just a bit, and the blue eyes sparkled a little brighter.

Feeling like she had done some sort of good deed, Savannah left the guest room, went into her bedroom, and got the phone.

A few moments later, she was lying in her claw-foot bathtub, up to her chin in bubbles that glistened in the light provided by the rose-scented, votive candles on the vanity.

She punched some numbers on the phone, then smiled when she heard the soft, Southern accent on the other end.

"Hey there, Savannah, darlin'. How's my sweet girl?"

"I'm fine, Gran. Fine and dandy. I just wanted to call and tell you that I met somebody who puts me in mind of you."

"And who might that be?"

"A lovely lady named Helene. Oh, and I just spoke to an old friend of ours. Valdosta says to tell you, 'Hi, Granny.'"

Savannah had just drifted off to sleep, Diamante curled beneath her right arm, Cleopatra snuggled at her feet, when her bedside phone jangled her awake.

She jumped and grabbed at the phone, her heart pounding.

With a growl of indignation, Diamante relocated to the foot of the bed to lie beside her sister.

"Hello?" Savannah said, staring at the darkness outside her window, trying to orient herself.

She squinted at the clock on her night table. It was only 11:02. No wonder she felt less than refreshed.

"It's me, Ryan," said a voice on the other end. A voice that sounded worried. Very worried. "I'm sorry to wake you."

"No problem. What's up?"

"You've got to come over here . . . to Helene's estate."

Her pulse rate soared. She could feel the blood pounding in her temples. "Why?" she said. "What have you got?"

She heard Ryan draw a long breath, then let it out. "Honestly, Savannah, we're not even sure what we've got. But you have to come over here right now. I've already called Dirk. He's on his way."

"So am I."

Savannah hung up the phone and leapt out of bed so fast that it made her lightheaded. As she ran to the closet to grab a pair of jeans and a shirt, she fought down the sense of panic that was rising along with her blood pressure.

She knew, whatever it was, it had to be really bad.

Ryan had called *Dirk* first.

Chapter 11

By the time Savannah had arrived at the Strauss estate, Dirk was already there. She parked her Mustang next to his old Buick and jumped out, cell phone in hand. As she hurried to the mansion's front door, she phoned him.

"Where are you?" she barked when he answered.

"Where are *you?*"

"In front of the main house," she said, looking up at the windows, which were nearly all lit.

"Wait there. I'll send Ryan to get you." He hung up.

Impatiently, she did as she was told, standing at the front door, listening for sounds from within. But the house was silent.

When Ryan did appear, it was from a path that led into the woods to her right.

The solar lights that lined the stone walkway were bright enough for her to see his expression. And it was grim.

"What in tarnation's going on?" she asked, hurrying down the porch steps and running to him.

He pointed back in the direction he had come. "We've got two down," he told her.

"Two? Down?" She did a quick mental tally of the residents of the estate. Helene, Waldo, Tiago, and Blanca. Two was a disturbingly high percentage for a place that was home to only four people.

And Emma, she thought. *Emma said she'd be spending the night here, too.*

"Down as in *hurt?*" she asked. "Or . . . ?"

"They're gone, Savannah. I'm sorry. When we found them, we tried to help, but . . ."

He turned and hurried back down the path he had come, with her trotting alongside.

"Who is it?" she asked breathlessly

"We don't know for sure. A male and a female."

Savannah's throat felt like it was closing so tightly she could hardly speak the word, "Helene?"

"Helene's accounted for. She's in the house. John's with her."

"Good."

Ahead, through the trees, Savannah could see lights and a figure moving about.

She would know those broad shoulders and the lumbering gait anywhere.

She and Ryan hurried through the trees and emerged into a small clearing.

Soft blue lights illuminated a large whirlpool spa surrounded by rock paving and several thick-cushioned, wicker chaise longues with matching accent tables. But it wasn't the water gently swirling in the tub or the comfortable furniture that caught Savannah's eye.

It was the two bodies lying, faceup, on the stone pavement beside the spa.

Dirk stood next to them, arms crossed over his chest, a mixture of sadness and anger on his face.

Savannah had seen that look and that stance many times. And she knew what he was feeling. He was trying to shield himself from the harsh reality of what he was seeing—a futile attempt that law enforcement officers everywhere couldn't help making.

Of course, it never worked, but that didn't stop anyone from trying.

She felt herself doing it as she approached the bodies. Emotion clicking off; logic and intellect taking over.

And that worked for five seconds, until she recognized the face of the young woman.

"Blanca," she whispered. "Oh, no."

"Yeah, it's her," Dirk said, reaching over and placing a hand on Savannah's shoulder.

Savannah didn't have to ask if the housekeeper was dead. Her eyes were staring sightlessly into the night sky. Her torso was covered with a white towel, and there was no natural rising and falling of her chest.

Her beautiful, long, black hair was wet, spread out on the stones around her head, and her skin that had glowed with golden health looked ashen in the blue light.

Long ago, Savannah had realized that not every dead person had the peaceful look of sleep on their faces, like the corpses on television and in movies. Some looked as though they had died in a moment of horror.

Sadly, Blanca was one of those.

Savannah walked around her body to get a better look at the face of the male lying near her. "So, who's the other one?" she asked.

"His name is Victor Odell," Ryan replied. "John and I recognized him right away."

Savannah knelt on one knee beside the male's body and tried to see his features, which were in shadow.

She saw enough that she, too, recognized him.

"Victor who?" she said. "That's Vern Oldham. Ada's boyfriend."

"Well, I don't know what name he's using now," Ryan said, "but John and I had the misfortune of crossing paths with him several years ago, and back then, he was Victor."

"At least he kept the initials the same," Dirk added.

"Yeah," Ryan replied, "good old Victor had everything he owned monogrammed. I guess he didn't want to change wardrobes every time he changed aliases."

"I had the new gal at the station run a check on him today," Dirk told them. "She couldn't find anything past a year ago."

"How did you two know him?" Savannah asked Ryan as she stood and brushed off her knee.

"He belonged to our boat club and—"

"Your *yacht* club," Dirk corrected him. "You can say 'yacht.' We know you've got one. I have a fifty-footer myself . . . keep it parked behind my house trailer."

"Okay." Ryan gave him a half smile. "He was a member of our *yacht* club, courtesy of a dear friend of ours, Melissa Hamilton. He did everything he could to cause Melissa to fall in love with him . . . and succeeded . . . and then robbed her of most of her fortune and broke her heart."

Savannah shook her head. "One of your favorite people, no doubt."

"Let's just say, John and I offered to administer some Georgia-style, Savannah justice to him, but Melissa just wanted to put the whole sorry affair behind her."

Savannah looked down at the still body, the lifeless face. "Looks like Lady Justice might have knocked hard on our boy Victor/Vern's door tonight."

"Yeah," Dirk said, "I'm not gonna cry over that one." He pointed to Blanca's body. "That one there, I feel really bad about. Something tells me she didn't deserve what she got."

Savannah looked around, taking in the details of the scene. "And what, exactly, *did* she get? What happened here?"

"John and I were making an evening round," Ryan told her. "Just wanted to check everything one more time before we went to bed. John walked down toward the gardener's cottage, and I checked the pool area and then back here."

"You were the one who found them, lying here by the spa?" Savannah asked.

"No. As I was walking by, I saw something strange in the water. As it turns out, it was her hair, floating at the top. Both of them were submerged there in the tub."

"You dragged them out of there yourself?" Savannah noticed for the first time that the front of Ryan's shirt and his trousers were wet.

"Yes, and I phoned John and told him to get over here. The two of us could see right away that they were both gone. We tried, but no amount of resuscitation was going to work."

"Looks to me," Dirk said, "like they've both been dead a couple of hours at least."

Savannah pointed to the white towels, one covering Blanca's body and the other lying over Vern's groin area. "You and John put the towels over them?"

Ryan nodded. "I know. Dirk already mentioned that wasn't the best choice, forensic-wise. But it seemed like the decent thing to do."

Looking around, Savannah spotted a towel valet, stacked with snowy white towels. "Did you take them from over there?" she asked.

"Yes," Ryan replied. "We deliberately used clean ones, so that we wouldn't cross-contaminate any evidence."

"And the towels beside the spa were there already?" Savannah asked with a wave toward a couple of crumpled ones on the edge of the whirlpool.

"Yes," Ryan said, "and their clothes are over there." He pointed to a woman's sundress, a man's slacks and shirt, and a pair of panties and some men's briefs draped across one of the chaise lounges. On the pavement nearby were two pairs of sandals.

Savannah noticed something else on a table near the spa—a tray laden with sumptuous goodies. The remainders of their feast included giant shrimp, a couple of lobster tails, various cheeses and fruits, chocolate-dipped strawberries, a champagne bottle, and two wineglasses.

In an ashtray next to the food was a half-smoked marijuana joint.

"Wow," she said. "That was quite a spread. Something tells me that Blanca couldn't have afforded a layout like that."

"Like I said"—Ryan shook his head—"Victor—or Vern, as you call him—was good at seduction."

Dirk walked closer to the bodies, took a flashlight from inside his jacket, and shined it slowly from one end of Vern's body to the other, lifting the towel and looking beneath it as he searched. "I don't see any signs of trauma at all," he said. "The guy's clean as a whistle."

Savannah borrowed his light and did the same to Blanca's. "I don't see anything on her either. Did anybody look at their backs?"

"John and I both did, after we dragged them out and before we covered them," Ryan replied. "Nothing at all."

"What do you suppose killed them?" Savannah wondered aloud. "You hear all the time that you aren't supposed to drink alcohol in a hot tub, for fear of heat stroke. But what're the odds they'd both be overcome like that at the same time?"

She walked over to the whirlpool and looked in. There was nothing, not even a floating leaf or soap bubble in the crystalline water that gently swirled inside.

"The jets weren't on when you found them?" she asked.

"No. It was just like that," Ryan told her. "Both of them inside, completely submerged . . . except for her hair that was floating on the surface."

Savannah pointed to the buttons on the side of the spa. "It's on a timer. So, even if they'd been using the jets, it would have probably shut off on its own."

Dirk put his flashlight back into his jacket. "Obviously, they were having a little hanky-panky out here. Romantic snacks, smokin' a joint, having a moonlight skinny dip . . . Where's the hubby, Tiago?"

"More importantly," Savannah said, "where's he been all night?"

"John and I asked Helene earlier where everyone was. She said that Waldo went out for a drive to some unknown destination . . . to 'settle his nerves,' she said. Apparently, he does that a lot."

"Probably went to the bad part of town to score," Savannah surmised.

"And," Ryan continued, "she said the gardener and his wife had gone to La Rosita, like they do every Saturday night, to visit his brother and cousins."

Savannah looked down at the young woman on the ground. "Blanca should have gone to La Rosita to visit her in-laws instead of staying behind to fool around with Vern the Skunk. She'd probably still be alive."

"I checked their place, the gardener's cottage, before you got here," Dirk said. "The house was dark. Nobody was there."

"Did you go inside . . . without a warrant?" Savannah asked.

"Of course."

"My bad habits are rubbing off on you, boy."

"Heaven forbid."

They heard someone coming down the path and turned to see a disheveled Emma emerging from the woods. She was wearing a tank top with pajama bottoms, and she was dripping wet from head to toe.

"There you are," she said. "I was looking all over

for you guys. Oma said there's been some sort of accident out here, and—oh, my God!"

She gasped and clapped her hand over her mouth, staring at the bodies.

Savannah hurried over to her and put her arm around her shoulders. Her skin was wet and clammy, and she was shivering violently.

"Girl, you're cold as a cucumber," Savannah told her. "Dirk, fetch us a couple of those towels over here."

Dirk delivered the towels, and she wrapped one around Emma, like a shawl.

"How'd you get so wet?" she asked her. "You look like a drowned rat."

"I took a shortcut across the lawn to get over here," Emma said, teeth chattering. "The sprinklers came on when I was halfway across. I was drenched before I could get to the other side."

Emma took the second towel and began to dry her hair with it. "I wasn't expecting the sprinkler system to come on so early. It's set for three in the morning."

"You know when the sprinklers come on?" Dirk asked her.

"I grew up here. I was a teenager here. When you sneak into the house late, you keep track of things like that."

"Yeah," he said, "I guess you do."

"Who is that over there?" she asked, nodding toward the bodies. "What happened to them?"

"It's Blanca," Savannah told her.

"Oh, no!"

"And Vern."

"*Vern?* It can't be! Blanca and *Vern?*" Her body sagged, and for a moment, Savannah thought she might faint. "Blanca would never go into a hot tub with Vern."

Dirk sniffed. "I don't wanna argue with you, ma'am, but it looks like she did more than just take a tub with him."

Emma took one tentative step toward the bodies. "Are they . . . Are they both dead?"

"Yes, I'm sorry," Ryan told her.

"Are you sure?"

"We're sure, darlin'," Savannah said. "Ryan here pulled them out of the water and tried to resuscitate them. They were already gone."

"This is going to just kill my grandmother," Emma said, starting to cry. "Because of Blanca. Not because of Vern."

Savannah looked over at the gigolo's body and thought of all the things she'd heard about him in the past twenty-four hours.

"It's a cryin' shame about Blanca," Savannah agreed, "a young woman paying an awfully high price for her foolishness. But call it a hunch . . . I don't think anybody's gonna get all that tore up about ol' Vern."

Chapter 12

Savannah hadn't even poured her first cup of morning coffee when there was a knock at the kitchen door. She opened it to a sunbeam of a gal who looked a lot like her assistant . . . only much happier than the last time she had seen her.

"Tamitha, get your butt in here," she said, throwing the door wide and pulling her inside. "You're a sight for sore eyes, girlie."

And she was a sight.

With her long, silky blond hair, sun-kissed skin, and athletic, runner's form, Tammy was a lovely girl on any day. But today she seemed her buoyant, vibrant self as she bounced into the house, all smiles.

"Want a cup of coffee?" Savannah asked her.

"You know I don't drink that poison, and you shouldn't either." Tammy hurried to the refrigerator and opened it. "Got any wheatgrass juice?"

Yes, Savannah thought, *our Tammy's back and as annoying as ever.*

"Oh, sure," she said, shuffling in her fluffy slippers to the coffee pot. "I keep the wheatgrass juice right there in the door . . . next to the cabbage nectar and essence of broccoli. Help yourself."

Tammy grabbed a bottle of apple juice and peered at the label. "Is this organic?"

"Are you a pain in the ass?" Savannah grinned at her. "You're chipper as a chipmunk this morning . . . even more than usual. What's up?"

" 'Who's out' is more like it."

"Oh?"

"I broke up with Chad last night. Gave him his walking papers, sent him packing."

It was all Savannah could do not to dance a wild backwoods Georgia jig right there in her Beauty and the Beast pajamas and fuzzy house slippers. But, instead, she pasted a totally false look of heartfelt concern on her face and said with all due gravity, "I'm so sorry it didn't work out."

Tammy snorted. "Oh, you are not. I saw the way you looked at him when you met him the other day. You hated him."

"That's true. I hated him."

"Dirko, too."

"Dirk loathed him."

"And that's enough for me. If you two don't like him, he's out."

Savannah paused, the half-and-half carton in her hand. "Don't tell me you got rid of him because Dirk and I didn't approve of him. I mean, it had to be your decision and—"

"Pleeezzz. I love you two and trust your opinions of people. But I broke it off with him because I overheard a dirty message some bimbo had left on his answering machine. We'd agreed to be exclusive, and he was messing around on me."

"Then he's lucky he's alive."

"Exactly."

Savannah poured a generous portion of the half-and-half into her coffee. There was nothing quite like a good cup of cream with your coffee to get the day started. Except, of course, hearing that your girlfriend had dumped her jerk boyfriend.

Life was worth living after all.

The phone rang, and Tammy rushed to answer it.

"Moonlight Magnolia Detective Agency," she breathed. "Oh, it's you. Just a minute." She passed the phone to Savannah. "It's Pee-Pee Brain," she whispered.

"You really have to stop calling him that," Savannah told her. "It's just so . . . immature . . . so juvenile."

"Poopy Pants."

"That's so much better." Savannah walked into the living room and over to the windowsill, where Diamante and Cleopatra were sitting on their kitty perch, catching their morning rays.

"What did the ding-a-ling just call me?" Dirk wanted to know on the other end.

"Nothing. She was telling me that she dumped Turkey Butt."

"Awesome! I take back everything I ever said about her. She's got two brain cells to rub together after all."

Savannah sighed and sipped her coffee. "Granny Reid would not approve. If she were here, we'd all be gnawing on bars of Ivory soap."

"Have you had your coffee yet?" he wanted to know.

"Just started it. Why?"

"Dr. Liu called. She's finished with the autopsies."

"You're kidding! Already?"

"Yeah. She stayed up all night. Says this is the most interesting case she's ever had. Never seen anything like it. She wants to show me what she found."

"Okay. Are you on your way to the morgue?"

"Soon as I get one cup in me. Wanna meet me there?"

"You bringing the donuts?"

"Uh . . . yeah, I guess."

"Make mine maple bars. See ya in twenty."

There was nothing whatsoever cozy or inviting about the county morgue. And Savannah thoroughly hated the place.

Though not as austere as the industrial complex where the forensic lab was housed, the plain stucco building was equally generic and dreary in its own way. Cutbacks in county funds had taken its toll on the place, which hadn't been painted or re-roofed since the Carter administration . . . and even back in Jimmy's heyday, the county had used cheap paint.

Utility, not style, continued to be the primary concern of the local officials. Whether the national economy was booming or taking a dive off the end of the pier, the politicians holding the county's purse strings squeezed every nickel.

So, the morgue remained in need of a paint job, and the flower beds in front of the building remained empty, year after year.

But then, Savannah mused as she drove up to it,

maybe a morgue shouldn't be overly festive. Not a lot of happy things happened inside its walls.

And as Savannah parked her car and walked up to the front door, she recalled that some of the least happy occasions in her memory had occurred right inside that door, at the desk of Officer Kenny Bates.

Kenny had once been madly in lust with Savannah, though why, she had never been able to figure out.

Everyone, with the possible exception of Kenny, knew that she despised him. She had never given him any reason to think he had a strawberry ice cream cone's chance in hell with her. But the more she abused him and made poignant suggestions about painful ways that he could exit this world, the more he adored her. For years, she had been unable to walk through those doors without receiving some lovely invitation to either watch X-rated movies at his rancid apartment or hit the sheets of the local no-tell motel with him.

Until the centerfold incident.

Since the day, not long ago, when she had beaten him half to death with his own rolled-up porn magazine, he had gone from perverted to pouting.

"Show me an ugly centerfold and tell me she reminds you of me," Savannah muttered as she walked through the front door. "It's a wonder you still have breath in your body."

When she entered the reception area, and Bates looked up from his desk, he didn't appear to be all that grateful to be among the living. In fact, he looked downright disgruntled to see her.

He grumbled under his breath as he managed

to dislodge his girth from behind the desk, where his breakfast of sausage and egg burritos and a giant chocolate milk shake was spread.

As he trudged over to the counter and shoved a clipboard at her, Savannah caught the strong and most unpleasant odor of onions and sausage, mixed with an overpowering dose of his cheap cologne. She attempted to breathe through her ears until she could exit his personal space.

She glanced down and saw that Dirk had signed in only three minutes before her. Good. She'd rather not have to wait for him here in Hell's Antechamber.

She signed in as "U. McMee Sik," and shoved the clipboard back at him. As usual, he didn't look at it what she'd written but returned to his desk, sat down, and buried his face in his burrito.

She headed toward the hallway that led to the coroner's office. But as she left the room, she couldn't help saying over her shoulder, "Hey, Bates . . . read any good *magazines* lately?"

When she was halfway down the hall, she could still hear him cursing her. Although, considering he had a mouthful of burrito, his ranting was pretty garbled.

She didn't need to understand every word to catch his drift. And she didn't stop giggling until she was at the end of the hallway and standing in front of the swinging double doors of the autopsy suite.

The sight of those doors always sobered her in an instant.

While the work inside those rooms was sacred, because it was a search for truth, it was sad work.

And Savannah didn't envy people who had to do it, day in and day out.

However, when she pushed one of the doors open a few inches and peeked inside, the woman standing next to Dirk, beside the long, stainless steel table, looked anything but unhappy.

In fact, Dr. Jennifer Liu looked far more cheerful than Savannah had ever seen her. Wearing surgical greens and disposable paper booties over her shoes, her long, glossy black hair tucked into a scrub cap, Dr. Jen wasn't her usual hotsy-totsy self. Outside the autopsy suite she was far more likely to be wearing a black leather miniskirt and stilettos. But in this room, the county's first female coroner was all business.

And today, apparently, business was good . . . or at least, interesting.

"There she is," the doctor said as she looked up and saw Savannah at the door. "Come on in, Savannah. You arrived just in time."

Dirk seemed excited, too. "Yeah. She was just starting to tell me what she found here."

"Here" was the body of Vern Oldham, stretched out on the autopsy table.

It occurred to Savannah, as always, that the deceased always looked so vulnerable, lying on Dr. Liu's table. Death reduced them to nothing more than what they had been at birth.

When expounding about the follies of materialism, Granny had often said, "Naked we enter the world, and naked we leave."

Savannah thought about Vern's expensive watches and diamonds and suits.

What good did they do him now, when all he

was wearing was Dr. Liu's stitched vee incision across his chest and down his abdomen?

"Whatcha got?" Savannah asked as she walked over to stand next to Dirk. Not too close to the body, for fear of contaminating the evidence—and getting yelled at by the meticulous doctor—but close enough to see whatever she was about to show them.

"I was just telling Dirk that there was no sign of trauma of any kind on either body."

The doctor pointed to a gurney that had been wheeled against the far wall of the room. On it was a body bag, zipped closed. "I finished her earlier."

Savannah felt a wave of sadness, thinking about the pretty young woman whose life had been wasted. But she pushed the feeling down and concentrated on what Dr. Liu was saying.

"Not a scratch or a bruise on either of them," she continued. "Her internal exam showed no disease. His . . . some lung and liver damage, due to lifestyle, no doubt. But no natural cause of death."

"Did they drown?" Savannah asked.

"She had some water in her lungs. Not a lot, as you'd expect if drowning was the sole cause of death. His lungs were clear."

"Any idea on time of death?" Savannah said.

Dr. Liu shook her head. "As you know, TOD is hard to establish under the best of circumstances. But here you've got bodies that were in hot water, we don't even know how hot, for how long. My best guess would be eight, nine o'clock in the evening. But don't hold me to it."

"Then what do you think killed them?" Dirk wanted to know.

Dr. Liu walked over to a stainless steel tray and

picked up a large magnifying glass. "Of course," she said, "anytime someone dies in a tub of water and there's no sign of trauma, we suspect accidental drowning. But we've ruled that out."

"Heat stroke maybe?" Dirk said. "Hot tub and alcohol can be a deadly combination."

"But not both of them at the same time," Savannah added.

Dr. Liu switched on the light on the magnifying glass. "Yes, that's an unlikely coincidence. Besides, if they'd suffered heat stroke, they probably would have lost consciousness and drowned. Drowning would have been the actual cause of death."

She motioned them closer. "And if you have victims in a tub, whose lungs are mostly clear of water, you have to suspect electrocution."

"Electrocution? I saw an electrician one time who died that way," Dirk said. "He had burn marks."

"Yes, but when a victim is in water, marks aren't always present," Dr. Liu told him. "At least, not ones you can see with the naked eye. But look at this. . . ."

She held the magnifying glass over the body's chest, an area near his armpit. Dirk and Savannah leaned down and first one, then the other, peered through the glass.

"I don't see anything," Dirk said.

"Me either," Savannah added. "What exactly are we looking for?"

The doctor handed the glass to Savannah. "There's no distinct burn mark, but there *is* a mark . . . a pale stripe on the skin, right across the chest. And if you look closely, you'll see a row of small blisters there on the stripe."

Savannah leaned down and adjusted the glass

until she saw them. Exactly as Dr. Liu had described, there was a line stretching from just beneath his left arm across his chest to his right. And on that line she could see the tiny blisters.

"How strange. I've never seen anything like that." Savannah handed Dirk the glass, and he took a look.

"Me either," he said. "But there they are."

Dr. Liu took the glass from him and laid it back on the tray. "I've read about the pale stripe and blisters. But this is the first time I've ever seen them myself. It occurs when electricity is introduced into the water where someone is lying, sitting, whatever. And the line on the body appears parallel to where the surface of the water was at the time they were electrocuted."

"That makes sense," Savannah said. "A lot of people sit in a spa with their arms lying on the edge of the tub, the water up to their chest that way."

"Does she have a line like that, too?" Dirk asked, pointing to the body in the bag on the gurney.

"Yes, but it's across her neck."

"She was petite," Savannah said. "The water probably only came up to her neck."

"But where did the electricity come from?" Dirk asked. "There wasn't anything in the water. No hair dryers, radio, or other electrical appliances."

"It might have been removed from the scene . . . afterward," Savannah suggested.

"Or maybe there was some sort of problem with the spa itself," Dr. Liu said. "I don't know much about how they're wired, or what could cause a terrible shock like that. Perhaps you could get an electrician to check it out for you." She stepped away from the body, took off her surgery cap, shook her long hair free, and ran her fingers through it. She closed her eyes for a moment and took a deep breath. "Either way, I'm exhausted and headed home for a shower and a nap."

"So, just to sum it up," Dirk said, "on both of them, we've got electrocution as cause of death. And what would you say was the manner of death?"

"Might've been accidental." Dr. Liu looked as doubtful as she sounded.

"But you reckon it was murder?" Savannah said.

Dirk sighed. "Let's face it . . . we all reckon it was murder."

Chapter 13

As Savannah drove the Mustang out of Tammy's beach neighborhood and toward the foothills and the Strauss estate, she glanced at her passenger and was happy she had invited her along.

"I'm glad you called me," Tammy said, as though reading her mind. "I'd finished your book work and thought I was going to have to spend the rest of the day at home with nothing fun to do."

"You mean you'd rather do some serious investigating than stick around the house and extract juice from carrots?"

"Actually, I like juicing carrots, too, but I'd rather sleuth any time."

For the sixth time in less than five minutes, Tammy's cell phone chimed. And, once again, Tammy flinched but didn't answer it, just as she hadn't answered it the past five times.

Savannah had a good idea who it was, but she bit her tongue and said nothing.

It wasn't easy. Being a Georgia gal, she seldom

had an unexpressed thought. Where she was from, it was considered bad for the digestion not to speak your mind.

Tammy did glance at her phone. Then she shoved it deep into her purse.

They rode on in silence for a while, passing neighborhoods where tiny bungalows had glowing white stucco walls and red Spanish-tile roofs. Like Savannah's part of town, the yards in this area were lovingly tended and decorated with the occasional statuary—flowing fountains, majestic lions, fanciful fairies, and the beloved Lady of Guadalupe.

But as they climbed the hills and the ocean views became even more spectacular, the price of the real estate rose, as well.

The bungalows gave way to custom-built homes in every style imaginable, and yards that required full-time gardeners to maintain.

Long ago, Savannah had aspired to being a lady of the manor who employed a full-time gardener. But for now, she would settle for a lawn mower that worked.

As the highway led them into the valley where the Strauss estate was situated, Tammy's phone went off again.

This time, Savannah couldn't restrain herself. "Is it him?" she asked.

"Yes," Tammy reluctantly admitted. "He keeps texting me. One minute he's telling me how he loves me and will do anything to get me back. The next he's demanding to know who the new guy is and threatening to hurt him when he finds out who he is."

"New guy?"

Tammy shrugged. "Sure. There's gotta be a new guy. God knows, I'd never leave a great guy like him unless there was somebody else, right?"

"Of course."

Savannah felt her stomach do a flip-flop. "Tammy, I don't want to interfere here, or speak outta turn. But I don't like the sound of that one little bit. I have to tell you, I'm concerned about your safety, dealing with a man like that."

"It's okay. I know how he is. I can handle him."

"A lot of women think that, and then—"

"Savannah, I know you mean well, but I don't want to talk about it anymore."

Tammy reached into her purse, took out her cell phone, and read the string of texts. Then she turned the phone off and shoved it back into her purse.

Savannah fought down the mental flood of domestic violence scenes she had witnessed as a cop. The ones that had been minor—if you could call victims living in fear and pain, year after year "minor"—and the other ones that had ended in tragedy.

She cast a sideways look at the beautiful young woman sitting beside her, one of the smartest and sweetest women she'd ever had the pleasure to know and call "friend."

"Okay, sugar," she told her. "If you don't want to talk about it, we won't. But I'm here for you if you ever do want to talk, if you need me."

Tammy turned her head to the right, and all Savannah could see was the back of her head.

A moment later, Savannah heard her sniff. "I

know, Savannah," she said softly. "I know you're there for me. But some things, a woman has to do herself."

Savannah reached over, put her hand on her friend's knee, and gave it an affectionate squeeze. "That's true, darlin'. But she doesn't have to do it alone."

By the time Savannah and Tammy had made their way to the Strauss property and walked through the woods to the secluded spa area, Dirk was already there. And so was the electrician, along with Ryan, John, and the less-than-thrilled lady of the house, Helene.

"Don't tell me you didn't trample my petunias when I saw you do it with my own eyes," she was saying as she shook her finger in the face of the giant workman. He looked like a five-year-old boy getting yelled at by his great-grandmother . . . a boy who was six and a half feet tall and weighed at least three hundred pounds.

John walked over to Helene and placed a calming hand on her shoulder. "I'd be happy to replace those petunias for you, Helene."

"Of course, we can," Ryan assured her. "We have a friend who's a landscaper. He can drop some by this afternoon. We'll have them in the ground before sundown."

"I'll pay for them," the electrician said. "I didn't even notice your flowers there, ma'am. I was having a hard time getting to that junction box, and I've got these big feet. . . ."

He pointed down to his enormous boots that were covered with dirt.

"And look at the mud you've tramped all over my stones here!" she said. "Who's going to clean that up?"

Dirk had his exasperated look firmly in place, but Savannah could tell he was fighting to hide his annoyance. "Mrs. Strauss," he said. "I'll hose off the mud, but honestly, we have more important things to worry about here than just your flowers and—"

"Do not call me Mrs. Strauss!" she shouted at him. "Can't you see I'm very upset here? One of my employees has been killed. Maybe even murdered!"

Her voice broke, and it seemed all the strength went out of her. She reached for John's arm, then leaned on him for support.

For the first time, Helene Strauss looked frail to Savannah. She seemed unsteady on her feet as he walked her over to one of the chaise longues and sat her down.

Savannah hurried over to her. "Helene, are you okay?" she asked as she dropped to one knee beside the chaise.

Helene seemed to notice Savannah's presence for the first time. She looked up at her with enormous sadness in her green eyes.

"Savannah," she said, "how did this terrible thing happen? Right here on my property? Poor Blanca!"

"We don't know yet, Helene. But that's why we're here. We're going to find out."

Tammy hurried up to Helene, reached into her purse, and fished out a bottle of water. "Here," she said, unscrewing the top and handing it to her. "I always carry an extra."

"Who are you?" Helene said. "And what are you

doing on my property? Everyone's just coming and going on my property these days without my permission. I won't stand for it!"

"This is my assistant, Tammy Hart," Savannah told her. "She's also a friend of Ryan's and John's."

That seemed to mollify Helene, who actually gave Tammy a wan smile as she accepted the water bottle from her hand.

"Thank you, honey," she said. "I'm sorry. I'm just not myself today."

John pulled a chair close to Helene's and sat down. Taking her hand between his, he patted it and told Savannah, "Go do what you need to over there with Dirk. Ryan and I will take care of our dear lady here."

Savannah nodded, gave Helene what she hoped was a comforting smile, and walked over to Dirk and the electrician. Tammy followed close behind.

"What did you find out?" she asked Dirk.

"Don't know yet," he replied. "I was just starting to ask him when she got in our face about the friggin' petunias and the mud."

Savannah looked over at Helene, who was calmer now, talking softly with Ryan and John. "It's not about petunias," she said. "Two attempts on her own life, and then her maid is killed. She has to be scared to death."

Tammy said, "And from what you've told me about Helene, I'd bet that the last thing she wants is for anybody to realize she's afraid."

"Well, she sure scared me," the electrician said. "It's been a long time since anybody's yelled at me . . . let alone a little old woman like that."

"I wouldn't say that too loud," Dirk told him. "I hear she's handy with firearms."

"So, what did you find while you were tiptoeing through her prize petunias with those big clod-hoppers of yours?" Savannah asked him.

"I didn't find anything at all," he told them. "There's nothing wrong with the spa's electrical system. Everything's working fine—the heater, the blower, the lights, the GFCI breaker—all in good shape."

"What about that over there?" Dirk pointed to an electrical outlet box next to the towel valet. "Mrs. . . . I mean, Helene . . . said that's where they plug in a heater on cold nights and a boom box sometimes when they're having a party out here."

The big guy nodded. "I checked that, too. It's on a different circuit than the spa. It runs to a breaker box in that shed back there in the trees." He cast a tentative look over at Helene, who was still talking to Ryan and John. "I was going to warn her that she needs to have somebody put a GFCI breaker on that circuit. The sprinkler system's on that line, too, and wherever you've got water, you need a GFCI for safety, just in case there's a—"

"Sprinkler system?" Savannah's brain started to whir. "You say that plug there and the sprinkler system are on the same circuit . . . a different one than the spa?"

He nodded.

She looked over at Dirk. He was all ears, too.

"Why does that matter?" Tammy asked.

"It might not matter at all, but . . ." Savannah turned back to the workman. "If somebody plugged some sort of electrical appliance into that outlet over there, and then tossed it into the spa, what would happen?"

"There'd probably be some fireworks, and the circuit breaker in the box in that shed would trip."

"And what would happen to the automatic timer on the sprinkler system?" she asked.

"It could blow it out completely, but it would probably just reset."

"To twelve o'clock?"

"Yeah. Like your digital clock does when there's a power outage in your house?"

"Right."

Tammy looked from Savannah to the electrician to Dirk. "Why does that matter? Somebody tell me!"

"It matters," Savannah said, "because, according to Emma, who grew up here, the automatic sprinklers are normally set to go off at 3:00 a.m. But last night, they started watering a little after midnight."

"So," Dirk said, "if somebody caused that circuit to trip about, say, nine last night, the sprinkler timer would have reset to twelve midnight and start counting from there."

"And when it got to 3:00 a.m.," Savannah added, "it would have started the sprinklers. Only, it was really only midnight, because nobody reset the timer to the correct time after the outage."

Tammy looked over at the outlet, then turned back to the electrician. "Is there current to that plug right now?" she asked.

He nodded as he gave her a quick, typically male, once over and smiled, apparently liking what he saw. "Yes, ma'am," he said. "It's live."

"Then, if what Dirk suggested really happened, somebody must have reset the circuit breaker in that shed. And if they did, that person was probably the murderer."

"And their fingerprints might be on the panel box or the breaker switch," Savannah added.

Dirk was already punching numbers on his phone. "Coulter here," he said into the phone. "Send Michelle over to the Strauss place with her kit. Right away."

Savannah felt a surge of claustrophobia sweep through her as she stood in the tiny, cluttered shed with Michelle, the fingerprint expert of the county's CSI team, Dirk, Tammy, and the electrician—whose name they had discovered was Corey.

In the corner, shoved up against a shelf that held spa chemicals, she could feel a leaf blower poking her in the ribs . . . or was it a leaf skimmer?

"Do you all have to be in here?" Michelle asked over her shoulder as she swirled her thick brush across the outside of the panel box. "I'm running out of air."

Savannah chuckled as she watched the petite blond tech elbow Dirk and then Corey out of her way. She had seen Michelle at work many times and knew she was a woman after her own heart.

Michelle didn't suffer fools. She didn't even suffer smart folks, if they got in her way.

Tammy's phone jingled for the third time since they had gathered in the shed. She glanced down at the caller ID and shot Savannah an uneasy look.

"I'll go out," she offered.

Savannah couldn't help wondering if Mr. Peckerhead Numb Nuts had anything to do with it.

"I'll go, too," Corey said, following Tammy out the door like a hound in search of a T-bone steak.

"There's nothing on the front of this box," Michelle announced. "The lid is completely clean."

"Not even a partial?" Dirk asked, leaning over her shoulder and looking for himself.

"Nothing at all. As in, wiped clean."

Dirk gave Savannah a look. "That could be telling," he said.

She glanced around the shed. "Yeah, as in . . . nothing else in this place has been cleaned in fifty years."

"I do well to dust my coffee table," Michelle said. "I doubt this thing was wiped down out of fastidiousness."

She opened the lid to the panel box and began to brush her fine dust onto the line of switches inside, all of which were in the "on" position.

"Something tells me those are going to be just as clean as the lid," Dirk said.

He and Savannah leaned over Michelle's shoulders, watching closely, until she said, "You two bring whole new meaning to the phrase, 'breathing down my neck.' Dirk, you're making me hungry. You smell like apple pie."

"That's from his cinnamon sticks," Savannah told her. "He smokes those instead of cigarettes now."

"You can smoke cinnamon sticks?"

Dirk shrugged. "Sorta." He pointed to the circuit breakers and seemed eager to change the subject. "See anything?"

"Absolutely." Michelle leaned back, surveying her handiwork. "I see *nothing*. And that tells you something."

"An old box like that should have smudges all over it," Savannah said. "The only reason it would be clean is if someone deliberately cleaned it."

"And why would they clean it," Michelle added, "unless they'd touched it?"

Savannah looked at the shelf beside her that had half a dozen rags stuffed here and there. It certainly wouldn't have been difficult to find something to wipe away the evidence. "And why would they reset the switch on the sneak like that, unless they wanted to hide the fact that it had been thrown in the first place?"

Michelle leaned down and placed her brush back into her kit. "And your killer's pretty familiar with the property here," she said. "Not everybody would know that the circuit panel is out here in this little storage shed."

"You've got someone who knows the property," Dirk said, "knows a little about electricity, and knows enough to try to make an electrocution murder look like some sort of accidental drowning."

"Which makes them halfway smart." Savannah shook her head. "Dadgummit. I hate it when a bad guy's got smarts. Even a little. It makes him a lot harder to catch."

Dirk shrugged. "Oh, well. They can't all be like the Murphy brothers."

When Savannah, Dirk, and Michelle left the shed and returned to the spa area, they found that Ryan, John, Helene, and Corey had gone. Tammy sat on one of the chaises, talking on her cell phone.

Savannah couldn't help but notice that when Tammy saw them coming, she looked uncomfortable and brought her conversation to a quick close.

Shoving the phone into her purse, she jumped up from the chaise and hurried to meet them.

"Find anything?" she asked, a little too brightly.

"No, nothing at all," Savannah told her. "Where's the rest of the gang?"

"Helene was feeling a little tired. Ryan and John took her back to the house, so she could lie down for a while."

"I don't like the sound of that. And I don't like the way she looked or the way she was acting earlier."

"This sort of thing would upset anyone," Tammy said, "and she's been through a lot lately, with the motor scooter accident and the sleeping pill overdose, and now two people dying on her property. That's a lot for anybody to go through."

Having walked Michelle back to her car and sent her on her way, Dirk joined them.

"What I want," he said, "is to get my hands on my number one suspect."

"The husband?" Tammy asked.

"Ain't it always?" Savannah shook her head. "Any woman dies, you look at her significant other. A married woman dies with her lover, you just about know it's gonna be the husband."

"And he would know the property better than anybody other than maybe Helene herself," Dirk added. "So, he'd know where the breaker box was."

Savannah nodded. "And being a handyman, he'd probably know a little about electricity."

"Not to mention," Dirk said, "that nobody's seen him since before his wife met her nasty end."

Savannah nodded. "Oh, yeah. We've just gotta lay hands on Mr. Tiago . . . have a little talk with him."

"Hey, did you hear that?" Tammy asked.

"Hear what?" Then Savannah heard it, too. Through the trees . . . the puttering of a vehicle's out-of-tune engine coming toward them, then passing and heading on, the sound dying away.

"That's going toward the gardener's cottage," Savannah said.

But Dirk was already on his way.

Savannah and Tammy scrambled down the forest path after him.

As they hurried through the woods and passed the chicken coop, they startled the birds, who squawked and flapped their wings.

"Damn chickens," Dirk said. But he kept running, Savannah and Tammy right behind him.

A few moments later, they entered the backyard of the gardener's cottage. Savannah felt a rush of excitement when she saw an old, rusty pickup beside the house . . . and Tiago getting out of it.

As they approached, he turned, and looked surprised to see them. But not as surprised as Savannah was to see him . . . especially, his face.

"Holy cow," she said to Dirk. "Looks like our number one suspect got his clock cleaned by somebody who knew how to do it!"

With his two black and swollen eyes, the bumps and bruises on his forehead, and his fat lip, the gardener was the most unhappy-looking guy Savannah had laid eyes on in a long time.

And if, perchance, he didn't kill his wayward wife and doesn't know she's dead, Savannah thought as they caught up with him at the front door of his house, *he's about to become even more so.*

Chapter 14

If there was one thing Savannah knew about Dirk, it was that he hated notifications.

And she couldn't blame him. One of the worst aspects of being a law enforcement officer was having to inform people of the passing of their loved ones—almost always under tragic circumstances.

If the relative was female, Dirk could hardly bring himself to do it at all. Savannah had performed the hated task for him many times over the years. Not that it bothered her any less than it did him. But she knew she was better at it.

When it was a male who was the recipient of the bad news, Dirk could handle it better.

So, she left this one to him. And he waded right in.

"Tiago, my man," he said, when they intercepted him on the front porch of his cottage. "We gotta talk."

Tiago looked like the last thing in the world he wanted to do was converse with anyone. He shook his head and held up one hand. "I can't talk right now. I'm sick. I need to sleep."

"Yeah, looks like you were on the bad end of a bad tussle," Dirk said. "You wanna tell us about that?"

"Not really. I want to take a shower and go to bed."

He put his hand on the doorknob, but Dirk reached out and put his hand on his shoulder. "Tiago, *mi amigo*, have a seat over there."

Dirk pointed to a wicker rocking chair on the porch and gently pushed him toward it.

He resisted at first, but Dirk gave him a look that strongly suggested he should comply.

"Okay," he said. "I didn't do anything wrong. Nothing against the law."

"I didn't say you did," Dirk told him.

"I just had a little fight with my brother. And I got the worst of it, so it's no one's business but my family's."

"What was the fight about?" Savannah couldn't resist asking as Tiago sank into the rocking chair.

He gave her a wary look. "Nothing important. We just drank too much, and we fought, and it's over now."

"When and where did this fight take place?"

"Last night, about nine o'clock, at El Lobo Loco."

"Is that a bar?"

"Yes. A bar in La Rosita. Why are you asking me this? It was just a fight between brothers."

"What's your brother's name?" she asked.

"Sergio . . . Sergio Medina."

"Does he live in La Rosita?"

Tiago nodded. "Why are you asking me all these questions?"

"Because," Dirk said, "we're gonna have to talk to him, to make sure you were where you say you were."

"Why?" Tiago looked at Dirk through swollen eyes, then at Savannah, and back at Dirk. "Something's wrong," he said. "Why are you here? Why are you talking to me?"

Dirk drew a deep breath. "We got some bad news for you, buddy."

"What bad news? Is Miss Helene okay? She's not . . . ?"

"No. She's fine." Dirk put his hand on the man's forearm. "It's Blanca."

Tiago leaped to his feet and headed for the front door. "Where is she? What's wrong with her?"

He threw the door to the cottage open and stepped inside. "Blanca!" he yelled. "Blanca! *Donde estas?*"

Savannah hurried after him and intercepted him in the living room. "Tiago," she said, grabbing him by the arm. "She isn't here."

"Where is she?" he said, his black, swollen eyes wild. "Where is my wife?"

"She's gone. I'm so sorry, Tiago. She's *muerto.* She's dead."

"No!" He pushed her away and ran into the kitchen, then the bedroom and bathroom. "Blanca!"

Savannah waited quietly for him to complete his futile search, her heart aching.

She looked back at the doorway, where Dirk and Tammy stood, their expressions as dark as the emotions washing through her.

Finally, Tiago returned to her, tears streaming down his face.

"What happened to her?" he demanded to know. "What happened to my wife?"

"She died in the spa," Savannah told him, knowing she was about to make his hell even worse.

He looked totally confused. "The spa? What? She fell into the spa?"

"She was in the water. Taking a hot tub."

"She never does that."

"She did last night."

Dirk walked into the room and stood between her and Tiago. "This is gonna be hard for you to hear, man," he said softly. "But you're gonna find out sooner or later. Blanca wasn't alone in the hot tub."

"Who? Who was with her? Helene?"

"No. It was Vern," Dirk said. "Vern Oldham."

Savannah could feel the wave of rage that swept through the young man. It seemed like a palpable force that filled the room.

"Blanca was in the tub with *Vern?*" he asked, his voice shaking, his fists clenched. "My wife and Vern?"

"Yes," Dirk said.

"And he killed her? He killed my Blanca?"

"No," Savannah said. "He died, too. They were found in the tub, and both of them had already passed. I'm really sorry, Tiago."

Suddenly, Tiago turned and ran across the room and out the front door, nearly knocking Tammy off her feet as he passed her.

They hurried after him, but when they saw he wasn't heading for his truck, but down the path into the woods, Savannah said, "Leave him alone. Give him a few minutes."

"But he's our prime suspect," Dirk protested. "I wanna know where he's going."

"I know where he's going." She watched as Tiago disappeared among the trees. "He's like everyone else who hears that someone they love has died suddenly, unexpectedly. He has to see the place where it happened. He has to be there and try to feel what she felt . . . no matter how much it hurts."

Half an hour later, Savannah found Tiago exactly where she thought he would be, sitting on the edge of the spa, staring into the tub.

The CSI team had emptied it and strained the water, searching for evidence, but the look on Tiago's face couldn't have been any more somber than if he were seeing his wife there inside the enclosure.

She approached him slowly, watching for any signs that he resented her intrusion. But when he finally noticed her, he gave her a faint half smile and a small nod.

"Are you okay?" she said, sitting a few feet away from him on the side of the tub.

"No." He closed his eyes for a moment. She couldn't imagine what he was seeing in his mind's eye. "I'm not okay."

"It must be god-awful, what you're feeling."

"It is."

"I've lost loved ones," she said. "And I've been betrayed by people close to me. But not both at the same time. That's a double blow."

He nodded, still staring into the empty tub.

"Is there anything I can do for you?" she asked. "Anything at all?"

"Tell me what happened."

"We don't really know, beyond what Dirk already told you. They were here in the tub, and both of them died. We're pretty sure it was from some sort of an electric shock."

He thought that over for a moment. "How could that happen? Is something wrong with the spa?"

"No. An electrician just checked it. It's working fine."

Tears spilled from his swollen, black eyes and streamed down his cheeks. Savannah reached into her pocket and pulled out a tissue. She offered it to him, wondering how a man could be so unlucky as to have his wife murdered and get a nasty beating all in one day.

The coincidence seemed unlikely.

He appeared genuinely surprised and deeply upset to hear of his wife's passing. But Savannah reminded herself that she had been fooled many times before.

Contrary to popular opinion, it wasn't easy, even for professionals, to always know who was lying and who was telling the truth.

"Maybe you're wrong," he said. "Maybe they were here, but not together . . . in that way."

"Maybe," she replied. "Anything's possible. You probably knew her better than anyone, Tiago. What do you think happened?"

He passed his hand over his face and shook his head. "My wife was beautiful. Any man would want her. And Vern wanted every woman. Some men are like that."

The rage and pain that flashed across his face made Savannah think that, if he could lay hands on a living Vern at that moment, Vern would be murdered a second time.

"Blanca was smart," he continued. "But she wasn't smart in that way, like he was. She was like a child in her heart. She trusted everyone. A man like him can take advantage of someone like her."

Savannah nodded. "That's true. There are wolves in this world . . . and lambs."

"I wish I could punish him, but I can't punish him for hurting her, because he's already dead."

"We can catch the person who killed them. Will you help me do that, Tiago?"

He considered her words carefully, then said, "Yes. Blanca was foolish to be with him. But she wasn't a bad person. And she didn't deserve to die. What can I do?"

"Answer some questions for me."

"Okay. I will if I can."

"Miss Helene said that sometimes, when the weather is cold, people plug a portable heater in over there." She pointed to the outlet by the towel valet.

"Yes, we do that sometimes."

"Where is that heater now? I didn't see it in the shed with the spa supplies."

"We keep it in the garage. Sometimes we use it on the patio by the house and beside the pool, too."

"And how about the boom box . . . the one that you use out here sometimes? Is that in the garage, too?"

"No. That belongs to Waldo. He keeps it in the tool shed behind his house."

"Okay. Now, try to think hard, Tiago. Has anything different, anything unusual happened in the past few days?"

"Miss Helene fell over the cliff. And she had the problem with her medicine."

"Yes, of course. But anything else? Anything at all?"

He appeared to be thinking hard for a long time. Then he said, "This isn't important, but you said anything."

"Yes, what is it?"

"A few days ago the shovel disappeared. The one I use to clean the chicken coop. I always put the tools away in their places. I hang the shovel on the wall in a shed by the coop. But when I wanted to use it the other day, it was gone. I looked for it everywhere, but I haven't found it yet."

"What does it look like?"

"It's small and the blade is flat."

She nodded. "Down South we call that a spade. It's the perfect thing for cleaning a chicken coop."

"And one corner of the blade is broken off." He shrugged. "I was trying too hard to dig out a rock for Miss Helene."

"Thank you, Tiago," she said. "And now I have one last question to ask you. . . ."

"Okay."

"This isn't a time when you can have any secrets. The police are going to uncover everything there is to know about you and Blanca and your life together. Eventually, they'll figure out what really happened to you last night, to your face. So, you might as well tell me. Who were you fighting, and what was the fight about?"

"I'm sorry, *señora*," he said. "It doesn't matter now. I've told you enough. We're done talking."

And with that, he stood and walked away, heading back toward his cottage.

Savannah watched him leave, surprised by his sudden change in attitude and wondering what it meant.

Well, Tiago, she thought. *The fact that you won't answer that question means it's the one I have to get answered first . . . right after I look for the heater, the boom box, and that shovel.*

"So, what did you squeeze out of him?" Dirk wanted to know when Savannah found him and Tammy standing by the cliff where Helene had fallen days before.

"Not a lot," she replied. "I couldn't get him to tell me about the fight. What are you two doing here?"

"I thought I'd show the kid where Mrs. Strauss took her tumble."

"I think you're right about the dirt there in the path, Savannah," Tammy said. "Looks like somebody dug a hole there to me, too."

"Speaking of digging . . . we've got a runaway shovel to locate."

"Get Dirko here to put out an APB," Tammy said, gouging him in the ribs with her elbow.

Savannah waved a hand in the direction of the main house. "How about you two shake some tail feathers and help me look instead?"

"Yeah, okay," Dirk grumbled, "but no more chicken references."

"I'd like to have a four-car garage," Tammy said, looking around the cavernous interior.

"I'd like to have a garage," Dirk added.

"I'd like to find a heater with water inside it and big, fat fingerprints all over it." Savannah walked along the wall, searching the shelves that held everything from luggage to boxes of seasonal decorations in well-organized and clearly labeled boxes.

"Helene has six boxes of Halloween stuff," Tammy said. "I'll bet this place makes a great haunted house."

"And Easter must be pretty festive, too." Savannah pointed to a stack of clear, plastic bins filled with colorful rabbits and egg decorations. "But so much for the fun stuff. Where are the tools and patio equipment?"

"I see a rake and some chair covers over there." Tammy pointed to a far wall.

They headed that direction, and it didn't take them long to locate several different types of patio heaters, including a large fire pit hanging on a hook from the wall next to a big propane gas heater.

Savannah pulled a surgical glove from her purse and slipped it onto her hand. "I think this is what we're looking for," she said, reaching behind a folded chair cover and pulling out a small, portable, electric heater.

Dirk donned a pair of gloves himself and took

the heater from Savannah. He turned it this way and that, as they all three looked it over.

He gave it a little shake.

"No water that I can see," he said. "But I'll bag it and take it to Eileen. See if she can find anything wrong with it."

"Or any prints or fibers or other forms of evidence on it," Tammy added in her most officious, Moonlight Magnolia tone.

Savannah was already moving down the wall, looking at the Peg Board wall where the large garden tools hung, all in a neat row. If one tool had been missing, there would have been a noticeable gap. Or if there had been an extra one, it would have been obvious.

Everything had a place and was neatly arranged accordingly.

"Helene runs a tight ship," she said.

"Just like my trailer," Dirk replied with a self-satisfied smile.

Savannah marveled at how thoroughly he could deceive himself. Having a tidy, well-organized home was a far cry from knowing where all your junk was in the midst of a cluttered mess, like his house trailer.

Just because a guy could lay his hands on his bottle opener at a moment's notice, didn't make him Martha Stewart.

"I don't see our missing shovel," Savannah said. "Not that I was really expecting to. I'm sure Tiago searched here already."

"You act like you believe everything he told you." Dirk was wearing his highly suspicious, cynical look. The one he wore most of the time. Savannah suspected he wore it in the shower and to bed.

"I wouldn't say I believe everything that *any*body tells me, but—"

Dirk looked wounded. "You don't believe everything *I* tell you?"

"Nope. You lied to me once. Trust is a fragile thing. And it was broken."

"What did I lie to you about?"

"Breaking the wing off my fairy statue in my rose garden."

"Oh, God. I'm never gonna live down that stupid fairy."

"Hey, it's my fairy, and I love her. Don't call her stupid."

Tammy giggled and walked away. She was always smart enough to know when to make a graceful exit.

"I tripped over it," Dirk protested. "It was an accident!"

"I know. And I forgave you for the accident. But lying to me, blaming in on poor little Cleopatra—who's an indoor kitty—*that* I'll hold against you till the day I die."

"Apparently so. Sheezzz."

After locking the electric heater in Dirk's trunk, the three checked the shed by the chicken coop, looking for the missing shovel.

Dirk was clearly eager to leave the area as soon as possible. So eager, in fact, that Tammy's curiosity was piqued.

"This phobia thing you've got about chickens," she asked him as they headed in the direction of Waldo's cottage, "does it have anything to do with that awful cock-fighting ring we busted some time back?"

"Uh, yeah," he replied. "That's it. That's when it started."

Savannah nudged him with her elbow. "And you wonder why nobody trusts you?"

"*Nobody* trusts me?"

"Nobody who actually knows you."

"That's cold, girl."

"Okay, I trust you a little. But only because I'm a sucker for a cute ass."

"You think I have a cute ass?"

"Yeah, but don't let it go to your head. We'd all have to start calling you butt head, and I don't want that sort of immature talk going on at the office."

"Of course not."

As they approached Waldo's house, they could see a building behind it that was too small to be a garage.

"His car's still gone," Dirk said. "When I told Helene I couldn't find him here on the property, she said he's often gone all night."

"Doing what?" Savannah asked.

"She was a bit vague about that. Deliberately avoided the question."

"I wouldn't be surprised if he's out trying to score one of his recreational substances. Emma told me that's pretty much his main pastime— doing the drugs or looking for his next high."

"Sad way to live a life," Tammy commented.

Her cell phone beeped again. She pulled it from her pocket and looked at her latest text with a look of dread on her face.

It occurred to Savannah that jumping every time your phone rang was a pretty sad way to live a life, too. And it took all of the fine, Christian, Southern upbringing that Granny had given her for her not to curse Chad the Cad and wish he would fall down a flight of steep stairs into a pit of rabid crocodiles.

Just regular crocs will do, she decided with all the charitable kindness she could muster.

Tammy texted something back, and Savannah wondered if there was any point at all in suggesting that interacting with a fool was foolhardy.

Probably not.

Savannah had realized long ago, that was something a woman had to learn on her own . . . the hard way. And it was heartbreaking to see how long and how hard that way had to be in most cases. *When it comes to matters of the heart,* Savannah thought, *these processes take time.*

And as she watched her beautiful young friend, so full of life and love . . . so trusting that both life and love would bring her only good things . . . she hoped that hard road wouldn't be too long or too rough for her.

"These are the only outbuildings that Tiago mentioned?" Dirk asked as they approached Waldo's shed.

Savannah nodded. "The only ones where they store tools—the garage, the one behind the spa, the one near the chicken coop, and this one."

"So, if we don't find that shovel here," Tammy said, "it's God-knows-where."

"Yeah." Savannah sighed. "Then we start looking in bushes and the Dumpster for it. Unless the

garbage service has collected the trash since Helene's cliff accident."

"One can always hope," Dirk said. "I'm dedicated to my work and all that hooey, but whenever
possible, I avoid Dumpster diving. Kitty litter, wet
coffee grounds, and rotten potato peels . . ." He
shuddered.

"And this one would probably have chicken
coop scrapings in it, too," Savannah added, grinning at him.

"Shut up."

"Okay."

When they reached the small shed, they found
the door was secured with a padlock.

"What's ol' Waldo got in there that he needs to
hide from the world?" Dirk said.

"More like from his grandma," Savannah replied. "With that big fence around the property, I
can't imagine they get a lot of unwanted visitors."

Savannah was already rummaging in her purse.
A moment later, she produced her lock pick.

Dirk gave her a look.

"What?" she said. "Helene gave me permission
to search her property. If you don't want to see
this, Detective Sergeant Coulter, avert your eyes."

"Hell, no. I'm gonna watch. You're way better at
that lock picking business than I am, and I'm always trying to figure out why."

He didn't learn much, because Savannah had
the lock opened in five seconds.

"Some women knit while they watch their soap
operas. I practice picking locks." She shrugged
and grinned. "Hey, for a while there I was totally
hooked on *General Hospital.*"

She opened the door, and they stepped inside.

This shed was a bit larger than the one by the spa, and that was a good thing, because it was overflowing with junk.

"This is the least organized, dirtiest place I've yet to see on this property," Savannah remarked as she looked up and down the teetering stacks of magazines, bags of old clothes, and boxes overflowing with discarded computer equipment, CDs, and the occasional piece of drug paraphernalia. "The rest of the estate is neat as a pin . . . though I never could figure out what was so gall darned neat about a pin."

"Expensive looking bong." Tammy pointed to a large piece of fanciful, colorful blown glass . . . a marijuana bong with a broken stem.

"Hey, spare no expensive for your favorite vices," Savannah said. "That's why I put only the best chocolate and ice cream on my backside."

"High brow reading material here." Dirk held up a handful of porn magazines, mixed with some periodicals promoting the cannabis culture.

"How old is Waldo?" Tammy asked.

Savannah replied, "Old enough to have moved on."

Tammy moved a big, empty cardboard box that, according to the logo printed on its side, had contained a large, flat-screen television. Pushing it aside, she peeked behind it and said, "Hey! I think I've got a shovel here!"

"Don't touch it!" Savannah said. "And let's get a picture of it first, hidden behind the box."

"Any good defense attorney would say the box was just set in front of it," Dirk replied.

"Not if we prove he used the shovel a few days ago and bought the TV last summer."

"Good point."

Savannah pulled a small digital camera from her purse and snapped several photos of the box and the hidden shovel. Putting the camera away, she grabbed a couple of the disposable gloves that she always carried in her pocketbook and handed them to Tammy.

"You found the evidence—or, at least, we hope it's evidence—so you can retrieve it," she told her.

It did Savannah's heart good to see the wide grin on Tammy's face as she donned the gloves, then reached behind the box to get the shovel.

Until Tammy had met Chad, she lived for her work. Investigation and everything remotely related to it was Tammy's chosen career, and had been since she'd been a child. All little girls might go through a Nancy Drew period, while growing up, but Tammy Hart had never outgrown the dream. And there was no happier person on the planet than someone who was living their childhood fantasy.

Until she meets a controlling numbskull, who hijacks her life, Savannah thought as Tammy's cell phone chimed once again. *What's that been, thirty texts in the past two hours?*

Once Tammy had the shovel out of its hiding place, Savannah said, "Hold it up here. I want to see its blade."

Tammy tilted it, bringing the business end of the tool even with Savannah's face.

There it was. The flat blade, which proved it was a spade, not a shovel, as Tiago had described. And better yet, there was the damaged corner.

"It's chipped, just like Tiago said," she told them. "He explained that he'd broken it trying to dig a rock out of the ground for Helene."

"So, this is definitely the shovel that Tiago claims went missing?" Dirk asked.

"I'm sure it is," Savannah said. "And the fact that it was obviously hidden, and in a locked shed, points a finger right at Helene's favorite great-nephew."

Dirk was still looking, moving boxes aside, searching inside miscellaneous jars and cans. "Bingo," he said, showing them the contents of an old, wooden, cigar box. Inside were at least a dozen tiny glassine envelopes containing white powder.

"Waldo's cocaine stash," Tammy said. "That's got to be helpful."

"Oh, it will be," Dirk said. "This means, as soon as I lay hands on our man Waldo, I can hang on to him as long as I want."

"It's going to break Helene's heart," Savannah said softly.

Dirk sighed and nodded. "Something tells me this guy's going to be a source of heartbreak for a long, long time . . . for everybody that loves him."

Chapter 15

While Dirk and Tammy properly packaged, labeled, and stowed the spade and cocaine evidence in the Buick's trunk, Savannah decided to take a stroll to the main house and see if she could find Emma.

She hadn't spoken to her since last night's tragic activities, and Savannah wanted to find out how Helene was doing.

As Savannah approached the front of the mansion, she saw Emma standing behind her BMW, putting an overnight bag into the trunk.

When she opened the driver's door and started to get inside, Savannah called out to her. "Hey, Emma. Got a minute?"

Emma tossed her handbag onto the passenger's seat, then closed the car door and walked over to Savannah. "Sure," she said. "How's it going?"

"Okay. Can we sit a spell?"

Emma motioned to a couple of comfortable chairs in the shade of a large, leafy oak tree. They strolled over to the chairs and sat down.

"I saw you throw your bag in the back of your car," Savannah said. "Are you going somewhere?"

"I figured I'd go back home."

"Oh, really? So soon?"

"Well, the main reason for me coming over here was to keep an eye on Oma, but your friends, Ryan and John, are doing a good job of that."

"I'm sure they are, but . . ."

Emma shrugged and looked a little sheepish. "Kyd called me, and he really wants me to come home. He misses me. He's not good at being on his own."

When Savannah didn't reply, Emma added, "He's just so crazy about me, adores me, you know. Can't stand it when we're apart even for a second. It's really true, true love. Soul-mate stuff."

Sounds more like having a giant, parasitic, blood-sucking tick on your butt, Savannah thought. But she decided to keep her opinions to herself. Something told her that Emma wouldn't appreciate her observations about soul mates who couldn't allow you a moment to yourself.

"Kyd hated going to his gig without me last night," Emma continued, as Savannah tried to picture what a giant tick with spiked hair and a Poison Nails logo on its back would look like. "Sometimes, I go along to offer support and also to keep an eye on him. You know how those groupies are . . . always after the musicians . . . throwing their panties at them . . . stuff like that."

Savannah shrugged. "Can't say that I understand that. Don't see the point in hurling your bloomers at a guy unless you're in them."

"What did you want to talk to me about?" Emma

asked. She crossed one leg over the other and toyed with the lace of her sneaker.

"Waldo."

"Oh, must we?" She sighed and slouched in her chair, like a five-year-old protesting the fact that she had to eat a beet and liver sandwich.

"You don't like him much, do you?" Savannah commented.

"No. I really don't."

"Would you tell me why?"

"Because he's a spoiled little brat who takes everyone and everything around him for granted and always has."

Savannah nodded. "That's upfront and honest. Thank you."

"Waldo was pretty much raised here, too, you know. Just like I was. Oma took better care of him than Ada did. He had all this given to him." She waved an arm, encompassing the gracious mansion, the lush, sweeping grounds. "Even back when Ada was married, she and her husband would drop Waldo off here for months at a time, when they were globe hopping, or even when they just didn't want a kid around."

Savannah thought it over for a couple of moments, then said, "That might lead a kid to feel pretty rotten about himself, fancy digs or no."

"Oma made up for it. She showered him with love and attention. Anything he didn't get from his mother, he more than got from my grandmother. She gave him everything he ever wanted. Still does."

Seeing Emma's bright green eyes flash and her pretty face contort with anger, it occurred to Savannah that Emma and Waldo had a bit of pseudo-sibling rivalry going on. And it appeared to be a pretty intense battle . . . at least on Emma's side of the chess board.

"How does Waldo support himself?" she asked.

"Stealing money from Oma's purse every time her back's turned. Begging from his mother. Oh, and dealing dope."

Savannah thought of the bundles of cocaine in the shed. "A lot of it?"

"Enough to support his habit. He keeps getting arrested. Oma spends a fortune on attorneys to keep him out of jail. He's off to rehab for a while . . . again, at my grandmother's expense . . . and then the cycle repeats itself."

"Why doesn't Ada pay for all the legal bills and rehab, since he's her kid?"

"Ada doesn't have any money. She spends it all on plastic surgery and toys to keep her boys happy."

"Boys? She has more than Vern?"

"Please. She has more boyfriends than shoes. Apparently, when you're Ada, it takes a lot of stud service to keep your mind off the fact you're not as young as you used to be."

"Has anybody told her about Vern yet?"

"Not that I know of. I didn't call her. I don't think my grandmother did."

Savannah was pretty sure Dirk hadn't. The last she'd heard, Dirk had the gal at the station trying to track down Vern's next of kin. And it was proving to be a challenge, considering that he gave out false addresses and changed aliases more often than he did his socks.

She made a mental note to talk to Ada and see

how broken up she was, or wasn't, about losing this great, or mediocre, love of her life.

"We can't find Waldo," Savannah told her. "We looked in his house, around the property, in his shed. Couldn't find him anywhere."

"He leaves without saying anything to anybody. That's nothing new. He goes into Hollywood, cruises around until he scores."

"Drugs . . . sex . . . ?"

"Yeah. Whatever."

"Any particular places he goes?"

"There's a bar on Sunset in West Hollywood called Rattlesnake Tom's. He hangs out there a lot."

"And you say he doesn't have any sort of job?"

"Not unless you call getting high and playing video games a career."

"Does he ever do any work around the estate here? Digging, for instance?"

"Digging? You mean, like with a shovel?"

"Exactly."

Emma sniffed. "You've got to be kidding. Waldo never used any kind of tool or did an hour's work in his life."

"When did you last see him?"

"I saw him yesterday afternoon, as soon as I got here. I was pulling into the garage and nearly ran over him."

"What was he doing?"

"He said he was looking for his boom box . . . the one he likes to listen to when he's outside. He accused me of taking it, sweetheart that he is. Like I'd want the ratty old thing."

"His boom box?" Savannah's mood lifted considerably. All of a sudden, the flower gardens around them seemed more colorful, the birds' songs sounded sweeter, the sun shone brighter. "And did he find it?"

"Don't know. I didn't hang around to find out. That was the last time I saw him, and if I don't run into him again soon, that's fine with me. I avoid Waldo as much as possible. Everyone does."

Except Dirk, Savannah thought. *If Dirk's anxious to get his hands on him now, just wait till he hears about this!*

After Savannah sent Emma on her way, she gave Dirk a call. "You guys still messing with that shovel and dope?" she asked him.

"Just finishing up," he replied. "The stuff from the shed tested positive for cocaine. What are you up to?"

"I had a conversation with Emma. She told me Waldo hangs out at Rattlesnake Tom's, a bar on Sunset in West Hollywood."

"I know the place," he said. "A real spit-on-the-floor dive. I'll call Hollywood, and see if they can send somebody over there to pick him up for me."

"Oh, yes, I'm sure the HPD has nothing better to do than to run that little errand for you. And if they nab him, see if they'll drag him back to San Carmelita for you, too."

"Brothers in blue, banding together in the never-ending search for law and order."

"Uh-huh. Be sure and use that phrase when you talk to them, too. I'm sure it'll go a long way." She walked up to the door and rang the bell. "I'm going to see if I can talk to Helene before I leave. Make sure she's okay."

"Gotcha. Me and the kid, we'll meet you back at the cars."

"Bye."

The door opened, and Ryan was standing there, looking immaculate, as always, in a pale blue shirt and navy slacks.

"Hi," he said, holding the door open for her. "How's it going out there?"

"We found the spade," she said, keeping her voice low. "It was in Waldo's shed."

"Grandnephew Waldo?"

"Yeah. And a stash of cocaine big enough to get a herd of elephants buzzed."

He glanced over his shoulder toward the back of the house. "That's not good. Helene's going to hate hearing that. She has nothing but good to say about him."

"She's too kind," Savannah told him. "Really, from everything I've heard and observed myself, she's way too kind where he's concerned. Where is she now?"

"In the kitchen, baking a German chocolate cake. John's watching and getting tips."

"Waiting to lick the spoon and the bowl is more like it."

"That, too."

"I want to talk to her, say 'bye' before I leave."

"I think she'd like that. She's got some pretty nice things to say about you, too."

"The feeling's mutual."

Ryan led Savannah through the house to the kitchen, where they found John standing at the stove, stirring something vigorously in a heavy saucepan. Sweat was beading on his forehead.

Helene sat on a stool at the island, watching him with a critical eye.

"Don't let it burn!" she was telling him. "If it sticks at all on the bottom, it'll scorch and be ruined!"

"Looks like she's working you to the bone there, good buddy," Savannah said as she walked over to the stove and peeked into the pan.

One smell of the heavenly, caramel-colored aroma told her that John was doing the down and dirty part of cooking the buttery base for the coconut and pecan frosting. As she recalled, the boiling mixture had to be stirred vigorously and continuously for twelve minutes.

It was a long twelve minutes with the sticky, hot liquid spattering all over your hand. And that was why she only made German chocolate cake on holidays.

"If I'd known you were that good at stirring that stuff," she told John, "I'd have given you the job last Christmas."

"Sorry, love," he said, "but I only do this for Helene."

Savannah sat down on the stool next to Helene's. "Do you have this effect on all men?" she asked her.

"All." Helene's green eyes twinkled. "I crook my little finger, and they come running."

"It's not your little finger that caught my attention," John said, stirring, stirring, and stirring, "it was your clenched fist that got me moving."

Ryan laughed. "More like the promise of a prize-winning recipe."

"How are you doing?" Savannah asked, putting her hand on Helene's forearm.

"Better. Cooking always makes me feel better. Especially if someone else is doing it for me." A sadness passed over her face. "Though when I think of poor Blanca, even the baking doesn't . . ."

"I understand," Savannah said. "It's a terrible thing."

Helene shook her head and closed her eyes for a moment. "Tiago will be heartsick when he hears."

"He's already been notified," Savannah said. "He arrived home earlier, and we told him."

"Is he okay?" Helene asked.

"As okay as could be expected under the circumstances."

Helene's face hardened. "If it weren't for Blanca, I must admit, I'd almost be glad to hear that Vern's gone. I guess that sounds coldhearted."

"From what we knew about Victor, I mean, Vern," Ryan said, "I don't blame you very much for feeling that way. It's a shame, anyone losing their life that way, but he caused a lot of misery in this world. I don't think too many people are going to miss him."

"Does Ada know?" Helene asked Savannah.

"I haven't heard. We haven't told her yet. I suppose we should," Savannah said, thinking it wasn't a job she wanted, but she'd probably get stuck doing it.

Someday, Dirk was going to have to find some really remarkable way of paying her back for doing all his dirty work.

"Ada might miss him," Helene said. "She saw something in him. God knows what."

"I don't believe she loved him for who he was."

John turned the heat down a bit under the saucepan. "I suspect she loved him because he had a knack for making her feel better about herself. He was good at that . . . and therefore, at seduction."

"Poor Blanca, falling for that crap." Helene shook her head. "And look what it cost her."

"Do you think that's why she was killed? Because she was with him?" Savannah asked.

"No, I don't," Helene replied. "I think she was in the wrong place at the wrong time."

"Then, you think that Vern was the intended target . . . the one the killer was after?"

"No, I do not." Helene seemed grim and more than a little certain. "I think I was the intended victim."

"You?" Savannah asked. "Why do you think they were trying to kill you?"

"Because every single night, I go take a soak in that tub. It helps my arthritis. Everybody knows that. I've been doing it for years." Savannah saw her shudder, ever so slightly.

Then Helene Strauss lifted her chin a notch and continued, "If I hadn't been at your party last night, Savannah, I would have been in that spa, just like I am every night. It's quite dark down there after sunset. And there are a lot of shrubs on that one side of the tub. If someone had thrown something electrical into the water, the way you think they did, they probably couldn't see who was in it for sure. They just assumed it was me."

Savannah didn't want to believe her. She would much, much prefer to think that someone wanted to murder a womanizing swindler than a dear woman she had grown to like and admire greatly.

She tried to picture the spa, the way it had looked last night. And she had to admit that if someone had plugged an appliance into that outlet and sneaked around behind the bushes, where they grew very close to the tub, they wouldn't have had a clear view of the water. At least, not until the moment they were tossing their item in.

Helene's theory was plausible. This double murder could have been yet a third attempt on the matriarch's life.

She looked at Ryan and John, and the solemn looks on their faces told her that they, too, believed that Helene could be right.

"I'm glad you have Ryan and John here with you," Savannah said. "Very glad."

"Me, too," Helene replied. "Otherwise I'd have to stir my own frosting."

A few moments later, Ryan walked Savannah back to the front door.

"Keep an eye on her highness," Savannah told him, tiptoeing to give him a peck on the cheek.

"Every moment of every day," he said.

"And while you've got your eyes open, keep tabs on our friend, Tiago. He seemed sincere to me today, but he's got a passel of bruises he doesn't want to talk about."

"And a deceased wife who was fooling around on him."

"Exactly. And if Waldo shows his mug around here . . ."

"Call you or Dirk right away, and keep him here. Got it."

Savannah paused, her hand on the doorknob.

"And just one more thing. We're looking for what's been described as a ratty old boom box. It belonged to Waldo, was sometimes used for background music beside the spa . . . and it's gone missing."

"Gotcha."

"Thank you, Ryan."

"For you, Savannah, anything."

"A piece of that cake when it's done?"

He gave her a knee-melting grin. "Even that."

By the time Savannah made her way back to the spa area where her car was parked, Dirk and Tammy were waiting for her. Dirk, as impatient as ever, was leaning against his car, arms folded over his chest, scowling.

Tammy stood nearby, talking on her cell phone, her back to them, her voice low.

"I talked to Ryan, John, and Helene back at the house," she told him. "Ryan says they'll look for the boom box. And by the way, Emma says Waldo was asking her about it yesterday afternoon."

"Oh really?"

"Yes. And Ryan says they'll keep an eye out for him, too, and let us know if he comes back home."

"Good man, Ryan."

"So, what's next?"

"I'll take the spade to Eileen, have her dust it for prints or whatever. And then I'll drop the dope by the station. Then I'm off to West Hollywood. Woo-hoo."

"Want me to go to La Rosita, verify Tiago's alibi?"

"That'd be great. The only reason I'm not taking him to the station right now is because you say you believe he's clean."

"I wouldn't say he's completely off the hook. I just have a feeling about him, that he's told me the truth so far."

"Well, in my book, he's not in the clear until we find out for sure how he got those shiners."

"True. And I'm thinking a ride to La Rosita might settle that, once and for all." Savannah looked at Tammy, who was still on the phone and casting the occasional furtive glance their way. "Let me guess," she said, "she's talking to What's-His-Nuts."

"Yeah. And from what I heard, it sounded like the bimbo's making up with him."

"Tarnation."

"Yeah. What's the matter with you women? The worse a guy treats you, the more you stick around."

"It's complicated."

"Apparently so."

"And not all of us are like that. First time a guy looks cross-eyed at me, he gets kicked to the curb."

Dirk crossed his eyes and stuck out his tongue.

"Oh, pleeez," she said. "You've been camping out on the curb for years, boy. You just never noticed."

Chapter 16

Savannah had never noticed that the forty-minute drive to the tiny inland town of La Rosita was particularly long or boring. But with Tammy sitting beside her, staring out the passenger window and saying nothing, Savannah felt like she was driving to New York.

Tammy was known for her buoyancy, her effervescence, her nonstop chatter. Savannah hardly recognized this quiet, withdrawn person sitting in the passenger seat.

"I'm glad we live on the beach," Savannah offered. "When you come inland like this, you realize how much the ocean breezes really keep the temperature down."

"Uh-huh."

Savannah pointed to either side of the highway, where the brown, parched hills were covered with scrub brush and prickly pear cacti. "Not really a place you'd want to live, unless you were a rattlesnake or a coyote or a jackrabbit."

"Uh-huh."

Okay, Savannah thought, *so much for philosophical chitchat.*

"Tammy, are you mad at me?"

Tammy gave her a quick, wary look, then went back to perusing the view of the countryside from her passenger window. "No."

"Well, you could've fooled me. If I had a nickel for every word you've said since we left, I wouldn't have the down payment on a pack of gum."

"Sorry," Tammy said. "I've got a lot on my mind."

"Okay. Would you like to talk about it?"

Savannah turned the Mustang off the freeway and onto a two-lane highway that twisted through a canyon lined with citrus groves and miscellaneous oil pumps.

"I don't think we should," Tammy replied.

"Since when don't we talk about everything that goes through our minds?" Savannah asked. "Remember? You and I are the kind of gals who let it all hang out . . . especially with each other."

"I don't think Chad would like it, me talking to you about him," Tammy mumbled.

Another alarm went off in Savannah's head. Lately, she felt like she lived next door to a fire station with so many warning bells clanging.

"I reckon it's the right thing to keep a lid on how much you gossip," Savannah agreed. "But I'd like to think that if my best friend was having a problem, she'd feel comfortable sharing it with me. Even if somebody else didn't particularly like it. Nobody's got the right to tell a person what they can say and what they can't."

"It's not just that he wouldn't want me to," Tammy said after a long silence. "I don't want to

talk about him with you. You'd start telling me
how stupid I am to put up with him. And then I'd
have him telling me I'm stupid for dumping him,
and you telling me I'm stupid for not dumping
him, and I'm sick and tired of hearing how stupid
I am, when I'm just trying to—"

"Whoa! Hold on there! I'll have you know, I've
never, never called you stupid, and the day's not
gonna dawn when I do!"

"You won't say the word, but that's what you're
thinking."

"It is not!"

"So, you think it's just fine and dandy . . . me
reading his texts, talking to him on the phone,
agreeing to go out with him later to talk things
over?"

"You agreed to go out with that nasty, controlling bastard, after you got up the gumption to
break it off with him? What's the matter with you,
girl? Have you completely lost your marbles?"

Silence reigned supreme for at least a mile, as
more scenes of cacti and dried brush flew by the
window. Rattlesnakes slithered, coyotes prowled,
and jackrabbits hopped.

Finally, Savannah couldn't take it anymore.
"Yeah . . . thank God for those ocean breezes," she
said.

"Uh-huh."

El Lobo Loco wasn't the nicest bar Savannah
had ever been in by a long shot, but it wasn't the
worst. It didn't smell of stale beer or dirty bath-
rooms, and the mostly Latino clientele appeared

to be average working men, stopping by the cantina for a drink before going home to their families.

Only one other woman was in the bar when Savannah and Tammy walked in. She was sitting with a couple of guys in the rear corner, drinking a beer. She wore a pink dress and white apron with the name "Cecelia" embroidered on it—a waitress's uniform.

She, and every other patron of El Lobo, gave Savannah and Tammy thorough appraisals as they walked across the room and to the bar. From the looks on the men's faces, they passed muster. But when the woman saw the approval and interest on the face of the man sitting next to her, she seemed less impressed with the new arrivals.

She shot them a couple of dirty looks, then whispered something to her companion. When he turned his head to answer her, Savannah noticed that he had a black eye and bruised cheek.

He also bore a strong resemblance to Tiago— the same strong jaw, high cheekbones, and thick, black hair. And through his thin tee-shirt, his body looked as toned and muscular as the gardener's. Even more so.

Savannah figured this was the brother who had tangled with Tiago . . . and clearly won the fight.

The bartender, a small, older fellow wearing a beer-stained shirt, hurried over to take their order. "Two colas," she said.

When she saw the frown on Tammy's face, she quickly amended it to, "One cola and an organic water."

"Organic water? What's that?" he said.

"Just water," she told him. "If it's wet, it'll do."

"Wet water, we have."

As he walked away to get their drinks, Savannah sat on one of the stools, and Tammy took a seat beside her. The ten or so drinkers watched their every move and talked to each other in hushed tones.

"Reckon they don't see a lot of strangers in here," Savannah said.

"Obviously not," Tammy replied.

"Especially good-lookin' gals like you and me." Savannah gave her an elbow poke and a grin.

She got an anemic smile in return.

"Here you go, *señoritas*," the bartender said, sliding the two glasses toward them. "Welcome to El Lobo Loco, The Crazy Wolf."

"Thank you," Savannah said, laying a twenty dollar bill on the bar.

He picked up the bill. "I'll get your change for you."

"I don't need change," she said, leaning closer to him and lowering her voice. "I need some information."

The bartender glanced quickly in both directions. Then down at the bill in his hand. "This is enough for the drinks," he said. "I don't know how much information it'll buy."

"Well, you give me my money's worth, and we'll discuss how much more I owe you. Sí, senor?"

"Sí."

"I need to know about a guy who comes in here all the time, he and his wife. His name is Tiago Medina."

"I know Tiago." He glanced toward the corner, where the woman sat with the fellow with the black eye.

"When was the last time you saw him?"

"Why do you want to know?"

"I'm a friend of Tiago's."

"You aren't the police?"

"No. I'm not the police."

He glanced at Tammy.

"Neither am I," she said, reaching for her water. "We want to help Tiago. That's all."

He thought it over for a moment, then said, "The last time I saw him was this morning. When he left here."

"Tiago was here drinking this morning?" Savannah asked.

"No. He was drinking last night. He drank too much and"—again, he shot a look at the couple in the corner—"he had some problems."

"What kind of problems?"

"It doesn't matter. Family problems."

Savannah heard a buzz coming from Tammy's purse, which was sitting on the bar between them. Tammy started to reach for it but took one look at Savannah and withdrew her hand.

Savannah fought the urge to fish the phone out of her purse and dunk it into the glass of non-organic water.

"I know about the fight," Savannah told the bartender. "Tiago's looking a bit the worse for wear today. I was just wondering if you could tell me what you saw, how it started, stuff like that."

Suddenly, without saying a word, Tammy snatched her purse off the bar and headed for the front door.

Savannah pushed down the surge of anger she felt at such an unprofessional move. Tammy knew better. And if she didn't, she was going to hear all about it on their way home.

But for now, Savannah had to attend to her own business at hand. And her task at the moment was to get this bartender to tell her more.

Unfortunately, she knew the look on his face. Like a meter that had run out of time and needed more coins fed in, he had reached his limit and wanted more than the change from her twenty dollar bill.

She pulled another one from her purse and put it on the bar. When he reached for it, she held it tightly in place.

"So, Tiago had too much to drink last night," she said. "And he had a fight with his brother, Sergio, over there."

The barkeeper nodded.

"What did they fight about?"

"It doesn't matter."

"Tell me something that does matter if you want this money."

He hesitated. "Okay. Tiago was too drunk to drive home to San Carmelita last night. He was going to sleep in his truck. So, I told him he could sleep here." He pointed to a door in the rear of the room. "Back there . . . on a couch in my office. This morning he left."

"He was here all night?"

"All night."

"Were you here all night, too?"

"No, I went home to my wife."

"Then how do you know for sure that he didn't leave and come back sometime during the night?"

Suddenly, the bartender's eyes narrowed. "Are

you sure you aren't *policia*?" he said. "You sound like *policia*."

Savannah let go of the twenty. "I'm not the police," she said. "If I was a cop, I'd have a petty cash fund and be able to pay you more than that."

She picked up her purse off the bar and stood, intending to try her luck with the couple in the corner. But when she turned to head in that direction, she saw they were gone. The booth was empty.

"Damnation," she muttered. Glancing around the room, she didn't see anyone who looked eager to gab. They were all giving her highly suspicious and moderately hostile looks.

Savannah decided her welcome had run dry at El Lobo Loco.

When she exited the bar, she looked up and down the street, hoping to see Tiago's brother, Sergio, or his lady friend.

But all she saw was Tammy, who was half a block away, walking in her direction.

Annoyed at herself for having let an important contact slip away like that, Savannah rehearsed the little speech she was going to give Tammy. The basic theme was going to be something like, "What the hell were you thinking, girl, leaving in the middle of an interview to call your no-good, sorry-excuse-for-a-human-being boyfriend?"

She climbed into the Mustang, started the engine, and rolled down the windows to release some of the stifling heat.

When Tammy opened the door and got in, Savannah said nothing, not trusting herself to keep it civil. She didn't want to bite the kid's head off . . . just set her straight.

As she pulled onto the street and headed toward the highway, she said in the gentlest tone she could manage, "We were in the middle of an interview back there, Tammy, and—"

"Did you get anything out of him? Enough to confirm Tiago's alibi?"

"Not really, but that's not the point I was making. I—"

"Did you find out what the fight was about?"

"No, and—"

"I did."

"*You* did? How did you . . . ?"

"I saw them leaving—that couple in the corner. When they went outside, he got in a truck and drove away, and she walked down the road in the opposite direction. Turns out she was going to work at a café down there."

"Oh, okay."

"I chased her down and talked to her. Her name's Cecelia Medina. She's Tiago's sister-in-law."

"Yes, I figured she might be because he looked a lot like—"

"Turns out," Tammy continued, "she started the fight last night between the two brothers. She told Tiago that his wife was a loose woman, who was probably fooling around on him with other men. Seems Cecelia never really liked Blanca, always thought Tiago could've done better. But when she told him that last night here in the bar, Tiago got mad and started yelling at her, telling her that she had a bit of a past before she and his brother got married, too. Sergio had to defend his wife. And he and Tiago wound up in a fistfight. A pretty bad one. Tiago was too drunk and messed up afterward to drive, so the bartender let him sleep it off in the back room. Everybody made up this morning, and Tiago went over to their house for a breakfast of eggs and sausages. Then Tiago drove back home."

Tammy stopped to draw a breath. Then she turned to Savannah. "What did you find out?"

"Um . . . uh . . . pretty much the same thing."

They drove on in silence until they reached the freeway.

Then Savannah reached over and patted her young friend's thigh. "Tammy," she said. "Don't you ever, ever, ever let anybody on the face of this earth tell you that you're stupid, or make you feel like anything less than the wonderful, amazing woman that you are."

"What?"

"You heard me. Promise me, right now."

"Okay. I promise."

Tammy placed her hand on top of Savannah's and gave it a little squeeze. "Thank you, Savannah," she said with tears in her eyes. "I love you."

"You're welcome, kiddo. And I love you, too."

Chapter 17

Savannah pulled the Mustang into the driveway of Tammy's beach house and cut the engine.

The return trip from La Rosita had been more pleasant and chatty than the ride there. So, Savannah was reluctant to reopen any worm-filled cans. But she felt she couldn't let Tammy out of the car without some sort of warning.

"Thank you for coming with me," Savannah told her.

"Oh, come on. We both know you didn't need me. You're just babysitting me to keep me away from Chad."

"Actually, you helped more than you realize. But speaking of Chad—"

"We probably shouldn't."

"I know. But if I didn't do what I shouldn't, I wouldn't do much o' nothin'."

"Huh?"

"There's something I have to say to you, Tammy, and I know you don't want to hear it. But you know how I am. I'm the oldest of nine younguns, and that makes me a mite bossy. You're just going to have to sit still and listen while I say my piece."

Tammy folded her hands demurely in her lap and gave Savannah a long-suffering look. "Go ahead," she said. "But hurry, because I've got company coming over at six o'clock, and something tells me you don't want to run into him."

"Oh, no. Tell me he's not coming here, after you told him it was over. Tell me you're not going to let him into your house when he's been texting you and calling you like a maniac all day long."

"Savannah, you don't understand. At first, he was texting me because he thought I was out with another guy. But when I convinced him I was with you, he started apologizing like crazy, telling me how much he loves me and how he'll do anything to get me back. He just wants to come by here for a while tonight and talk. What can be the harm in that?"

"What's the harm? Tammy, you know the warning signs. You've only been dating him a few weeks, and look how much control he has over you already. He criticizes you, monopolizes your time, tries to separate you from the people who love you. He's demanding that you account to him for your whereabouts. Sugar, I am deeply concerned about your safety with this guy."

Tammy turned in her seat until she was facing Savannah. She reached over and took both of her hands in hers and gave them a companionable squeeze.

"Savannah, I know you mean well. But you're just going to have to trust me on this. I know Chad in a way you don't. Behind closed doors he treats me very sweetly."

"And that's how you deserve to be treated. *All the time*," Savannah replied, while the sinking feeling washed over her that, no matter what she said, she wasn't going to win this one.

And even though she didn't care whether or not she won the argument, she didn't want her friend to lose . . . too badly . . . and too much.

"I know what I'm doing, Savannah. I'm not going to let anybody take advantage of me." She released Savannah's hands and reached for her purse on the floorboard. "I have to go now. But thank you for your concern. I'll call you tomorrow."

"You do that," Savannah said as Tammy got out of the car. "You need me, you call. Any time. Day or night."

As Savannah watched her friend walk into her house and close the door, a feeling swept over her that she hadn't experienced since she was a child.

Years ago, while Savannah's trucker father was on the road, her mother had brought a drunken boyfriend home from a local bar. The guy had gotten violent with her mom, and the ten-year-old Savannah had fought him, trying to defend her.

She hadn't saved her mother then. And she had a terrible sinking feeling that, once again, she wasn't going to be able to save a woman she loved.

"If you hurt her, I'll kill you," she whispered to Chad, wherever he was.

But even as she muttered the words, she knew how empty the threat was.

Savannah had been a cop, and cops knew better than anyone: If someone was determined to harm another, there wasn't a damned thing you could do to stop it.

She pulled out her cell phone and gave Dirk a call. "I'm back from La Rosita," she told him. "Apparently, Tiago did have a fight with his brother, just like he said. Seems his sister-in-law made some disparaging remarks about Blanca, which led to the guys getting into it."

"Women." He sniffed. "Always starting crap we guys have to finish."

"I choose to ignore that bit of sexist baloney and continue with my debriefing," she said as she drove the Mustang halfway down the block and watched the front of Tammy's house in her rearview mirror. "The bartender says he let Tiago sleep it off in the back of the bar. Claims he was there all night, although there's no way to actually prove that, because Tiago was there alone."

"Could have run home, knocked off his old lady and her lover, then headed back to the bar to keep his alibi intact."

"May have, but I don't think so. What are you up to?"

"Dropped the shovel at the lab, the dope at the station . . . and I put out an APB on Waldo. I talked to the HPD, and if he drops by that bar on Sunset, they'll nab him for me."

"Good." She thought she saw a car slowing down in front of Tammy's. She cautioned herself against the idea of driving backward and plowing her vehicle into it at full speed. *One must be prudent about these things,* she thought. *Wait till he's out of the car and* then *run him over. Less damage to the 'Stang's fenders that way.*

"You sound preoccupied," Dirk said. "Where are you? What are you doing?"

"Watching the front of Tammy's house. That dirt bag is supposed to show up any minute, and I might get a notion to clean his clock."

"Well, get an un-notion. I had to pay my car insurance this month, and I don't have enough left in the bank to bail your cute butt out of jail."

She grinned in spite of herself. "And here I thought I was the only one noticing things like that. You think my butt is cute? Since when?"

"Since I first laid eyes on it."

"You never told me that."

"There's a lot of stuff I haven't told you."

The deep, sexy tone of his voice went through her like a fine cognac, warming as it flowed from her head to her toes.

"You're just talking dirty to me to keep me from worrying about Tammy."

She heard him chuckle. "Is it working?"

"No, but I surely appreciate the effort."

"You're going to have to leave that girl to her own devices, Van. This is her situation to handle. Not yours."

"I know." She sighed and looked at her watch. Five thirty-five. Was she really going to sit here and wait a half an hour, just to watch the creep get out of his car and walk into Tammy's house?

"You have to be sensible, babe," Dirk was saying. "You've gotta let it go for now."

"I think I'll pay Ada a visit," Savannah replied. "Find out if anybody's informed her of Vern's passing. And if they have, see how she's taking it. That'll keep my mind occupied for a while."

"Let me know what you find out."

"Will do. Thanks for the advice. And the butt compliment."

"I'd follow you anywhere, sweet cheeks."

She blew him a raspberry. And hung up.

Savannah had visited the high-rise apartment complex on the beach several times, but never socially. Other than Ryan and John, she had no connections to San Carmelita's upper echelons. She was far more likely to be invited to a cops' barbecue than a cocktail party on the eighth floor of this luxury building.

But that was okay with her.

She found all the stainless steel and smoked glass in the lobby a tad cold and off-putting. *A bit like a contemporary art museum,* she thought, *only without the art.*

But she had to admit the views were amazing as she walked down the lushly carpeted hallway toward Ada Fischer's apartment. From the window at the end she could see an ocean vista with the picturesque little town nestled in a gently curved beach.

With the sun setting on the water, staining the sea a rich coral and amber, the palm trees silhouetted against the turquoise sky, it was a soul-inspiring sight.

She wondered if the occupants here, seeing it every day, took such beauty for granted. She knew she never would.

When she knocked on Ada's door, there was no answer for a long time . . . long enough for Savannah to think she might not be home. She knocked again, and then was getting ready to leave, when the door opened.

Ada stood there in a negligee that was straight from vintage Hollywood, film noir. The fine satin wrap rippled from her shoulders to her toes in ivory elegance, the wide sash and low vee neckline accentuating her surgery-perfected figure.

Savannah thought of her own Minnie Mouse pajamas at home and felt terribly insecure. Until Ada breathed on her and nearly knocked her unconscious with whiskey fumes mixed with something resembling pepperoni.

There went the whole glamour image.

"Good evening, Ada," Savannah said.

"I wasn't expecting you. Why didn't you call first? I don't have time to talk to you."

"I'm sorry, but you should make time. It's very important."

Ada cast one quick, telltale glance over her shoulder, and Savannah knew: Ada had company.

And that made Savannah all the more determined to weasel her way inside.

"Really, Ada, this can't wait. It won't take long." Savannah all but pushed her way inside, much to Ada's annoyance.

"Are all you private investigators this rude?" she asked as Savannah stepped into her living room.

"Only the good ones." Savannah glanced around, noting the half-empty wineglass on the coffee table, where several candles flickered. The stereo was playing a pleasant version of the old jazz standard "Take Five" that she'd never heard before. "Nice music," she said.

Ada walked over to the stereo and clicked it off. "You said this wouldn't take long . . . ?"

So, Ada wants it short and sweet. Okay, Savannah thought, *that can be arranged.* "Ada, when was the last time you saw Vern or heard from him?" Savannah asked.

"Yesterday afternoon. Why?"

"Did he come home last night?"

"I don't know. He doesn't live with me. He's got his own place over on the east end."

Hmm, Savannah thought. *If Vern was a kept man, he wasn't kept in very high fashion.* The east end of town was definitely the wrong side of the tracks. Not that there were any actual tracks in San Carmelita, but the delineation was just as clear. Most folks didn't venture into that area without a concealed weapon and a leash with a big pit bull on the end of it.

"And the last time you saw him was yesterday afternoon?"

"No, that's the last time I talked to him. He called me to tell me he wasn't feeling up to going out to dinner. Said he was going to order a pizza and stay in."

Savannah thought of all the decadent goodies, laid out on platters beside the spa. Pizza? More like a buffet at the Ritz.

"Why are you here? Why are you asking me all this?"

"Maybe you should sit down," Savannah said.

"I don't want to sit down. I want you to leave so that I can relax and enjoy my evening."

Savannah looked into the woman's cold eyes, her hard face, and decided she'd been nice long enough. "Ada, there was an incident last night at your Aunt Helene's estate."

"What sort of incident?"

"Vern was sitting in her spa. And it seems, somehow, an electrical surge passed through the water. And he received a fatal shock."

Ada just stood there, staring at her, hardly blinking. Other than the fact that she appeared to pale a bit beneath her tan, she had no reaction at all.

"Your aunt's bodyguards found them—Vern and his companion—and pulled them from the tub. They did everything they could to resuscitate them, but they were already gone. I'm really sorry."

Ada turned away from Savannah and walked over to the coffee table. She took a cigarette from a pack and lit it. Savannah could see her fingers trembling, but aside from that, she seemed cool and collected.

"Do you have any idea who did it? Who electrocuted them? Or how they did it?"

"No. We don't. But we're working on it."

Ada drew long and hard on her cigarette, then released the smoke through her nose. "That's a shame," she said with about as much distress as a woman who's discovered that her two-week-old bouquet of long-stemmed roses is beginning to wilt.

"He and I were pretty much over anyway," she continued. "But still, it's too bad."

"Can you think of any enemies he might have had," Savannah asked. "People who would have wanted to do him harm?"

Ada waved a hand, spreading a cloud of cigarette smoke. "Oh, please. Who didn't want to do him harm? Vern was a jerk . . . didn't have a moral bone in his body . . . or a spine either, for that matter. He had more enemies than he had pairs of Italian shoes."

Savannah couldn't help asking, "So, why were you with him? Why keep him around?"

Ada shrugged, and just for a moment, Savannah saw a glint that might have been the beginnings of a tear in her right eye. "Vern had a way about him," she said. "He could make you feel like you were nineteen again, and at the beginning of love . . . not at the end."

She reached for the glass of wine on the coffee table and downed the last half in one draught. "You wouldn't think a girl could buy a feeling like that . . . but you can. Believe me. The going rate is a Rolex and a Ferrari."

Savannah got into her car and sat there, looking up at the high-rise complex, counting the floors, figuring out which one was Ada's. She didn't really think she'd be so fortunate as to see Ada walk out on the balcony, arm-in-arm with her other squeeze— whoever was sharing the candlelight and alcohol with her.

Savannah's sixth sense had told her there was someone in the bedroom, bathroom, or maybe the broom closet, while she'd been talking to Ada. And Savannah couldn't help but wonder why Ada had felt the need to hide another lover. She didn't appear to be shy about having the world know about her affairs. Why get secretive all of a sudden?

But although Savannah was curious and tempted to just wait in front of the building to see if anyone she might recognize came sauntering out, she was exhausted and in need of some companionship herself.

She didn't need a man to make her feel nineteen years old, or surrounded by the sweet springtime of love, or to make her forget those crow's-feet that had appeared out of the blue last week.

But she could use a friend.

She punched in some numbers on her phone.

Dirk's deep voice answered with a, "Hey, good-lookin'. What's up?"

"I'm pooped. Completely done for," she said. "Or, as Granny says, 'my hind end's draggin' my tracks out.'"

"Same here. Staying up all night and working all day, it'll do it to ya every time."

"Whatcha doing for dinner?" she asked.

"Is that an invitation to your house for a Savannah blue plate special?"

"No, it most certainly is not. The last thing in the world right now that I want to do is cook."

"So, meet me at my trailer, and I'll order us a pizza with everything on it."

She knew she was tired, because she very nearly burst into tears at the simple offer. "Oh, thank you, sugar," she said.

"You don't have to sound so grateful. It's just pizza."

"That's what you think," she said, after she hung up. "The pizza's the least of what I want. With the way this day's gone, what I really need is a friend's shirt to snivel all over."

Chapter 18

On the way from Ada's apartment building to Dirk's trailer park in the outer foothills of town, Savannah couldn't resist making just one quick drive by Tammy's house. And once she had, she wished she hadn't.

The sweet little house with its blooming flowers and perfectly manicured yard and bright pink Volkswagen Beetle in the driveway looked so very Tammy. The big red SUV with the flames painted down the side . . . not so very Tammy-ish.

Savannah hated the SUV on sight, reminding herself of how many serial killers had been pulled over during routine traffic stops, only to have dead bodies discovered in the backs of their vehicles.

She knew how ridiculous it was to despise an inanimate object, like an automobile, because of a strong distaste for its owner.

Nearly as ridiculous as thinking someone was a serial killer just because he drove an SUV.

"Duh, Savannah," she told herself. "Get a grip. You're losing it here."

But still, against her better judgment, she pulled over to the side of the road, opposite the house and dialed Tammy's home phone number.

As it rang, she formulated her lie: "I left my jelly roll pan there at your house last time I was over and just have to have it to make a raspberry jelly roll tonight. . . ."

Four, five rings. No one picked up.

She knew the machine was about to answer, so she hung up. She also knew that if Tammy were in her right mind—her normal, highly curious mind—she wouldn't have been able to resist a ringing phone.

When a phone rang in Tammy's presence, she answered it. Sometimes, even other people's phones.

Savannah stared at the living room window and was moderately consoled that it was lit and the bedroom window wasn't. And as soon as that thought registered in her mind, an unsettling, unsavory feeling swept through her, as if she knew she was doing something wrong, something disrespectful, spying on her friend like this.

If Tammy knew she was out here watching, she'd be angry, and Savannah wouldn't blame her.

By checking up on her like this, she was very nearly guilty of the same sort of controlling behavior that Chad the Creep had been doing earlier in the day, calling constantly to find out where she was and what she was doing.

"Damn," she muttered as she drove away. "Self-awareness can be a real bite in the ass."

The first time Savannah had visited Dirk's trailer park, she had been critical of the location.

She had made a snide joke about the name "Shady Vale," since it wasn't in any sort of valley and didn't have a single tree to provide even a bit of the advertised shade.

The country road leading to the park was lined with eucalyptus trees and orange groves. And as she got out of the car and walked to the mobile home parked in space number two, she could smell the intoxicating scent on the night air. The aroma added a bit of ambiance to an otherwise ambiance-free zone.

As she walked up onto the porch, she noticed that Dirk had left the outdoor light on, in anticipation of her visit.

She was touched. She knew how much it cost him in emotional suffering, leaving that light on and paying the one tenth of one cent's worth of electricity it used.

It made a girl feel so special.

She knocked the "Shave and a Haircut" cadence on the door, right below his Harley-Davidson decal. A couple of seconds later, he swung the door open and stood there, grinning down at her.

"This is a switch," he said, "me entertaining you. Why were you looking for a change of scenery?"

She walked inside and looked around at the worn, plaid furniture, the TV trays that served as end tables, the stack of *Bonanza* VHS boxes mixed with Clint Eastwood westerns, and the box beside the door brimming with empty beer bottles, waiting forever in Dirk purgatory before being taken to the recycler.

"I'm feeling a little weak and shaky," she said. "Guess I needed an infusion of testosterone and figured this was the place to get it."

"You got that right." He motioned her toward a love seat that had been a school bus seat in a former life. "Sit yourself down and breathe it in . . . all that manly man air."

Since in Savannah's experience "manly man air" wasn't all that fragrant, she resisted the invitation to breathe deeply. "Actually," she said, "it smells a bit like chili in here."

"Yeah, I warmed up a can for dinner last night."

"A warmed-up can of chili? No wonder you eat over at my house so much."

He pulled a plastic, molded lawn chair in front of the bus seat—an impromptu footstool. Then he moved the chair's mate closer to her and sat down. "The pizza'll be here any minute," he said. "But till it gets here, you just rest your dogs there. Can I get you a beer."

"No, thanks. I'll pass on the beer," she said.

"Why? We're both off for the night, and it's been a rough twenty-four hours or so."

"I want to keep my faculties clear . . . or at least not any muddier than they are."

"In case Tammy needs you tonight?"

"Something like that."

She kicked off her loafers and lifted her feet onto the chair seat. He leaned forward, lifted one foot and placed it on his knee. With hands that were surprisingly gentle, considering their size, he began to massage her sole, arch, ankles, and toes.

She felt herself melting into the bus seat, like a stick of butter left out in the summer sun.

"Oh, that's pure heaven," she said. "If I'd known you could do that, I'd married you a long time ago."

"Yeah, right," he said, a trace of sadness on his face. "You're going to marry a dude with an old rusty house trailer furnished from the junkyard just because he gives good foot rubs."

She nodded. "Any guy with a job can pay a mort-gage or the rent . . . but a man who gives delicious foot rubs . . . he's worth his weight in gold."

"That's an awesome compliment."

"From a woman with her priorities in order."

"So, how did it go with Ada?" he asked, working her pinkie toe.

"Ada wasn't surprised, shocked, or dismayed to be told that her lover had met the same fate as a lobster in that spa."

"She had to have been told already."

Savannah nodded. "And when I said the water had somehow become electrified, she instantly made the jump that someone had tossed some-thing electrical into the water."

"We didn't make that assumption."

"I don't think most people would. And the most telling thing of all"—Savannah nudged his arm with her toe—"when I said he'd been killed with someone else, she never asked who."

"Get outta here. If their lover's killed in a hot tub with someone else, who doesn't raise hell to find out who it was?"

"I sure would."

"I guess that doesn't leave us with much . . . other than a healthy suspicion of her, which we've always had. She stands to gain a lot in inheritance if her aunt dies."

"And her schmucky son, Waldo, too."

"Not to mention Emma," Dirk added. "I know

you like her a lot and she's your client, but still, we have to throw her into the pot and see who bubbles to the top when we turn the heat up."

Someone tapped at the door.

Dirk jumped up. "Pizza's here," he said.

"And not a minute too soon. I'm so hungry I'd gnaw the south end off a northbound skunk."

He gave her a disgusted look as he walked to the door to greet the delivery man. "You know," he said, "I find most of your quaint Southern phrases charming. But that one, I can do without. It's enough to put me off my pizza."

"Good. All the more for me!"

Later, when the heirloom fine bone china had been washed and carefully stowed away in the butler's pantry—or rather, when the pizza box and paper towel napkins had been tossed into the garbage—Dirk replenished her glass of iced tea and sat down beside her on the bus seat.

"Feeling better?" he asked.

"There's very little in my world that a foot massage and a thin-crust, everything-on-it pizza won't set right."

"Good," he said. "Because I've got a couple of things to tell you and—"

"No! Don't you dare spoil the first good mood I've had in weeks. You have no idea how rare good moods are to a perimenopausal woman!"

"That's true, I don't. But you're just gonna have to brace yourself, 'cause you have to know."

"Okay." Savannah sighed and slouched down in her seat. "Let 'er rip."

"Just before you got here tonight, I had a phone call from Eileen."

"All right. And . . . ?"

"And the water heater we found in the garage . . . it's perfectly fine. Hasn't been dunked in water, probably ever, and definitely not recently."

"Any prints on it?"

"Waldo's. But he's the one who used it most, so . . . that's sort of to be expected."

"Dangnation."

"I know. And the shovel . . . clean as a freshly diapered baby's butt. Not a latent, a smudge, or even a partial on it."

"Just like the circuit breaker box and the switches."

"Exactly like them. Wiped perfectly clean. Obviously no tool that's used frequently would be that pristine unless it hadn't been deliberately cleaned."

Savannah shook her head. "All that climbing around in spider-infested garages and sheds . . . it was all for naught. Shoot. I'm getting a little tired of living in this part of town called 'Square One.' Enough already. We need a break in this case."

She leaned her head wearily over on his shoulder and passed her arm through his. "I'm tired, big boy," she told him. "Between worrying about Helene and Tammy, too, I'm plumb worn to a frazzle."

"Skipping a night's sleep will do it to you, too," he said, kissing the top of her head.

"No, I've done that many times before, as you well know. I'm not even that concerned about Helene, now that Ryan and John are there, watching over her. Let's face it; it's Tams. You know I've always felt like a big sister to that kid. She's very dear to my heart."

"I know." He patted her hand. "But there's only so much you can do in that situation. You press her too hard, you'll damage your friendship. I had a friend a long time ago, a guy I'd known since junior high. He got involved with this gal who was a real piece of work. Everybody knew she was trouble . . . everyone but him, of course. I tried to tell him so, and he cursed me out and never spoke to me again. They got married, had three kids, she left him for another guy, and he's still handing over his paycheck to her every week."

"Sorry about your friend," she said.

"Learn from my mistake. Stay out of it. Let your friends work this stuff out on their own. That's my motto."

"Okay."

They sat in companionable silence for a long time with him stroking her hand and her soaking in the warmth of his body as she leaned against him. It always made her feel better, just breathing in the comforting smell that she always associated with Dirk—leather, Old Spice deodorant, and the underlying aroma of cinnamon.

Finally, she looked up at him, her heart in her blue eyes. "I want you to do something for me, good buddy," she said.

He looked down at her and smiled. "Anything."

"Run a check on that sonofabitch, Chad. Do it for me, and I'll cook you anything you want. I promise."

"Anything?"

"Name it."

"Pulled pork sandwiches, corn on the cob, cole-slaw, and homemade ice cream."

"You got it."

"Cool." He wrapped one of her dark curls around his finger and gave it a gentle tug. "I set you up, baby," he said.

"What?"

"I already ran a check on that guy."

She sat up, suddenly alert. "Well?"

"He's got a record."

"For what?"

"You really wanna know?"

"Damn. Yeah, yeah . . . I wanna know. Lay it on me."

"Three girlfriends, three ROs, two assaults."

She ran her fingers through her hair and shook her head. "No, no, no! He's had three girls take out restraining orders on him?"

Dirk nodded.

"And he assaulted two of them?"

"In violation of the ROs."

"Holy cow! Poor Tammy! That does it. I'm never, never going to sleep again."

But she did sleep. Two hours later, she was stretched across Dirk's sofa, and she was out like a street lamp on the east end of town.

Dirk walked out of the bedroom, a blanket in his hands. Gently, he spread it over her, tucking it around her shoulders, legs, and feet.

"Sleep while you can, sweetheart," he whispered. "It's the only break you get from worrying about everybody and their brother's cousin's uncle's dog."

He leaned down, brushed her hair back from

her face, and kissed her cheek. "Always the big sister, aren't you, Van," he said softly, "taking care of everybody but yourself. Good night, baby."

He patted her on the back, then turned down the lights and left the room.

She stirred slightly in her sleep, reached up and touched the spot on her cheek that he had kissed. "Good night, darlin'," she whispered back. "Sleep tight."

Chapter 19

When Savannah woke the next morning, for a moment, she thought she was back in Granny Reid's feather bed in the little shotgun house in McGill, Georgia.

Golden sunlight streamed through a nearby window, gently warming her face, and the heavenly aromas of coffee, bacon, and something that smelled a lot like pancakes filled her senses.

The smell of Granny's coffee and bacon was the only thing powerful enough to lure a body out of that feather bed. And even though she was pretty sure she wasn't in Gran's pillow-soft bed, the divine scent was the same.

"Hey, sleepy head," a deep voice said. "It's about time you rejoined the land of the living."

"What?" She sat up and pushed the old army blanket off her shoulders. Looking around, she realized she was on Dirk's sofa. A few feet away, he was puttering about in the kitchen. And through eyes that were still sleep-fuzzy, she was pretty sure she saw him flip a flapjack.

"Good morning," he said. "Your timing's perfect. Breakfast is ready."

"You cook breakfast?"

"Once in a while . . . on special occasions."

She ran her fingers through her hair and yawned. "What's the special occasion?"

He looked slightly hurt, then turned away from her to pour the coffee. "Let's just say I don't usually have company this time of morning."

"Oh."

She stood, smoothed her rumpled blouse and slacks, and walked over to stand behind him. She put her hands on his shoulders and said, "I'm not used to being anybody's company this time of day either," she said. "So, it *is* special. Thank you."

When he turned to face her, he had a large cup of coffee in his hand. On the front of the mug was a faded picture of the *Bonanza* gang: Pa Cartwright, Adam, Hoss, and Little Joe.

As he handed it to her, she said, "Wow! And out of your favorite cup! I really am getting the royal treatment."

He blushed and looked uncomfortable, as he always did when he got caught doing something nice.

"Go sit on the bus seat and pull up a TV tray," he told her. "Is there enough half-and-half in that coffee?"

"Yeah, it's perfect."

She took her seat and dragged a tray in front of her. And a moment later, he set a plate, laden with golden pancakes and crisp bacon, in front of her, along with a wad of paper towels and a fork with three bent tines.

Then he sat on the sofa across from her with a tray and heaped plate of his own.

"Chow down," he said. "Or bon appétit or whatever."

She took one bite of the pancakes and let out an orgasmic groan. "Oh, lawdy be! That is pure paradise in your mouth!"

"Just pancakes," he mumbled, again embarrassed to be on the receiving end of praise.

"No, these are not just pancakes. What are these things in the batter, mandarin oranges?"

He nodded, taking a big bite himself.

"And what's that special flavor I taste. Better than vanilla . . . It's . . . What is it?"

"I'm not telling you. You'll laugh."

"If you don't tell me, I'll put you in a headlock till you do!"

He laughed and lifted his own Elvis mug to toast her. "Here's to keeping a little mystery in every relationship."

The phone rang, and he groaned. "You want somebody to call you, just cook a decent meal and the damned thing starts ringing off the hook."

"Don't answer it," Savannah said. Then she thought of Tammy, and her heart jumped into her throat. "No, answer it. It might be—"

"It's Ryan," he said, looking at the caller ID. He picked up the phone and said, "Hey, man . . . what's happenin'?"

Dirk listened for a moment, then turned to Savannah, a big smile on his face. "Really? Wow! Good work, dude! We'll be right over."

Savannah sat with bated breath, holding a big bite of pancake, dripping with maple syrup, in front of her face. "What?" she asked, half excited, half annoyed.

"John and Ryan were taking Helene for a nice morning stroll on the beach just now."

"And?"

"When they got to the area where she went over the cliff, they looked up, and there it was."

"There was what?"

"The boom box. It's stuck there on the side of the hill, halfway up."

"Whoa! We've got to get our hands on that!"

"Yeah."

She looked down at her plate, the golden cakes, the crispy bacon. The scrumptious aftertaste of that first bite, her only bite, still lingering on her palate.

"I'm not going anywhere until I eat every morsel of this amazing breakfast you've made me," she told him.

"A team of mules couldn't pull me away from this," he agreed. "Friggin' boom box can just hang for a while longer."

"I'd give anything to be that agile again," Savannah told Dirk, Ryan, John, and Helene, as they stood on the beach and watched Tammy scale the cliff.

"Heck," Helene said, "I've given up standing on a step stool to get dishes out of my top kitchen cupboards."

"The only thing I hate worse than chickens," Dirk added, "is heights."

"I think you just say that so that I won't ask you to clean my gutters," Savannah told him.

"No, really. Three rungs up, I freeze." He glanced over at Ryan and John. "Yeah, yeah, I know . . . you guys parachute and bungee jump when you've got nothin' better to do on a Saturday afternoon. But you're nuts. The both of you."

"But we located your evidence for you, loonies that we are," John told him.

"Something tells me you've hit pay dirt," Ryan added. "Why else would someone toss that over the cliff, instead of just pitching it in the trash?"

"Obviously, they didn't think we'd find it." Savannah looked at the beach sand under her feet and the waterline on the cliff. "Last night the tide was in. If they threw it away then, they probably thought it would hit the water and be carried away."

Dirk gave her a grin. "Now we know something else about our suspect—he or she throws like a girl. They couldn't even clear the cliff."

Helene sniffed. "Let me tell you, sonny, in my day I threw a fast ball that you would have had a hard time hitting."

Savannah laughed, but she didn't take her eyes off Tammy, who was about a quarter way up the hill, about half the distance to her goal.

An avid rock climber, Tammy had been tickled pink when Savannah had called her earlier and asked her if she thought she could do this chore for them. She had scooted over to the Strauss estate and had arrived before Savannah and Dirk.

Of course, Savannah had been glad to have an

excuse to call her and check on her. And to see her young friend, practically jumping out of her shorts with excitement, thrilled to play an important part in the case, did Savannah's worried heart a world of good.

Apparently, Tammy's meeting with her troublesome ex-boyfriend had gone well. She seemed in top spirits on this, the morning after.

"She looks okay," Dirk said as he watched Savannah watch Tammy.

"Yeah. She does. For now," Savannah replied tentatively.

"Don't worry," Ryan told her. "Tammy's a very good climber. John and I couldn't keep up with her the last time we went to Mission Mountain."

"Doesn't she need some sort of safety rope?" Savannah said as Tammy found new footing and lifted herself a bit higher.

"Not for that one," Ryan said. "A beginner could scale it with no problem, let alone an experienced climber like Tammy."

"She has a natural knack for it," John added. "She's already far better than Ryan or I will ever be."

"She has a fearless spirit," Helene said, looking up the cliff at the young woman, who was within a couple of feet of her goal. "I like that in anyone, but especially a female."

"Yeah," Savannah murmured, "though sometimes fear is a good thing. You wanna have a little bit of 'scared spitless' in your bones, say, when you're wranglin' a rattlesnake."

"She's not going to run into any rattlesnake on

that hill," Helene said. "Not with all the racket we've been making down here. They've crawled into their holes or left a long time ago."

"I'm not worried about the snakes that live in holes in the ground," Savannah grumbled under her breath. "It's those nasty, two-legged rattlers that bother me."

"Hey, I made it!" Tammy yelled down from her perch on a rock that jutted from the side of the cliff.

With both feet firmly on the stone, she removed her climbing gloves and tucked them into her shirt pocket. Then she pulled a pair of surgical gloves from the back pocket of her shorts and put them on.

Reaching up, she gently dislodged the portable stereo from the branch where it had caught.

From the other back pocket of her shorts she took out a small nylon cord. Carefully, she tied one end around the handle of the boom box.

"Here you go," she said. "I'm sending it down."

"Let 'er rip, kiddo," Dirk called to her as he pulled out his own gloves and put them on.

Slowly, Tammy played out the cord, lowering it down until it reached Dirk's outstretched hands.

"Got it," he said and dodged the cord as she released it.

"Good girl! Careful coming down, sweetie," Savannah called to her.

Helene stepped up to Dirk and squinted, looking the boom box over carefully. "I don't understand all the uproar over a stereo," she said. "I agree my nephew should have put it in the garbage, instead of littering the property with it, but that's hardly a concern for the police, I should think."

Dirk was instantly alert. "Did you actually see Waldo throwing this away?" he asked her.

"Of course not. If I had, I'd have yelled at him and sent him down the cliff to get it. We know what to do with garbage."

"Then why are you assuming he was the one who pitched it?" Savannah asked her.

Helene shrugged. "I don't know. I suppose because it's his."

"Are you sure?" Dirk asked. "These things look a lot alike . . . black, rectangular, buttons . . ."

"Certainly, I'm sure. I gave it to him for his birthday a couple of years ago. I picked it out myself. I don't forget things like that. In fact, I don't forget much of anything."

"I'll bet you don't, love." John gave her a smile and patted her shoulder. He turned to Dirk. "If she says it's her nephew's, it is."

"Fine with me," Dirk said under his breath.

Savannah watched as Tammy made quick work of returning down the cliff.

Dirk was squatting on the beach, the stereo balanced on his thigh, when Tammy jumped down onto the sand.

"Excellent work there, girlie," Savannah told her, giving her a hug and a slap on the back.

"No sweat." Tammy brushed the dirt off her clothes, then removed her climbing gloves. "In fact, it was fun."

"Not as fun as beating us to the top of Mission Mountain," Ryan said, giving her a playful nudge.

Tammy poked him back and laughed. "No. Not nearly as much fun as that."

Savannah looked over Dirk's shoulder and watched as he pushed the eject button on the player and caused the CD drive door to open. A small amount of water trickled out.

"Oh, yes," he said, looking up at her with eyes twinkling. "We have water inside."

"Hallclujah," Savannah answered.

"What's so good about that?" Helene wanted to know.

Instantly, Savannah's mood plummeted. What was good news to them was going to cause a lot of pain to a nice lady. And Savannah wasn't sure how to tell her.

She didn't have to.

Helene's sharp mind processed the information, and she came to her own conclusion in an instant. "Oh," she said sadly. "I see. You're happy because you believe you've found the murder weapon . . . which happens to belong to my grand-nephew."

"Yes, Helene," Savannah said. "I'm so sorry."

Helene turned to leave. "Not as sorry as I am," she said as she walked away.

As Savannah walked Tammy along the beach and down the forest path, back to her car, she tried to get a reading off her young friend's mood.

She had seemed buoyant enough before the climb, and ecstatic afterward, while reveling in the praise of the team. But now, as they strolled through the sun-dappled woods, Tammy seemed worried and preoccupied.

"You did really well back there. Thanks again," Savannah told her.

Tammy took the ponytail scrunchy out of her hair and shook the glossy length free. It fell around her shoulders, looking like a golden, satin curtain.

Savannah couldn't help but think that Tammy could have her pick of men. Pretty, sweet, funny, and smart, she was a prize.

Far too good for the likes of that Chad creep, she told herself. *May he run into a grizzly bear with a big hunk of bacon fat in his back pocket.*

Savannah also realized that any mother, big sister, or adopted big sister would think the same thing.

Of course, in Tammy's case, it was true.

"I know why you're including me so much in this case," Tammy said with a bit of sadness in her voice. "You're trying to build me up, make me feel better about myself."

"You shouldn't have one blamed reason to feel anything *but* good about yourself, Tammy Hart. Don't underestimate yourself . . . or the contributions you've made to this case. Nobody waiting for you at the foot of that hill today wanted to climb it . . . or could have the way you did."

"You know what I mean."

"Yeah, I do."

They walked on down the path until they saw the front of the mansion through the trees and Tammy's Volkswagen Beetle sitting in the driveway in front of it.

"How did it go last night?" Savannah couldn't help asking.

"Okay. Nice actually. He brought me some pretty roses and a box of candy. Apologized like crazy for doubting me yesterday . . . for thinking I was with another guy."

Savannah felt her pulse quicken. If this kept up, she'd have to be on blood-pressure medication or tranquilizers before the end of the week.

"Um . . ." she said, knowing she was wading into quicksand. "If you broke up with him, it really wasn't any of his damned business who you were with or where you were yesterday, right?"

Tammy shrugged. "I guess we're sort of back together again. He asked me for another chance, and I said okay." She glanced at Savannah and quickly added, "I told him not to ever put me down like he did before in front of you or anybody else. He promised he wouldn't."

"It'd be nice," Savannah said, "if he was just a decent man, who wouldn't dream of embarrassing you in front of your friends in the first place. A respectful man treats you respectfully without you having to demand it from him."

Tammy stopped in the middle of the path, her arms crossed over her chest. Tears sprang to her eyes. "Not everybody's as okay about being single as you are, Savannah. I get really lonely sometimes. And when he's good, Chad's really good, you know? Yeah, we have our fights, like every couple does. But most of the time, he really makes me feel special."

"You're special *all* of the time, Tammy. *All*, not most. And that's how he should treat you."

"You really need to stay out of this, Savannah," she told her. "It's my business, my relationship. Not yours."

"I understand that. And believe me, I'm not saying half of what I want to. My tongue's bloody from biting it."

Tammy's face turned red with anger, more than Savannah had ever seen before. She hardly recognized her friend at all. And it shocked and deeply saddened her.

"Well, we don't want you to have a bloody tongue, Savannah. Say whatever you're dying to say. Say it once, and get it out of your system."

"He has a record, Tammy. He's had three restraining orders against him, from three different girlfriends. He assaulted two of them. This guy's a batterer!"

Tammy stood there, eyes locked with hers, hardly blinking. She said nothing, just lifted her chin a notch.

"Oh, my God," Savannah said. "You already knew!"

"Of course, I knew," Tammy replied coldly. "I run background checks for a living. I'm a detective, remember? You taught me well."

"But . . . then . . . how could you . . . ?" Savannah was totally flummoxed. "I don't understand why you . . ."

"I talked to him about it on our second date. He explained it all to me."

"How the hell do you explain away three ROs and two assaults?"

Tammy sighed. "If you must know, he was living with the first one—had been for a couple of years—and he came home and found her in bed with his best friend. And, okay, he lost it. He hit them both, her and him, once each, and then he walked out and left her. A crime of passion, Savannah. It could happen to anybody. You joke all the time about smacking people with skillets."

"Yes, but I don't actually *do* it. I'm quite protective of my cast iron cookware. Besides . . . threatening people with strange forms of violence is just a quaint, Southern custom."

The two women stared at each other for a long, terribly uncomfortable time. Finally, Savannah said, "How about the other one? Two assaults."

"That was his last girlfriend," Tammy replied. "She used to hit him all the time. One night, he just pushed her off him, and she called the cops. That's all there was to it."

"And if you believe that one, I've got some marshmallows to sell you. He can go roast them in hell, telling you some cock-a-mammy story like that one."

Tammy's eyes went even colder, her face harder than before. "Okay, Savannah. You've said your piece. Now, I'm going to ask you for the last time to stay out of my personal business."

Savannah felt her own temper rising and fought to keep it down. "You got it," she said as calmly as she could manage. "Just, please, think it over."

But Tammy was already walking away. And Savannah could sense the distance between herself and her beloved, long-time, best buddy widening.

In fact, Savannah felt like her friend was already a hundred miles away.

* * *

"Hey, Van," Dirk called out to her, as she made her way back to his Buick, which was parked on the path near the cliff. "Come here."

He was alone now. Ryan and John had left with Helene.

With his trunk lid up, he was rummaging around inside. She could see a large brown evidence envelope, sealed, and neatly tucked away on the left side of the interior. The right side was far less than tidy, housing an inordinate amount of Dirk's "manly man" junk—fishing poles, a tackle box, baseball bat, football, and a box filled with Elvis and Johnny Cash CDs.

"We got some news," he said, slamming the trunk closed.

He looked excited. She wished she could be excited. But after that encounter with Tammy, she felt lower than a hog with his chin on an auction block.

"What's up?" she asked, trying to sound like she gave a hoot.

"West Hollywood called. They picked up Waldo at that bar. They're holding him for me. I'm gonna go drop this boom box over at the lab and then drive down and get him. Wanna come along?"

She thought it over for a minute. "No, thanks," she said.

"Really? Since when don't you want to have your finger in the middle of the pie?"

"Sticking my fingers in other people's pies . . . that's been getting me in trouble lately," she said. "I think I'm going to go talk to Helene. I don't want her to hear about Waldo from somebody else first. Then I've got some fences to mend."

He reached over and tugged on one of her curls. "You sure? Are you okay?"

"No," she said, giving him a tired smile. "I'm not okay. And right now, I'm not sure about much of nothin'."

Chapter 20

John answered the door of the mansion when Savannah knocked and escorted her into the great room.

"Miss Helene, it's Savannah to see you," he said to the lady of the house. She was sitting in a large, wing-backed chair, combing a doll's hair, a wistful look on her face.

"Shall I get the two of you some refreshments before I go," he asked, his pale blue eyes full of concern for both of them, as he looked from one to the other.

"Nothing for me, John. Thank you," Savannah said.

Helene gave him a slight shake of the head, then went back to grooming the doll's beautiful, long red locks.

Quietly, John slipped from the room.

Savannah sat on a chair near Helene's and quietly waited to be acknowledged.

Eventually, Helene said, "This doll was fashioned after my granddaughter. Emma was such a beautiful child; I had to do a doll with her face and hair."

"It's gorgeous," Savannah replied. "And your granddaughter is a lovely woman. I'm sure she gave you a lot of joy as a child."

"She was very much like her mother. Both of them were sweet-natured. When my daughter died in that accident, I thought I would die, too. But, of course, I couldn't. I had a grandchild to raise. In some ways, I think Emma saved my life."

"I'm sure you were a blessing to each other."

"My daughter's husband was drinking that day, driving the car. He and my daughter were killed, and Emma was badly hurt." Helene laid the small hairbrush aside and passed her hand over her eyes, as through trying to erase painful images. Images, no doubt, just as vivid all these years later.

"My daughter couldn't say no to her husband. I warned her not to let him drive her and Emma when he'd been drinking, but . . . it happened anyway, in spite of my warnings."

Savannah fought back her own tears, and her fear, and imaginations too dark to bear. "They don't listen," she said. "I wasn't there, but I strongly suspect there's nothing you could have said or done to change what happened to your daughter."

"I wish I could believe you," Helene said, stroking the doll's cheek with her forefinger. "I'd sleep better, if I could."

"I have a similar situation," Savannah told her. "Someone very dear to my heart appears to be headed for a fall. But when I warn her, she gets angry with me. And after we argue, I have the sinking feeling that my words have only pushed her in his direction."

"Like my Emma." Helene held the doll close to her chest. "I know that boy she's seeing now is going to break her heart. I know this sounds elitist, but you can take one look at her and tell she's a quality person. And just as quickly, you can tell that he isn't. Why can't she see what's so obvious to everyone else?"

"She's in love, like my friend," Savannah said. "And when you're in love, especially when you're young, you don't always see a man for who he is, but who you want him to be."

"Probably the same way men look at us." Helene smiled.

"Yes, probably. Or else none of us would ever pair up. Thank goodness for love's shortsightedness."

"Have you ever 'paired up,' as you call it, Savannah?"

"No. I've never married. As I've been recently told, I don't mind being single."

Helene gave her a sly little grin that made her look at least twenty years younger. "I sensed a little something between you and that detective friend of yours. Am I mistaken?"

Savannah laughed. "No, you aren't mistaken. There's a little something there. We just haven't figured out what yet."

"Haven't figured it out, or won't admit it?"

"Maybe a bit of both. Or maybe we didn't move

on it back when we were still shortsighted and didn't know each other so well."

"Perhaps you should reconsider. Detective Coulter is a good man. My late husband was a good man. I can tell a good one when I see one."

"Yes, Dirk is a good guy. I won't argue with you about that."

Helene's sharp, green eyes studied hers for a long moment, then she said, "Don't wait forever, Savannah. Life goes by very quickly. It seems like only last week when I was your age."

"I'll bet it does."

"You mustn't take time or happiness for granted. Grab them with both hands and hold on to them whenever you have the chance, and don't let go."

"I'll remember that. Thank you."

Helene stood, walked over to her, and handed her the doll and the hairbrush. "Here," she said. "There are still a few knots at the nape of her neck. See what you can do . . . while you tell me what you came here say."

Savannah began to gently brush the auburn tresses as Helene walked over to the display case and took out another doll with blond hair and a blue velvet dress.

"I came to give you some bad news," Savannah said.

"I assumed that by the sour puss you were wearing when you walked in here. What is it?"

"Your grandnephew is in police custody. And he's going to be arrested. I wanted to tell you before you heard it from someone else."

"And what's the charge this time?" Helene asked, looking a bit tired, but not at all surprised.

"Cocaine possession."

"Is that all?" Helene asked.

"At the moment."

"Thank goodness. I was afraid you were going to say 'murder.'"

Long ago, Savannah had learned that when her spirits needed uplifting, performing one of Granny Reid's rituals usually gave her a boost . . . or a least, some degree of peace.

One of Gran's mood rescues was a bubble bath by candlelight, while nibbling a bit of chocolate. Countless times during her childhood, Savannah had heard her grandmother say to the nine grandchildren hovering around her, demanding a hundred things at once, "I'm gonna go take myself a soak. So, unless you can't get the fire out or the bleeding stopped on your own, heaven help anybody who comes knockin' on that door!"

Savannah had added the chocolate to the ceremony. After the first time, nibbling a chocolate truffle and sipping a bit of cognac, she had decided that if anybody thought it was unsanitary or déclassé to have food in the bathroom, they could just get over it.

But bubble baths weren't always practical. And they didn't help when the stone that was weighing down a body's spirit was a fight with a loved one.

That called for the basket ritual. A basket, laden with yummy goodies, delivered with a humble heart, went a long way toward restoring the peace after a conflict.

And since it had been a big fight, the situation called for the extra-large basket.

Savannah talked to Diamante and Cleopatra as she ladled some homemade soup—vegetables only, of course—into a mason jar, screwed the lid on tight, and placed it into the basket.

"Of course I used organic vegetables," she said to Cleo. "Even the peanut butter cookies are one hundred percent natural ingredients.

"Yeah, they taste like crap," she told Di, "but that's the way she likes 'em. Go figure. Girl doesn't know what's good . . . in men or cookies."

And then, to the ever-present grandmother in her head, she added, "I know, I know, Granny. Have a humble heart. You don't deliver a peace offering basket with an uppity, I-know-better-than-you attitude."

Maybe Tammy's right, Savannah told herself as she carefully placed the cookies into a decorative tin. *Maybe he's a good guy, and I'm overreacting to what I saw. Ex-cop, big sister . . . I'm being overly protective and alarmist. Yeah, that's it.*

She placed a loaf of her best onion-wheat bread into the basket and covered it all with a red- and white-checkered napkin.

Glancing down at the cats, who sat, looking up at her with big, innocent, animal eyes, she said, "I hear ya. I don't believe it either, but it's her life. All we can do is be there for her if she needs us, right, girls?"

She picked up the basket off the counter, grabbed her purse, and headed out the door. "Yes, Gran," she whispered to the voice in her head . . .

the one with the sweet, soft, Southern accent, "we do what we can."

As Savannah was driving down Tammy's lane, she practiced her speech and tried not to gag on the words. "If you say he's a nice guy, I'm sure he is," just seemed to stick in her craw.

Savannah was a good cook, she was an excellent shot at the target range, but saying something that was contrary to what she was thinking . . . that she wasn't so good at.

Lying to herself and others wasn't a new skill she wanted to develop this late in life. Being false took a toll on a person. She had seen too many people who had spent their life energy that way. And she had determined, long ago, not to be one of them.

"Be true to yourself," she whispered as she neared Tammy's house. "Don't lie to her, but don't give her any unsolicited advice either. This is hers, not yours."

However, when she saw the red SUV with its metallic flames sitting next to Tammy's pink VW Bug, her best intentions flew out the window.

"Damn," she whispered. "Who'd have thought he'd be here in the middle of the day?"

She parked across the street and sat there, debating about whether to knock on the door and hand Tammy the basket, leave it on her porch, or come back later.

Before she could decide, the front door of the house opened, and Savannah saw Tammy and Chad step outside.

As the two of them walked to his car, Savannah watched their body language and didn't like what she saw. He had his hand on Tammy's shoulder and seemed to be practically pushing her along. Once, she said something to him and stepped away from him. In a heartbeat, he had her by the arm and was holding it tightly while he answered her with what appeared to be some sort of long speech.

Finally, he put his hands on her waist and pulled her toward him. He kissed her roughly, which under other circumstances might have seemed passionate, but Tammy didn't seem that into it. Savannah noticed that she didn't even return his embrace, but let her arms hang limply at her sides until he was finished.

As he got into the car, pulled out of the driveway, and headed down the street, Savannah was both surprised and relieved that neither of them seemed to notice her sitting there. The last thing she wanted right now was a three-way, knock-down-drag-out. And she didn't want to waste a perfectly nice basket full of food, hurling it at a knucklehead on her friend's lawn.

Once he was down the road and out of sight, Savannah grabbed her peace offering and bailed out of the Mustang.

"Tammy!" she called out as she hurried across the street. "Tams! Hold on!"

Tammy had just stepped up onto the porch when she caught sight of Savannah. But instead of "holding on" as she had been requested to do, she grabbed at the knob and pushed on the door, trying to get inside as quickly as she could.

"Hey, where's the fire?" Savannah asked as she rushed up to her. "I just wanted to drop off a little something for you, to show you that there's no hard feelings, and I—"

"No, Savannah! Go away! Please," she said as she fumbled with the door. "This isn't a good time."

"Then I won't stay," Savannah replied. "I'll just give you this and go."

She held out the basket with the most humble-hearted look that she could muster.

Granny would have been proud. She was sure of it.

Tammy hesitated, her back turned to Savannah. Then, after what seemed like forever, she reached around to take the basket, her long hair covering the side of her face.

But when she grasped the handle of the basket, her hair slipped back over her shoulder, and Savannah caught a glimpse behind the hair.

"Oh, my God! Tammy!"

Savannah grabbed the basket and set it on the porch at their feet.

Her hands on Tammy's shoulders, she spun her around until she was fully facing her.

"What the hell happened to you?" Savannah asked her . . . as if she didn't already know.

Tammy's lower lip was split, her cheek badly bruised, and her left eye was swollen. And to make the horror even worse, she had blue and red lines discoloring both sides of her neck.

Savannah grabbed her, opened the door, and rushed her inside. "Oh, sweetie," she said as sorrow and rage swept over her in waves. "I'm going to kill him. How dare he! Oh, honey. I'm so sorry!"

She pulled back Tammy's hair and examined her face, every bump and bruise. "Where else are you hurt?" she asked, glancing over her body. There was a bit of blood on the front of her tee-shirt . . . probably from the split on her lip, Savannah guessed.

"I'm okay," Tammy said, bursting into tears. "Don't worry about it, Savannah. I'm all right."

"You aren't all right, and I *am* worried. You're damned right I am, and you should be, too. That jackass beat you!"

"It's my fault. I didn't tell him I was going to the Strauss place this morning. And I was climbing the cliff when he texted me," Tammy sank down onto the sofa and tried to smooth her hair in a pathetic gesture that went straight to Savannah's heart.

"And later," she continued, softly crying, "I was driving home and I didn't answer him when he called me. He was just so worried about me, that when he saw me, he exploded and—"

"Bullshit! Do *not* tell me this was *your* fault, Tammy! I won't listen to that kind of crap! He assaulted you, just like he did his other two girlfriends, and he's going to pay for it!"

Savannah fished her cell phone out of her purse and started to call Dirk.

"No!" Tammy leapt to her feet. "Don't call the cops. He said if I did . . . I mean . . . Don't call anybody, Savannah." She started to sob. "I'm so ashamed. I don't want anybody to know about this."

"Tammy, you know how this works. You have to have him arrested! Next time he'll hurt you even worse. This won't end until you end it!"

"And you know how it works, too, Savannah. They'll pick him up, and he'll be out on bail in a heartbeat. Only then he'll be a lot madder at me. If he did this"—she pointed to her face—"because I didn't take his phone call and tell him where I was, what do you think he'll do if I have him arrested?"

"You'll get a restraining order against him and—"

"And what good would that do? It's a piece of paper, Savannah. Do you really think a piece of paper is going to stop him?"

"So, what are you going to do, Tammy? Are you going to live in fear and let this guy use you for a punching bag any time he gets a notion to?"

"I don't know what I'm going to do, Savannah. I don't know." She sank back down onto the sofa and buried her face in her hands, sobbing. "I don't know what to do."

"The first thing is we've got to get you to a hospital and have you checked over and—"

"No! I'm not going to any hospital. They'll just ask me a lot of questions I don't want to answer. I'm not going."

"Please. You could have internal injuries. You need to see a doctor."

"I'm okay. Really. No hospital!"

Savannah battled her own emotions as she tried to switch into a more logical, professional mindset . . . and couldn't.

Finally, she bent down and kissed the top of Tammy's golden hair. "Don't cry, darlin'," she said. "I'm not going to make you do anything you don't want to do. But I think you should go pack yourself

an overnight bag, a couple changes of outfits.
Then get that basket full of goodies that's out
there on your porch, and drive to Twin Oaks.
Check into the Oak Dale Motel there under a fake
name and pay cash for your room. Put some ice on
that lip and eye. For now, don't come back here
and don't go to my house, and when that sonofabitch calls you the next time, do *not* answer
your phone!"

"Okay."

Savannah fished some bills out of her purse and
handed them to her. "This should cover the motel."

"I don't want to take money from you, Savannah. This is humiliating enough already."

"You have nothing in the world to be ashamed
of. Let me help you, Tammy. It'll make me feel better. Okay?"

Reluctantly, Tammy took the money. "And while
I'm at the motel watching a TV with a lousy picture, what are you going to be doing?"

"I've got some business to attend to."

Tammy stood and hugged Savannah, tightly and
for a long time. When she finally released her, she
looked up at Savannah with nothing but pure pain
and fear in her beautiful face.

"You're not going to get yourself hurt or make
this worse for me, are you?" she said.

"No, darlin'. I promise, I'll be okay, and I'm not
going to make it worse."

But as Savannah walked her friend out to her
car and tucked her inside with her basket full of
homemade goodies, she couldn't quiet that voice
in her head. It wasn't Granny's sweet, gentle voice.

It was the voice of a cop, the police woman Savannah had been for so many years. The voice of experience. A lot of really bad experiences.

And that voice was telling her that, no matter what promises she made to her friend, this situation was going to get a lot worse before it got better.

Chapter 21

As Savannah sat in her Mustang and watched Tammy's VW Beetle drive away, a strange feeling that she'd never experienced before washed through her. It was an icy, numbing sensation that was oddly calming.

For the moment, the image of her friend's battered face had been carefully, methodically filed away, somewhere in the recesses of her mind. The time would come to take that memory out and deal with it.

But this wasn't the time.

Tammy was going out of town, to a place he couldn't get his hands on her, so she was safe for the time being.

Savannah pulled out her cell phone and made a call to the police station house. She asked to speak to Iris, the desk clerk who did most of Dirk's background checks.

"Hi, Iris. It's Savannah," she said.

"Hey, girl," Iris replied. "If you're looking for

Dirk, he's gone to West Hollowood to pick up a prisoner."

"I know. I wanted to talk to you. I have a favor to ask you."

"Sure. What's that?"

"You ran a background check on a guy yesterday. His name's Chad."

"Chad Avery. That's right. Bad dude."

"Could you possibly look up that particular bad dude's address for me?"

"Yeah. Give me a minute here. . . . Let's see . . ."

While Savannah waited, she looked at the front of Tammy's cute little beach cottage. Buying that house was a dream come true for Tammy. She had literally danced for joy when she'd crossed over that threshold.

But then, Tammy was joy and dancing and sunlight all rolled into one amazing human being. She always thought the best of and hoped the best for everyone she met.

And now she wasn't even safe inside her own precious little home.

"I've got it, "Iris said. "He's at fifteen seventy Becker Street. It's over in that subdivision behind the mall, I think."

"Yeah, I know where it is. Thank you. And, Iris, could you just keep this call between you and me?"

"Absolutely. Us girls gotta hang together."

Savannah hung up and headed toward the center of town and the mall.

A few times in her life . . . very few . . . Savannah had actually hated someone. Usually the feeling was hot, intense, and fleeting.

Granny Reid had taught her a lot about not hanging on to the hot coals of anger, because you were the person most likely to be badly burned by them. So, she had always let her anger go as quickly as she could.

But this feeling wasn't disappearing any time soon. All she had to do was think of Tammy sitting on her sofa, sobbing, ashamed, saying it was her own fault that she had been stuck, and Savannah knew . . . this was a rage she was going to feel for the rest of her life.

When Savannah saw the tricked-out SUV sitting in the driveway at 1570 Becker Street, she was relieved. She wanted this to be over, one way or the other. Now.

Deep inside, the ex-cop was telling her that this was dangerous, coming here to confront him like this. This man was violent. Large, mean, and, obviously, no gentleman where women were concerned.

And she didn't care.

For the first time in her life, a switch had been flipped, and survival was no longer the primary motive.

Stopping him. That was her only goal.

She reached beneath her linen jacket and, for a moment, closed her hand around the butt of her holstered Beretta. She unsnapped the thumb break, drew the weapon, then slid it back into the holster.

You should have a plan, Savannah, the cop in her head whispered as she walked up the sidewalk to the house.

No plan needed, she told it. *This is pretty simple.*

She knocked on the door, resisting the urge to pound it with her fist. No point in alerting him.

She knocked twice more before he finally answered. And when he did open the door a bit and peek around it, the look on his face suggested he might have been expecting her. He gave her a half a smirk and said, "Savannah! How nice to see—"

She kicked the door with all her might. It flew open and the edge struck him, hard, in center of his face. Blood spurted from his nose as he stumbled backward, holding it and moaning.

"What the hell?" he said, snorting, trying to breathe through the liquid flow.

She let go with another kick, this one directly to his groin.

He forgot his broken nose as he grabbed his crotch with both hands, folded in half, and toppled to the floor.

In an instant she was standing over him, her foot on his throat. Her Beretta was in her hand, end of the barrel jammed against his forehead.

"You hurt Tammy," she could hear herself saying in a voice she didn't even recognize as her own. "Tammy is my family. If you ever hurt her, if you ever even speak to her again, I will kill you."

He looked up at her with a dark enmity she had never seen before. For two seconds, she was afraid. Deeply, terribly afraid.

So, she shoved the gun even harder against his skin, leaned down until they were nearly face-to-face, and bored him with her eyes. "If I hear that you came within a hundred yards of her, or if you even call her on the phone, I swear to God, I will hunt you down and blow your brains out."

When he said nothing, she dug her foot deeper into his neck. "You won't even see it coming. I'll break into your house and shoot you in your sleep, or I'll sneak up behind you in a dark alley, and you'll be dead before you hit the ground. Do you understand me?"

He gave her the slightest nod.

A sinking feeling in her gut told her that was all she was going to get out of him.

She straightened up and took her foot off his neck.

As quickly as she had entered the house, she left.

It wasn't until she was at least a mile away that it hit her, and she had to pull over to the side of the road as the adrenaline surged through her body. Arms crossed over her chest, she hugged herself tightly and waited for the shivering to stop.

She fought the nausea and the horrible, tight sensation in her chest, like a giant hand was squeezing her, and there was no air to breathe in the car at all.

The enormity of what she'd done hit her like a riptide, overwhelming her, dragging her under, carrying her out to sea.

Finally, the shaking subsided. She passed her hand over her forehead and realized she was drenched in sweat. And when she looked in the mirror, a woman with wild blue eyes stared back at her. A woman who appeared very nearly insane.

In that moment, her eyes looked just like the eyes of the guy lying on the floor, her foot on his neck, her gun to his head. And that was what frightened her most.

*   *   *

Savannah's knees were still a bit weak when she entered the police station an hour later. She came in through a seldom-used side door to avoid running into the brass. Having parted ways with them under less-than-amicable circumstances years before, she didn't want to come face-to-face with the chief or the captain.

She figured that, after the day she'd just had, a run-in with either one of them could prove fatal for somebody.

When she found Dirk, he was just getting ready to begin his official interrogation of Waldo Fischer. He had given her a call and told her he had returned with his prisoner. He'd invited her to come watch, and she decided it was a better plan than sitting at home, stewing about Tammy and Chad.

She walked up to Dirk, who was standing in the hallway, right outside Interrogation Room Two. It was the room with the lousy air-conditioning, and was commonly referred to as "the sweat box."

Dirk always stuck his hardcore cases in there.

"Hey, Van," he said, happy to see her . . . until he took a second look. "Babe, don't take this wrong, but you look awful."

She quickly ran her fingers through her hair, wiped the smeared mascara from under her eyes, smoothed her slacks with her palms, and buttoned her jacket so that the blood on her blouse wouldn't show. "There," she said. "Better?"

"Not really. You look like you've been through the wringer. What's the matter?"

"Nothing."

"A lot of nothing, I'd say."

"We'll talk about it later. Let's play a game of Lean on Waldo."

"Sure." He motioned for her to enter the room first. Then, as she walked by him, he peered at the front of her shirt. "Is that blood on you?"

"Might be."

"Yours?"

"Nope. But with the mood I'm in, if he doesn't cooperate, we might be adding some of Waldo's."

Dirk and Savannah sat on one side of the unadorned, utilitarian, metal table on chairs that were as hard and uncomfortable as the SCPD could find when they had "decorated" the room.

With stark walls, no windows, and the temperature set higher than any other room in the station, they had intended the space to be a no-fun zone . . . and they had succeeded.

On the other side of the table, on his own hard, overly upright chair, sat a disgruntled, disheveled Waldo.

Savannah took a mildly perverse pleasure in knowing that, no matter how bad she might look at the moment, blood on her shirt and all, he looked way worse. His stringy, blond hair was damp with sweat, hanging into his eyes. His tee-shirt's armpits were dark and wet. His tanned face was an ashen shade of gray, which complemented his red-rimmed eyes perfectly.

Yes, Waldo was a mess.

Quality, one-on-one time with Detective Sergeant Dirk Coulter could do that to a guy.

Apparently, it had been a rough ride from West Hollywood.

Dirk had told her on the phone that Waldo had been extremely uncooperative, answering none of his questions on the way to San Carmelita. But at least, in his silence he hadn't uttered the one dirty word that ruined a detective's day. "Lawyer."

Prepared to play the "good cop," Savannah pasted a fake smile on her face—the "I Understand What You've Been Through" one—and leaned across the table toward Waldo.

His green eyes, so like his aunt's, were dull and vacant as he tried to focus on her.

"What are you on, Waldo?" she asked him.

He thought it over for a while. A long while. Then he delivered his well-considered, deeply philosophical response. "Nothin'."

"So, we're going to start this interview with a big, fat lie?" Dirk said. "Okay. If that's the way you want it."

"Waldo," Savannah said, "have you spoken to anybody in your family lately?"

"No."

At least he answered that one right away, Savannah thought to herself. One lie, one truth. The score was tied.

"Do you know what happened on your aunt's estate?"

"What do you mean, 'what happened'?" he asked, obviously trying hard to concentrate. "What happened?"

"Some people died," Dirk told him.

He suddenly looked far more alert. "Who?" he asked. "Who died?"

"Blanca," Savannah said. She waited for that to sink in, then added, "And Vern Oldham."

"Blanca? Oh, no." He seemed genuinely sad,

though Savannah couldn't tell for sure through the haze of the drugs. She hated interviewing someone who was under the influence. It often dulled their responses and made them harder to read.

"What was Vern doing there?" he asked.

"Apparently, he was doing Blanca," Dirk replied. "Did you know they had a thing going?"

"He used to drop by once in a while, when my aunt was gone somewhere. I guess he could have started something with her then."

"What did he drop by for, Waldo?" Savannah's wheels were turning fast. She remembered the half-smoked marijuana joint in the ashtray next to the chocolate-dipped strawberries and champagne. "Did Vern come to the property to score his pot from you?"

"Naw, he had a 'script for it, from his doctor, you know."

"You seem to know a lot about Vern's habits," Dirk said. "Were you his connection? Did you sell him what his doctor wouldn't give him? Like his coke?"

"Uh, no. I wouldn't deal."

"You've got a record for dealing," Dirk said, standing up and walking around to stand next to him. "And we found your stash in the shed behind your house, so don't tell me you're above it. That's just gonna piss me off."

Waldo held up his cuffed hands. "Okay, okay. I used to. But that stuff you found, it's not mine."

"Let me guess," Dirk said, leaning over him. "You were holding it for a friend of yours. Some guy who sits next to you in study hall."

"Waldo, buddy," Savannah said, "you need somebody to write you some new material. That one doesn't fly once you're wearin' big-boy britches."

"Did Vern come by your aunt's place to score from you?" Dirk asked again. "I don't care if he did. I'm investigating a murder here, not your drug dealing. But you're gonna tell me the truth, or you're going away for dealing. Got it?"

Waldo peered up at Dirk, whose face was less than a foot from his. He looked like he wanted to crawl under the table and hide.

"Tell him, Waldo," Savannah said. "You've got nothing to lose. The drug charges are the least of your concerns right now."

"What do you mean?" Waldo asked, starting to shiver. "The least of my concerns? What other concerns have I got?"

"Detective Coulter has evidence that you did those murders."

"No way!"

"You own the murder weapon," Dirk told him. "And the lab says that your prints are the only ones on it."

Savannah knew that, no matter how much Dirk might have leaned on Eileen, they wouldn't have processed the boom box that quickly. But then, contrary to popular belief, during an interview, it was perfectly legal for a cop to lie like a dirty dog on a cheap rug to a suspect. Many times, she had left an interrogation swearing that she could smell her own pants burning.

"What murder weapon?" Waldo was really shaking now. "I don't even own a gun."

"Who said it's a gun?" Dirk returned to his chair and sat down.

"You don't need a gun to kill somebody," Savannah told him. "Haven't you ever played the game Clue? Even a candlestick will do in a pinch."

"I have no idea what you guys are talking about," Waldo said, slouching down in his chair.

"We've got your boom box," Dirk said, "full of chlorinated water . . . with your prints on it. "

Waldo shook his head vigorously, which caused him to lose his balance and nearly fall off his chair. "You guys are crazy. How the hell would anybody kill somebody with a boom box? I mean, if you were going to smack 'em in the head or something, you'd use a brick or a rock. A boom box . . . that's just plain nuts."

As Savannah watched him and listened to him, she had a sinking feeling that he was telling the truth.

And that was always bad . . . when you had to admit that maybe your primary suspect wasn't all that suspicious after all.

"Where were you night before last, Waldo?" she asked. "We know you weren't home. So, where were you?"

He shrugged. "In Hollywood, with some friends of mine."

"You told me you didn't have any friends," Savannah reminded him.

"Well, not great friends. Acquaintances, you know."

Dirk took out a pad and pen. "Gimme some names."

Waldo gulped. "No. It doesn't matter who I was with."

"It matters a lot," Savannah told him. "It might make the difference in you going away for a couple of years for that coke in the shed, versus a capital murder charge for the premeditated killing of two people."

Waldo thought about it, then shook his head. "No, I'm not gonna tell you who I was with. But I'll say this . . . you're looking at the wrong person for the murder thing. I didn't try to kill my aunt, and I didn't do anything to hurt Blanca or Vern."

"Then, who do you think did?" Savannah asked.

He searched his brain for a long time. Savannah could tell it was a strain. "I don't know. Maybe Emma."

"Why would Emma want to kill her grandmother?"

"Because she's dying to get her hands on all that money. Emma's boyfriend, he's made it clear he's not going to marry her until she gets her inheritance. And Emma's scared to death she's going to wind up an old maid."

"How much money are we talking about?" Dirk asked.

"I don't know. Aunt Helene never tells anybody personal stuff like that. But it's a helluva lot. And Emma's getting sixty percent of it."

"Who's getting the other forty percent?" Savannah asked.

Waldo squirmed in his chair and cleared his throat. "Well . . . I guess . . . me."

Dirk smiled. "That's good to know. Very good to know. Thank you, Mr. Fischer. You've been most informative."

When Savannah and Dirk stepped out into the hall, Dirk was practically rubbing his hands together with glee. "It's him. He did it. And all that money he's going to inherit, that's the motive."

Savannah shook her head. "If you were trying to prove he made the attempts on Helene's life, maybe. But what does that have to do with killing Blanca and Vern? Those murders don't get him any closer to the money."

"But he did it! Why else wouldn't he tell us where he was? He doesn't have an alibi."

"Isn't he still on probation from his last drug charge?"

"Yeah. So?"

"So, he was probably hanging out with his druggie friends . . . a violation of his parole, right?"

"Oh."

"Yeah."

Dirk sighed. "Well, maybe Eileen'll find his prints on the boom box."

"*His* prints on *his* boombox? The one that belongs to *him*? Dude, if that's what you're hanging your hat on, it's a sad situation."

Dirk reached out and ran his finger lightly down her cheek. "So, enough about Waldo. Tell me . . . what's going on?"

Chapter 22

As Savannah stood in the hallway, looking up at Dirk, she could see the concern in his eyes and it went straight to her heart.

And when he touched her cheek, it went straight to her eyes, and the tears she had been holding back for hours started flowing.

She backed away from him a step and said, "Don't. Don't be nice to me. If you're sweet, I'll lose it for sure."

"You'll lose what? What's going on, Van? Why the hell do you have blood on your blouse, and why are you crying?"

She turned her back to him and headed for the rear door of the station. By the time she exited, she was running.

He caught her in the parking lot, next to her Mustang. Grabbing her by the shoulder, he spun her around. "Savannah," he said, pulling her close. "Talk to me, honey. What happened?"

For half a dozen reasons that immediately sprang to her mind, she didn't want to tell him.

First, he was a police officer, and she didn't want to put him in the position of knowing about even one assault, let alone two. But the main reason she didn't want to tell him was because she had a feeling that, if she did, there would be three felonies committed before the day was over.

Dirk had a protective streak just as wide as hers. And for all of his bickering with Tammy, he loved the kid dearly.

"You don't want to know," she said.

"Are you kidding me? You're standing here crying with blood on your clothes, and you're telling me I don't want to know." He hugged her to his chest and kissed the top of her hair. "Van, you are the most important person in the world to me. I *have* to know."

All of a sudden, her legs felt very shaky beneath her. She put her hands on his shoulders to steady herself.

It felt foreign, but good, to have someone to lean on, even for a moment.

"It's Tammy," she said. "That guy . . ."

Instantly, Dirk's face clouded. He gripped her shoulders so tightly that it hurt. "How bad?" he said.

"A split lip, some bruises and swelling on her face."

"Is she at the hospital?"

"She wouldn't go. I sent her to a motel out of town."

"Will she press charges?"

"No."

He turned away from her and walked over to a garbage bin. He kicked it so hard that the side caved in. The sound reverberated like an explosion across the parking lot.

He stood there for a while, spewing obscenities, then strode back to her. "I don't care if she's willing to press charges or not," he said. "You've got her blood on your shirt, and that's enough for me. I'll—"

"It's not hers. It's his."

He stared at her a moment, then nodded as the truth dawned on him. "Oh, okay."

"I think Lady Justice has already visited Chad Avery today, so to speak."

"Gotcha." He reached down and pulled her jacket lapels open, studying the front of her shirt. "That looks like medium velocity spatter. Do we need to get a shovel, take a long drive, and find a quite, secluded, wooded area?"

"No. The dirt bag's still sucking air."

Dirk gave her a dark, humor-free smile. "I'll bet he's hurtin'."

"Oh, he's in a world o' pain."

Savannah felt a bit guilty, taking any time to herself with two homicide cases open, a couple of unsolved attempted murders, not to mention three assaults—if she counted Tiago's, Tammy's, and the one she'd given Chad.

So much for peace on earth and loving your fellow man, she thought as she turned the water on in the tub and poured in a generous amount of rose-scented bath gel.

As the bath filled, she called Tammy.

"Hi, Savannah," said the tentative voice on the

other end. Tammy sounded like she had been crying.

"Hi, darlin'. How's it going over there?"

"Okay, I guess. I've just been sitting here on the bed, thinking about things."

"Unless you've got a bottle of whiskey and a lot of good country music to listen to, that's probably not a good idea . . . the thinking, that is."

Savannah heard her sniff, then blow her nose. "I need to figure out what I did wrong, how I let things get so out of hand. How did I ever get involved with a guy like that?"

"Tammy, there are women a whole lot smarter and stronger than you and I will ever be—and men, too, for that matter—who've found themselves in that situation. Abusers are hard to spot and even harder to get rid of."

"He's stopped calling me."

"Oh?" Savannah pulled the shades down in the bathroom.

"Yeah. I got a couple of texts from him right after he left, but then they stopped. All of a sudden."

Savannah lit a votive candle and stared into the flame. "Really? Huh. Imagine that. Maybe he broke one of his texting thumbs."

"Did you break one of his thumbs?"

"Nope."

"Would you tell me if you did?"

"Nope. But I can honestly say, the last time I saw him, I'm pretty sure his thumbs were where they're supposed to be."

"How long do I need to stay here in this place?"

Tammy sounded a bit better than she had at the

beginning of the conversation. Stronger. No longer crying. And for that, Savannah was grateful.

"I'm pretty sure he's done bothering you," Savannah said, "but you're already checked in there. Why don't you stay the night and then come over here tomorrow morning bright and early? You can help me decide what we're going to do next on the case."

"I love you, Savannah."

Again, Savannah heard sniffling, but it sounded like "good" crying . . . the kind of tears that healed.

"I love you, too, puddin'. I'm in for the evening now. So, you call me if you have a mind to. About anything."

"I will. Good night."

"Sleep tight. Don't let the bed bugs bite."

"Hey, don't joke about that. In a flea-bag motel like this one, it could happen!"

Savannah hung up the phone, took off her dirty clothes, and slipped her aching, exhausted body into the glistening suds.

She smiled as she settled in for a long soak.

The kiddo was going to be okay. Not right away, to be sure, but with enough love and support . . . eventually.

A couple of hours later, Savannah was in heaven . . . or, at least, the closest thing she had ever found to heaven on earth. She was sitting in her comfy, rose-print, chintz chair, her feet on the ottoman, a cat on each side, keeping her toes warm. She was wearing one of her favorite white, Victorian nightgowns and on the table beside her was a box of Godiva chocolates.

On her lap was a romance novel with her favorite male model on the cover, chest exposed, a maiden draped backward over his muscular arm, her bosom spilling from the front of her unlaced bodice.

So far, she had been staring at the first page for half an hour and hadn't read a paragraph yet. But the night was still young. And she held high hopes that eventually her mind would stop spinning like a chipmunk on an exercise wheel, and she could actually concentrate on Raif the Pirate Rogue and Lady Cumberley.

She reached into the box and selected a French vanilla truffle. Ah, heaven, indeed.

But as she raised it to her lips, a "Shave and a Haircut" knock sounded on her door.

She froze. "Dirk," she told the cats. "Dang it!"

She shoved the chocolate back into the box, replaced the lid, and slid the container into the magazine rack beside her chair.

Long ago, she had decided that Granny Reid wasn't always right. One didn't have to share *absolutely everything* with those around you. Some things were sacred, and one's chocolate stash definitely fit that category.

Experience had taught her that Dirk could mow through a box of chocolates in five minutes flat. And to a connoisseur like herself, that was pure blasphemy . . . and to be avoided at all costs.

When she opened the door, he looked her up and down, taking in the nightgown.

"Should I have called first?" he said. "You're ready for bed already?"

"No. I just needed to get out of out my . . . um . . . school clothes and get comfortable."

He gave her a mischievous grin. "Wash them in bleach yet?"

"No bleach. But they're definitely in the washing machine, even as we speak."

She stepped aside and ushered him in.

"Want something to drink or eat?" she asked, feeling only slightly like a hypocrite, considering the hidden chocolate.

"No. I'm good."

Since when did Dirk turn down food? Especially at her house.

"Everything okay?" she asked as she motioned him toward his usual spot on the end of the sofa, next to her chair.

"Yeah. I just thought I'd drop by and give you a few tidbits of juicy gossip."

"You know what Granny always says: 'If you don't have anything good to say about anybody, come over here and sit by me.'"

Dirk sat down, lifted his feet to put them on her coffee table, then thought better of it, and lowered them.

Taking pity on him, she reached into her magazine rack, pulled out a newspaper, and tossed it onto the table. "There," she said. "Go ahead . . . this once."

Gratefully, he propped his sneakers on the paper and slid down into a semi-reclining position. "The lab called. Turns out I lied to Waldo. There weren't any prints at all on the boom box."

"Wiped clean like everything else?"

Dirk nodded.

"Why am I not surprised?" Savannah said. "You better have some better gossip than that."

"I do. I looked into our friend, Waldo, a bit more," he said. "Found something interesting."

"Besides the drug busts and assaults?"

"Yeah. I was looking over his sheet and found a familiar name."

"What name?"

"Kyd Butler."

"Kyd . . . as in Emma's icky boyfriend, Kyd?"

"That's the one. Last year, they were busted together at a club in the valley. Apparently, Kyd was Waldo's coke connection. Helene hired a good attorney for Waldo, he and Kyd pled guilty to a lesser charge, and they each served three months."

Savannah thought of the disdain in Helene's voice when she had spoken of her granddaughter's boyfriend. "No wonder she doesn't like him."

"Who?"

"Helene. She can't stand Kyd. The first time I met her, she was fixin' to shoot me in her driveway because she thought I was him."

Dirk gave her a searching look. "I guess some women don't take it well when their female family members get mixed up with the wrong guys."

She cleared her throat. "I hear it can be worrisome."

"But before I found out all that stuff about Waldo," Dirk said. "I checked on another friend of ours."

"Oh?" Savannah cut him a sideways look.

"Yeah. I thought I should have a little talk with Tammy's former beau . . . Chad What's-His-Face."

Savannah scooped Cleopatra up from the ottoman and put her in her lap. "And how did your, um, talk go?"

"Didn't actually get to speak to him. Had a hell of a time finding him."

"He wasn't at home?"

"No. So, I went down to the warehouse where he works as a night watchman. And they told me he'd called in sick."

"Fancy that."

"Actually, he'd called in from the emergency room of Community General. Seems he took a tumble off his bike."

"Poor baby."

"Broke his nose and did severe damage to his groin. Sorta like Helene did to Vern. Kinda like Jesse Murphy the other day."

"A lot of that going around these days. Maybe it's a virus."

"Yeah, I think I'm gonna start wearing an athletic cup." He cleared his throat. "Seems Chad's right testicle was a mess."

"Only the right one? Damn."

Dirk laughed and shook his head. "Remind me never to piss you off, girl."

"We were talking about Chad, and I was really enjoying it. Get back on topic."

"When I left the warehouse and went to the hospital, they said he was in surgery, getting things put back where they belonged."

Savannah sniffed. "I feel plum awful about that. Let's take up a collection and send him a fruit basket."

"So, I never got to talk to him. But after hearing what a day he'd had, I figured it might be sorta redundant."

They sat in companionable silence for a while as she stroked Cleopatra's silky black ears.

"Are you ever going to tell Tammy about Chad's . . . uh . . . bicycle accident?" he asked her.

"No. She'd probably be overwhelmed with remorse that he'd suffered on her account. Sometimes, Tammy's just way too sweet for her own good. She's got too big a heart."

"Unlike you and me."

"Yeah. Us old, nasty farts don't suffer from that particular affliction."

Chapter 23

When Savannah woke the next morning, she felt like a new woman.

It was amazing what a good night's sleep could do to recharge a gal's batteries . . . or so she thought until Tammy arrived.

Savannah was pouring her usual cup of coffee, adding the standard, obscene amount of creamer, when she saw her young friend standing there, looking through the glass in the upper half of the door.

The forlorn expression on her face, combined with the heavy makeup that Tammy never wore, twanged Savannah's heart strings.

She hurried to the door, opened it, and pulled her inside.

"How are you today, sugar?" she asked, giving her a hug and a big-sister once-over exam at the same time.

"Okay," Tammy said, managing a feeble smile. "Considering."

Savannah tried not to look too much at her

swollen eye, her cut lip, or the bruised cheek that showed through the makeup. She also decided not to mention the turtleneck sweater . . . the first high-necked top she had ever seen Tammy wear in all the years she had known her.

Savannah hurried to the refrigerator and took out a bottle of organic apple juice. "Did you get any sleep at all? Or did you lie awake all night worrying about bedbugs?"

"I had a few nightmares," she admitted. "Not about bedbugs."

Savannah handed her the glass of juice. "I'll bet you did. I'm so sorry, sweetie."

Tammy shrugged. "Unfamiliar bed."

"Right."

Savannah watched as she sipped the juice. "I've got some granola cereal, if you want breakfast," she told her. "Or I'd be happy to make you an egg-white omelet."

"No, thank you. The juice is enough. I'm not really hungry."

Savannah took a drink of her own coffee and thought how flavorless it seemed all of a sudden.

She looked at her friend, sensed her wounded spirit, and thought it might be nice to go dislodge old Chad's other testicle.

"You haven't heard from him, have you?" she couldn't help asking.

"No. Not a word."

"Good." Savannah forced a smile. "So, are you ready to hit the road with me? I'm going to go talk to Emma Strauss about some new stuff that Dirk found out about her boyfriend and—"

"No. Thanks, Savannah, but I can't. I have an

appointment in an hour. Something I really need to do. I'm sorry. I hate letting you down."

Savannah set her mug aside and took Tammy's empty glass from her. "That's fine. Really, it's okay. If you have something you've got to do, then by all means, you attend to that. I understand. More juice?"

"No. I've got to get going."

"Okay."

Savannah set the glass in the sink, then stood there as an awkward, tense silence built between them.

Finally, Tammy said, "I'm going to a counselor, a psychologist who specializes in . . . this stuff." She pointed to her bruised face. "I know what you said, Savannah, about how this wasn't my fault. I thought about it all night, and you're right . . . I didn't deserve what happened to me. I didn't cause it."

Savannah nodded. "That's absolutely correct, Tammy. You're a victim of a crime, just like a man who's mugged walking down a street or a woman who's raped or a store owner who's robbed."

"I realize that. Really, I do." Tammy choked back tears as she reached for Savannah's hand and held it tightly. "But I want to talk to someone, a professional. I want to do everything I can to make sure this never happens to me again."

Savannah pulled her into her arms and held her, like she had her younger brothers and sisters when they had been hurt in a thousand different ways.

"I think that's a great idea, darlin,'" she told her. "It's very brave and smart, and I'm proud of you for making that decision."

No sooner had Savannah let go of her than they heard a cell phone ringing. They both cringed when they realized it was coming from Tammy's purse.

She opened her bag, took out the phone, and looked at the caller ID. "It's Dirk," she said. "Never thought I'd be so happy to hear from *him*."

She answered with a cheery, "Hi, Dirko." She listened for a moment, then said, "I'm okay, thanks. I'm at Savannah's."

Savannah poured herself another cup of coffee, pretending not to listen as Tammy said, "Oh, that's so sweet of you. A really nice offer. Can I let you know later? Okay . . . yeah . . . you, too."

She hung up. "Dirk just told me that if I want to stay over at his trailer and sleep on the couch, I can . . . for as long as I want to."

"An old bear like him, who growls when anybody even gets near his cave door? Wow, that *is* a nice offer."

"He told me that the door key is under that old Hudson hubcap he's got nailed to the porch. Like I didn't know that's where he keeps it."

Savannah laughed. "Like everybody who knows Dirk doesn't know that's where he keeps it."

"He also told me that he loves me."

Savannah was taken aback. "Really? I mean, I know he does, but . . . he actually said it?"

"Well, his exact words were: 'Stay out of trouble and keep your nose clean, fluff head.' But I know that's what he meant."

Savannah was hoping she could catch Emma at home alone without Kyd around. Not that she didn't enjoy his scintillating conversation. Not that she didn't welcome the chance to glean fashion tips and philosophical insights from this prince among men.

But she could swear her ears were still bleeding from listening to his so-called music the last time she'd been there. She wanted to give them a little time to heal before the next exposure.

And she was hoping to talk to Emma about him behind his back.

So, when Emma invited her into the little beach cottage, and she asked, "Is Kyd around?" and Emma said, "No," it was all she could do not to break into joyful song right there in the living room.

"Is there something new on the case?" Emma said, motioning for her to take a seat.

"You mean, something besides the fact that we're no longer just trying to find out about your grandmother's 'accidents,' but also trying to solve two murders?"

"Yes, something like that."

Savannah studied the redhead sitting on the chair across from her. She thought how many different versions of Emma she had seen since she had met her. There was the impeccably dressed, conservative woman who had hired her. The seemingly carefree beach bum in men's boxers and a tank top, explaining the fine points of death metal rock to her. And this woman, who looked as though she hadn't showered for days or slept for several nights.

Something about the jittery way she raked her fingers through her short hair, the way she ran her hands up and down her arms and constantly shuffled her feet, made Savannah wonder if Waldo and Kyd were the only ones with drug habits.

In spite of the fact that it was a cool morning at the beach, Emma was sweating, and Savannah was sure that her pupils were dilated.

"Are you okay?" Savannah asked her.

"Sure. Fine." She fidgeted in her seat, toying with her hoop earring. "You said there's a new development?"

"We found out something that might be important. That's why I thought I'd drop by and talk to you about it."

"Yeah. Okay. What is it?"

"We just found out that Kyd and Waldo are good buddies. Have been for a while now."

"Well, I wouldn't say they're good friends. They know each other. We've been out to my grandmother's for social events."

Savannah didn't like being lied to. It was one of her pet peeves. And being lied to by clients who were supposedly paying you to uncover the truth was particularly inconvenient and irksome.

"You've taken Kyd to a lot of tea parties at Oma Helene's, have you?" she asked.

Emma squirmed a bit more. "I don't see why it matters, if Kyd and Waldo know each other."

"It matters because they were busted together . . . for dealing drugs together. That matters, Emma."

"Kyd's clean now. He goes to meetings to stay straight and sober."

"The last time I was here, he was having beer for breakfast. So much for his sobriety. And how straight has he been? As straight as you are now?"

Emma stood, her arms crossed over her chest. "I

don't know why you're talking to me like this, Savannah. I thought you and I were friends."

"So did I. But you weren't truthful with me, Emma. And I know why. You didn't want me to look at Kyd . . . to think he's anything other than this great, talented musician, a real standup guy."

Emma shrugged and hugged herself tightly. "I'm sorry, Savannah," she said. "I admit it. I was afraid that if you knew Kyd had a record, you might think he had something to do with what happened to my grandmother. But he didn't. He loves her."

"Who are you kidding, Emma? I'll bet you he doesn't even like her. If she died tomorrow, how long do you think it would take him to march you down the aisle?"

"No! It's not like that! Kyd loves me for who I am!"

"Maybe he does and maybe he doesn't. But, Emma, a woman in your position has to be careful, discerning. Hell, we all do, but a future heiress like yourself . . ."

"I think you should leave. I'm sorry I ever hired you."

Savannah stood and looked deeply into the young woman's eyes. "Tell me the truth, Emma. Why did you hire me? And don't lie to me. I'll be able to tell."

"To protect my grandmother. That's why. I swear it."

"Then answer two more questions for me. And again, you better answer me truthfully."

"Okay. What do you want to know?"

"Where does Waldo keep the key to his shed . . . the one behind his house?"

"What?"

"Don't pretend you don't know. You lived on that property for years. You've known Waldo all your life. Where's the key to that padlock he has on the door?"

Emma swallowed hard. "There's a rock with a peace sign painted on it, on the ground to the right of the shed door. He keeps it under that. Now, what's your other question?"

"Does Kyd know where the key is?"

Emma closed her eyes for several seconds. When she opened them, they were filled with tears. "Yes," she said softly. "Yes. Kyd knows."

Usually, Savannah found Dirk's company to be a simple comfort, a bit like an old, well-worn, much-loved house slipper. Occasionally, he was highly annoying, more like having a grass burr on the seat of your pants.

But once in a while, when she was sitting next to him in the passenger seat of his old Buick, smelling his cinnamon sticks and Old Spice shave lotion, listening to an Elvis classic, an expanse of some Southern California freeway stretching into the distance before them, Savannah felt like life was pert nigh perfect. And his presence was a large part of the feeling.

"This better pay off," he grumbled in the middle of her blessing counting. "If we drag our candy asses all the way to the stinkin' valley for nothin', I'm gonna fly into a blind rage."

She sighed. *Back to the burr on the britches again.*

"Did you have a lot of other leads to follow up on?" she snapped back. "Calls pouring into the tip line? Witnesses lining up to say they saw a guy with a long, black cape and a big, black mustache sneaking around the spa, carrying a boom box? "

"All right, all right." He gave her a sideways grin. "That's quite enough out of you."

She sniffed. "*I'll* decide when enough's enough. I've got a really strong feeling about this Kyd guy. I want to make sure he was where he said he was that night. And if that means going to a club called Hell's Inferno in the stinkin' hot valley, so be it."

"A phone call wouldn't do it?"

"I told you, they didn't answer. You don't listen to me."

"You talk too much. My ears get tired. They say women speak twice as many words in the course of a day as men do."

"That's because men don't listen and we have to repeat everything."

He craned his neck to watch a gorgeous, classic Harley that was weaving through traffic. When it was out of sight, he turned back to her. "What?"

"Exactly."

Hell's Inferno was everything it promised to be. The bar was blood-red, as were the tables and the chairs. It looked as though the so-called decorator had walked through the door and tossed buckets of red paint on everything, then told some second-rate cartoonists to paint the walls with flames and cheesy little devils dancing around with pitchforks.

"What would you call this?" Dirk asked as they stood in the middle of the room, looking around. "Décor by Dante? Staging by Satan?"

Savannah looked at him with mild amazement.

"Did anybody ever tell you, you aren't the run-of-the-mill blue-collar dude?"

"All the time."

They walked over to the bar, where a gal with hair the color of the walls, tables, and chairs was slicing a pile of lemons and limes.

Savannah sidled up to the bar. "Hi."

"We're not open yet," the girl said.

"No problem. We're not drinking yet," Savannah replied. "But I'll bet you make a wicked Bloody Mary in here."

"Huh?"

"Never mind. Can we ask you a couple of questions?"

Dirk pulled out his badge and passed it under her nose.

Her eyes lit up. She pushed the fruit away. "You mean, like, when cops walk into a bar and ask the bartenders about people who come into the bar and the cops pay them money for answering? That kind of questions?"

Dirk scowled as he dug a couple of bills out of his pocket and laid them down. "Yeah. The kind where the bartender spills her guts and gives the cop his money's worth."

"Okay, shoot."

Savannah pointed to a poster on the wall behind the bar with the same hideous Poison Nails logo she had seen on the side of Kyd's van. "They play here often?" she asked.

"Oh yeah. They're everybody's favorite! They're here every weekend and sometimes during the week. We sell their CDs and everything." She reached behind the counter, pulled out a CD, and slid it across the bar.

Savannah picked it up and scanned the list of titles. It read like a roster of slice-and-dice horror
flicks.

"Were they here this past Saturday night?" Dirk
asked.

"Sure. They play here every Saturday night. And
even when they're not playing, they come by and
hang out."

"How often does Kyd drop in?" Savannah asked.

"Oh, he's in two, three times a week with his
girlfriend. He's so cool. I love his hair. He likes
mine, too. He's into redheads."

"Apparently so," Savannah said. "Emma's isn't
as red as yours, but—"

"Who's Emma?"

"His girlfriend."

"His girlfriend's name isn't Emma, and she's certainly not a redhead. She's a blonde . . . very proud
of all her highlights . . . and her fake boobs . . . and
her expensive, old-lady clothes. She stands out like
a sore thumb in this place."

She made a face like she had just sucked on one
of her freshly cut lemon wedges. "I don't know
what he sees in her. She's old enough to be his
mother and then some. It's probably her money.
He said she's coming into some big money soon,
and she's going to finance his career. She's already
produced a CD for them."

Savannah felt something rising in her spirit that
felt effervescent, like a nice champagne. She
glanced at Dirk and saw a smile on his face that
told her he was feeling the same thing.

"You wouldn't happen to know the name of this
older girlfriend of his, would you?" she asked.

"Sure. Her name is Ada." She looked under the

bar and found yet another CD. She handed it to Savannah. "This is the one she produced. It's a completely different style than they usually do. I hate it. Figures she'd produce something stupid like that."

Dirk leaned halfway across the bar, giving the gal one of his gunfighter glares, as Savannah called them. "Are you absolutely, positively sure that Kyd was here last Saturday night. All night?"

"No."

"No, you aren't sure?" Savannah asked.

"No, he wasn't here."

Savannah's thoughts spun around in a circle. "But you said Poison Nails played."

"They did. But Kyd called that afternoon and said he had an upset stomach and couldn't make it. Antonio sat in for him."

Savannah turned to Dirk, a smirk on her face. "So, tell me, big boy," she said. "Are you glad you came to the stinkin' valley now?"

Chapter 24

This time it was Kyd's turn to sweat in the no-air-conditioning interrogation room of the San Carmelita police station. And he wasn't doing any better than his buddy, Waldo, had.

Even copious amounts of ultra-gel weren't standing up to the heat. His hair was plastered flat against his head, and he was as wet with perspiration and as fidgety as his girlfriend had been earlier that morning. Though Savannah was pretty sure his condition wasn't the result of a narcotic high.

Kyd of the Poison Nails didn't appear high at all. Apparently, being suspected in a double homicide was a major buzz kill.

"You can sit there and lie all day long and piss off Detective Coulter here if you want to, Kyd," Savannah was telling him. "But your sugar momma already gave you up. We just interrogated her in a room down the hall, and she told us the whole thing."

"Well," Dirk said, "that's half true. She told us

what you did. She didn't come clean about how she was involved."

"She left you holding the bag, Kyd, my man," Savannah told him. "She's saying it was your idea from the first."

"It was not!" Kyd's eyes were practically bugging out of his head.

Savannah loved it when they looked like a fly that had just been swatted.

"She says it was." Dirk leaned back in his chair and crossed his hands casually behind his head. "Yes, she's saying you tried to kill the old lady. You dug the hole with the shovel so that she'd hit it and go off the cliff."

"Pretty smart," Savannah added, "wiping off all the prints and then sticking it in Waldo's shed, so that if anybody got blamed for it, it'd be him. By the way, we're processing the rock with the peace sign and the hidden key. Did Ada remind you to wipe your prints off those, too?"

"She didn't tell me . . . I . . . never mind."

Savannah stifled a chuckle. From the moment he had sat down, they had told him nothing but lies. But he was buying it all. It was like shooting catfish in a barrel, only without feeling sorry for the fish.

"She told us you tried to kill her aunt for her," Dirk said. "She even gave you up for murdering Blanca and Vern. But she said you just killed them for the fun of it, because you're nothing but a cold-blooded bastard."

"I am not!" Kyd shot up out of his chair.

Dirk reached across the table, put a big hand on his shoulder, and shoved him back down.

Savannah never ceased to marvel at how, no matter how vicious and cold-blooded certain criminals might be, they never wanted to be thought of as such. Over the years, she had heard the most contrived, totally illogical rationalizations for the most heinous crimes. But those who embraced their flimsy excuses did so with a passion.

Savannah suspected it had something to do with being able to sleep at night and look in a mirror every morning. Even cold-blooded bastards had to live with themselves.

Dirk turned to Savannah. "See there? He's not as bad as you thought. I told you it was all Ada's idea. I knew she was no-good the moment I laid eyes on her."

"She's not!" Kyd agreed, sensing an ally. "She's the one behind this. It was all her idea!"

"I told you so," Dirk said to Savannah, a twinkle in his eyes. "I told you she was laying it all on this guy, when it was her who talked him into it. She's the primary offender here. He's just a secondary offender at most."

She nodded solemnly. "And you should remember that when you write up your report, Detective."

"Oh, I will." He turned back to Kyd, who was looking much encouraged at his turn of good fortune. "So, Kyd, the only thing left to clear this whole thing up is why she had you throw that boom box in the spa in the first place. You know her better than we do. Help us out here. What would you say was her motive for that?"

Kyd looked right and left, as though expecting a vengeful Ada to appear over one of his shoulders.

"I think," he said, "it was because she thought it was her aunt in the tub with Vern. Helene was always in the tub at that time of night."

"Ah, that makes perfect sense," Savannah said.

"It does. Thank you." Dirk gave him an encouraging, grateful smile. "And if Ada had already planned for you to electrocute her aunt, even before she caught her boyfriend in the tub, too, that would be premeditated murder on Ada's part."

"Oh, come on. She's not *that* cold," Savannah said. "She told me that Kyd here decided to do it on the spot."

"I did not! She was planning that for days, telling me to get an extension cord for the boom box and where to plug it in and how to stand behind those bushes there by the spa so her aunt wouldn't see me."

"Then what was Vern, a bonus?" Dirk asked. "She wanted you to do her aunt, but then when she realized her boyfriend was in the tub, too, she figured, what the heck? Kill two birds with one boom box?"

Kyd gave him a suspicious look. "If that's what she did, would that be better for me, or worse?"

"Oh, much better," Dirk assured him. "Then she'd be even more of the primary offender, and you'd be like . . . a tertiary offender. That's a lot better than a secondary offender."

"Okay. Then, yeah . . . that's what happened."

Dirk stood, walked over to a file cabinet and opened the top drawer. He took out a yellow legal pad and a pencil. "But," he said, "for me to be able to make this all a matter of record, you need to get it down on paper. Otherwise, she could still dispute everything you've told us and blame it all on you."

"All right. I will. But you have to show it to her after I write it. I want her to know I was too smart for her."

"Oh, we'll show it to her," Savannah said as she watched him start to scrawl his words across the paper. "We certainly will."

Half an hour later, much to his surprise, Kyd was behind bars, and his written confession was securely sealed in an evidence envelope . . . having first been photocopied for Ada's sake.

Savannah and Dirk were strolling down the hallway, on their way out of the station.

"What the hell," she said, "is a tertiary offender?"

He shrugged. "I don't know. I just made it up. Pretty good for your run-of-the-mill blue-collar sorta guy, huh?"

She laughed, shook her head, and laced her arm through his. "Do you ever check to see if your nose is growing?"

"I file it down every morning when I shave."

When Dirk knocked on Ada Fischer's apartment door, he used his most officious, San Carmelita Police Department knock. It was the one that could be heard the first time, through every room of any residence. When Dirk used his cop knock, even the neighbors heard.

Savannah couldn't blame Ada for leaving the security chain on when she answered.

She peeked out of the five-inch opening and looked quite dismayed and annoyed when she saw them.

"What do you want?" she snapped.

"Oh, Ada," Savannah said. "We want you."

"Are you going to take the word of a drugged-out rock musician with a record over mine?" Ada stood in the middle of her living room, hands on her hips, glaring at Savannah and Dirk.

Even under the strained circumstances, Savannah couldn't help noticing the formfitting purple leopard jumpsuit she was wearing. Savannah couldn't recall seeing an outfit like that one for the past twenty years. And she hoped that after today, she'd have another fortunate twenty-year stretch without seeing another one.

It did show off Ada's nipped and tucked body to perfection though.

Savannah glanced at Dirk and saw that he was staring straight at Ada's face, his eyes not wavering one bit. She had seen him do that many times and admired his self-control. He would watch a cute bikini priss by on the beach, like any other guy, but when he was on duty, Detective Sergeant Dirk Coulter was the consummate professional and refrained from ogling.

"Hey, some of my favorite people are rock musicians," Savannah told her. "And a lot of them are probably drugged-out half the time. Doesn't make them liars."

"We have evidence that this particular rocker is telling the truth about your involvement in those murders," Dirk told her.

"I don't even know Emma's idiot boyfriend. I think I met him once when she brought him to the offices to see Helene."

"Oh, you've met him way more than once," Dirk said. "I'll bet there's a ton of Hell's Inferno customers who would testify they saw you two smooching in there."

"One little red-haired bartender in particular who's got her eye on Kyd and is wondering what he sees in you," Savannah added. "And that reminds me . . ."

She reached into her purse and pulled out the CD the barkeep had sold her. She held it out to Ada, who reluctantly took it.

"The fifth song on that," Savannah said, "is 'Take Five,' which just happens to be my favorite jazz tune of all time. It's actually a very nice version of it. That nitwit Kyd is a halfway decent guitarist after all."

Ada shoved the CD back at her. "What does that have to do with me?"

"You were playing it on your stereo system when I was here the other day," Savannah said with a smile. "You were playing a song on a CD that you produced, performed by a guy you've met maybe once? I don't think so."

"People don't lie to the cops unless they have a reason to," Dirk told her. "And when they do, it's usually because they're guilty of something."

"I've had nothing to do with Kyd or anything illegal that he may have done," she protested, flipping her hair—and hair extensions—over her shoulder.

"Funny," Dirk said as he pulled out a pair of handcuffs, "that's what he said about you . . . at first . . . before he gave us a full written confession."

"I want a lawyer!" Ada said as he clamped the cuffs onto her wrists. "I want to see that damned confession."

"Then get yourself a lawyer," Dirk said. "Maybe we'll let him see the confession."

Savannah walked along with them to the waiting patrol car in the apartment building's parking lot and watched as Dirk tucked an unhappy Ada into the backseat.

"He was so quick to sell her out," he said as they returned to his Buick.

"So much for true love. And once it sinks in on her that we've really got her, she's gonna blame everything on him."

"Sure makes our job a lot easier."

"Yeah," Savannah said, watching the unit drive away with its prisoner glaring at them through the back window. "If people ever start treating each other decent in this world, Lord help us. We'll actually have to work for a living."

They looked at each other and in unison said, "Heaven forbid."

The next morning, when the receptionist at Strauss Doll Works escorted Savannah back to Helene's office, he was far more polite, even personable.

"I hear that Ms. Fischer was arrested last night," he whispered as they walked down the hallway, passing one office door after another. "I even heard that she tried to kill Ms. Helene. Is that true?"

"Now, how would I know a thing like that?" Savannah said, raising one eyebrow.

"I heard you're the private investigator who solved the case."

"Don't believe anything you hear and only half of what you see. I'm only one of several people who solved this case."

"Then Ms. Fischer *was* arrested?"

"I'm nothing if not discreet. You're just going to have to read your newspaper, young man." Savannah reached over and patted him on the front of his well pressed shirt. "Now, if I can find a murderer, I can find my way to an office I've already visited. Thank you for your company."

She left him and hurried on down the hallway to Helene's office. When she knocked, she heard an instant and cheerful, "Come in."

Entering, she saw Helene rising from her desk.

The lady hurried to her and folded her close in a warm hug. "My dear Savannah," she said. "I don't know how to thank you!"

"So, you've heard?"

"My extremely repentant granddaughter called me first thing this morning and filled me in on all the details." Helene invited her to sit at the desk's side chair.

Savannah took the seat and watched as Helene glided back to her desk. She couldn't help hoping that she would be that graceful when she was Helene's age.

"I told Emma," Helene continued, "that guy was a no-good bum. But of course, the youngsters never believe us old-timers."

"Did you believe your grandmother when you were Emma's age?"

"Not on your life. I was sure she was cracked." Helene's green eyes glowed with an affectionate warmth as she looked into Savannah's. "But you revere your grandmother, don't you?"

"I do. I have to. If I didn't, she'd take a hickory switch to my behind."

Both women laughed.

Then Helene grew somber. "I still can't quite believe they actually tried to end my life . . . and wound up killing two people in the process. I'm not a young thing, you know. Ada couldn't have just waited until I died?"

"Ada is—what's the new term for it?—troubled."

"Yes, she's been troubled for a long time now. And the ironic thing is, I'd already rewritten my will and left everything to Emma and Waldo." A look of sadness swept over her face. "I'm going to rewrite it one more time. They'll have to address their substance-abuse problems to receive their inheritances. And even then, it's going to be in installments. I refuse to finance their addictions."

"I understand."

They sat in companionable silence for a few moments as Savannah looked around the enchanting room with its beautiful furniture, the shelves of beautiful dolls, and the large, black-and-white photograph of the little girl.

She studied the picture, and again, she was curious about the child, standing on the quaint, European street, holding a doll in her arms.

"If that isn't a picture of you," she said, "do you

mind telling me who she is? She's so lovely, such a sweet little face."

Helene turned in her chair and looked at the picture that dominated the wall behind her. When she turned back to Savannah, her eyes were filled with tears. "I don't talk about her. Hardly anyone is still living who knows her story. But because of what you've done for me, I'm going to tell you."

Helene rose and walked over to the large window, overlooking the city, and stood, her back to Savannah.

"Her name was Esther. She was my cousin, one year younger than I was. We lived in the same village in Bavaria, and we played together every day. She had a doll, the one in the picture. It was so beautiful, and I wanted it so badly. She would let me play with it, but I didn't want to play with it. I wanted it for my own."

She paused in her storytelling, and Savannah could tell she was crying.

Savannah took some tissues from her purse, walked over to the window, and handed them to her. "That's understandable, Helene," she said softly. "Every child wants what others have."

"Not like this. We aren't supposed to covet, and I truly coveted that doll. It's all I thought about night and day . . . how I could take it away from her, how I could have it for my own."

Helene dabbed at her eyes with the tissues. "Then one day, Nazi soldiers came to our village. They stayed for a week. And when they left, there were no more Jews in our town. My family was Catholic. Esther's was Jewish. My aunt and my uncle, and all their children were gone. In one night, they vanished. I remember going with my mother to their house. It was empty."

Savannah reached for Helene's hand and held it tightly. "I'm so sorry, Helene. For them. For you."

"My mother told me to keep the doll to remember her by. But I didn't want it anymore. All I wanted was my playmate. I left the doll there on the floor that day and walked away. I never saw it or my cousin again."

Helene turned and waved a hand toward the shelves overflowing with the beautiful creations of her company. "So, for over fifty years I've made dolls, dolls for little girls like Esther all over the world . . . to remember her by."

"And what a wonderful legacy that is for her," Savannah said, wiping away her own tears as she looked at the picture on the wall. "Thank you for sharing that with me."

"You're welcome, Savannah. Thank you for listening."

Helene walked over to her desk and picked up a white box that was lying there. It was a bit longer than a shoe box and tied with a pink ribbon.

"I want you to have this," she said, holding out the box to Savannah.

Savannah took it, touched the soft pink satin ribbon. "What is it?"

"It's the first prototype of our new doll."

"I thought you threw it in the trash."

Helene smiled through her tears. "This is a new one. See what you think."

Savannah untied the ribbon, lifted off the lid, and pulled back several layers of white tissue, revealing the most beautiful doll she had ever seen.

It was exactly like the one she had at home, but the black hair was even softer than Valdosta's, the bright blue eyes more lifelike, and the powder blue dress was covered with exquisite lace and trimmed with white satin edging.

"Oh, Helene! She's absolutely stunning! Are you sure you want me to have her?"

"Absolutely sure." Helene gave her a shy, child-like smile, and for a moment, Savannah could see the little girl she had been in Bavaria, so many years ago . . . before her innocence had been destroyed.

Savannah kissed the doll's cheek and held her close. "I'll cherish this gift forever."

"Good. I'm glad you approve," Helene said, re-arranging things on her desk, suddenly all business. "Because we're releasing her in time for Christmas, and we're naming her 'Savannah.' "

Chapter 25

As Savannah's guests sat in her living room, digging into the hot molten-lava cake, topped with Chunky Monkey ice cream, they all had looks of pure rapture on their faces. Even Tammy, who had decided to be "wicked" for one evening and indulge in "evil" carbs.

"The only thing that would be sweeter than this," Dirk said, between bites, "would be if I was using Ada Fischer's written confession for a napkin."

"I can't believe you got her to confess," Ryan said.

"I can't believe her barrister allowed her to," John added.

Tammy leaned close to Ryan on the sofa and whispered, "A barrister is a lawyer, right?"

Ryan nodded and sighed. "I'm going to be translating Limey to Yank for the rest of my life."

Dirk took a big bite of the ice cream, started to say something, then looked at Savannah and swallowed it first. "We had Ada good," he said. "Besides

Kyd's confession, we searched her house and found a prescription sleep-aid bottle in a bottom drawer in her bathroom."

"That doesn't sound particularly incriminating," Ryan said.

"It does if you filled the prescription for the first time on the day your aunt got poisoned, and if the lab finds your prints in cocoa powder on it."

"Woo-hoo," Savannah clinked her spoon on the side of her bowl. "Go Eileen and the lab kids!"

"And then there's the extension cord." Dirk grinned. "The one she put on the boom box so that it would reach from the plug to the tub. We found it rolled up in Helene's garage, where Kyd said it would be. The female end was partly melted, and it was discolored around the prongs. And it had Ada's fingerprints on it."

"And they were so careful to wipe everything else down," Savannah said. "No matter how smart a killer is, they can't think of everything. And those two aren't nearly as smart as they think they are."

Dirk agreed. "They're more worried about sticking it to the other one than they are about protecting their own backsides."

Tammy finished her cake and set the bowl on the side table next to her. Savannah saw her reach up and touch her cheek. The swelling had gone down, but the bruise was spreading and turning an ugly shade of brown and green that no makeup could hide.

Tammy glanced Savannah's way and the two friends looked into each other's eyes for several moments.

"I'm okay," Tammy said. "Stop worrying, big sister."

There was an instant hush in the room. Everyone stopped talking, even eating. No one had mentioned the elephant in the room all evening.

"I'm glad you're okay," Savannah said finally, breaking the awkward silence. "I knew you would be."

"Yes, me, too," Dirk added.

"I had no doubt, love," John told her.

Ryan reached over and patted her on the knee. "It'll take time, Tammy. But we're all here for you. Don't you forget that."

Tammy placed her hand over his. "Thank you. All of you." She drew a deep breath. "My counselor is really helping me. And I've joined a support group for people who've been in abusive relationships. They're so helpful and understanding. One of the women is a doctor, another's a judge. There are some guys there, too. This happens to all kinds of people."

John nodded solemnly. "We had a close friend whose partner battered him. It took him years to end the relationship. He could have used a group like that."

"Anyway, I'm starting to feel a little better. I'm going to go back home."

"Do you think that's wise, dear?" John asked. "I don't mean to be overly protective here, but . . ."

"I checked on old Chad today," Dirk interjected. "I drove by his house. He was out in the yard. When he saw me pull up, he ran into the house." He snickered. "Well, 'run' might be overstating it a bit. He hobbled, limped, did this strange little crab dance across the lawn to his door. I hear he took a bad spill off his bicycle and injured his naughty bits."

In unison, they all turned to look at Savannah, who was suddenly fascinated by a particular chunk of chocolate in her Chunky Monkey.

"Anyway," Dirk said, "I think our buddy Chad has a lot of other things on his mind right now besides Tammy."

"Good," Tammy said. Then with a note of sadness in her voice, she added, "Eventually, I hope to have other things on my mind besides him."

When Tammy, Ryan, and John had left, and only faithful old Dirk remained, faithfully polishing off the last of her ice cream, Savannah sat quietly in her chair, feeling the effects of the past few days sweep through her body.

"I'm not as young as I used to be," she told Dirk, as she massaged an aching muscle in her thigh . . . probably the leg she had used to smash Chad's door open. "I don't spring back from this crap as quickly."

"Avoid more of the crap," he replied, offering Diamante a taste of the ice cream off his fingertip.

"How? Retire from my work?"

"You'd have to retire from the human race."

"Sounds good. Wanna go find a deserted tropical island somewhere? It'll just be you and me."

He brightened. "Sure. With a big coconut tree and—"

"Two coconut trees."

"Two?"

"One for your side of the island and one for mine."

"Oh, of course. What was I thinking?"

She grinned at him. "You can come over to my side once in a while."

"Gee, thanks." He returned the smile. "No need to. I'll be able to hear you jabbering at me from the other side of the island."

"But you'll only hear half of it."

He set his bowl aside, picked up Diamante, and cradled her against his chest. She rubbed her whiskers against his cheek.

Savannah watched them, thinking that any guy who loved cats as much as dogs couldn't be all bad.

"You know, Van," he said softly, "you're so tired, because you take care of the whole world. At least, everybody in your world, and that's a big job."

"No, I don't."

"Yes, you do. I know where it comes from, you being the oldest of nine kids, your mom not taking care of you guys when you were little, and you having to grow up quick."

"Granny stepped up."

"Yes, but you went through a lot before the court gave you guys to her."

Savannah shrugged. "I just did what I had to. Still do."

"No, honey. You don't have to. That's what I'm trying to tell you here. I'd be the first to admit that, at any given time, in any given place, you're the strongest person in the room. But that doesn't mean you have to take everybody and their problems onto your own back."

Savannah stared at him, considering his words. "Do I do that?"

"Sure you do. Most of the time, you think you're the only one who can handle a situation or that you can handle it better than anyone else. And that's usually true. But it's also good for people to solve their own problems. That's how they learn."

She watched him stroke the cat's ears, heard her purring. "Granny used to tell me the same thing."

"Well, there ya go. If Granny said it, it's just a plain fact."

"Are you telling me that I shouldn't have gone after Tammy's creep?"

"No. I'd never second-guess you on something like that. But I wish you'd come to me, asked me to help you with it. That was a really dangerous thing for anybody to do alone. You could have been hurt or killed, Savannah."

She shrugged. "I didn't want to bother you with it."

"It wouldn't have been a bother. It would have been my honor to stand by you, behind you, in front of you, whatever you wanted. But you never ask me for help, Savannah. You never need me." He looked at her with his heart in his eyes. "I need you. I depend on you a lot. And it would mean the world to me to think that, at least once in a while, you needed me."

"Oh, Dirk." She jumped up from her chair, hurried over to him, and sat down on the sofa beside him. She picked up the cat and unceremoniously set her on the floor. Then she grabbed him in a bear hug . . . one of the no-frills, rib cracking kinds he usually gave her.

"I will next time," she told him, kissing his cheek.

"You will not." But he looked pleased as he ruffled the top of her hair with his big hand.

"I'll try. I promise I'll try."

Dirk had been gone less than a couple of minutes—just long enough for Savannah to change into the white, flannel nightgown that had once been Granny Reid's and settle into her book-cat-chocolate ritual—when the phone rang.

It was Dirk. "I think I left my sunglasses there," he said, sounding totally disgusted. "That or I've lost them again."

"It's dark out. How did you notice your sunglasses are missing?" She sighed, replaced the lid back on the chocolate box, and slid it into the magazine rack. At this rate, these truffles would last her until Christmas . . . or at least next week.

"A dude's gotta keep tabs on his shades," he said. "They make you feel like a man."

"They make *you* feel like a man." She set her cats and her book aside and started walking around the living room, searching his usual spots where he tended to plop things down and forget them. "Do you know where you left them?"

"You always ask me that. And I never do."

"Where are you?"

"Lester Street. I'm almost there."

"I'll keep looking." She hung up and went to the kitchen, muttering, "Dang boy'd lose his head if it weren't sewn on. . . ."

She opened the freezer door and checked inside, figuring that any guy who would leave his car keys in there might also stick a pair of shades inside. Nothing. *Not even ice cream,* she thought, thanks to her pack of ravenous guests.

She smiled and closed the door, thinking she wouldn't have it any other way.

Glancing around the kitchen, she spotted them . . . black Ray-Bans camouflaged on top of her black coffeemaker. "There they are, you turkey butt," she said to the forgetful, soon-to-arrive Dirk. "I'm gonna get a piece of scratchy, itchy twine and tie these onto your head."

She heard the knock at the door and hurried back through the living room and into the foyer, nearly kicking over a cat. "Sorry, Di," she said. "Go get back on the footstool. Mommy'll be there in a minute. Just let me give Uncle Dirk his sunglasses, so that he can look like a man."

She turned the deadbolt and swung the door open.

Looking into the semi-darkness—she had forgotten to flip on the porch light—she saw something that confused her.

Dirk had something on his face, she thought. Something white.

Her mind spun, trying to figure out what she was seeing and what it meant.

"What are you wearing there?" she said.

He was playing some sort of silly joke, like he did on Halloween when he thought it was hysterical to appear at her door wearing a mask that looked like a decomposing corpse.

He stepped closer to her and raised his hand. "It's your fault, you bitch! You didn't like me! You told her to leave me!"

In an instant, she knew. This wasn't Dirk.

The thing on his face was a bandage. And he was pointing a gun at her head.

"No!" She raised her arms and crossed them over her face. "Don't!"

Fire flashed through the darkness.

A sound like thunder crashed around her.

Smoke filled her lungs, and her wrist stung as though someone had stabbed it with a red-hot poker.

She tried to grab at the gun, but it was just out of her reach.

Another thunderous sound and blaze of flame.

More choking, blinding smoke.

It felt as though someone had slammed her in the chest with a huge fist. Then came the fiery pain.

And another blast.

It all seemed like a terrible dream, in slow motion, where something horrible is happening, but the dreamer can't run, can't speak, and can't wake up.

"She loved me. But you told her I was no good. It's all your fault."

Gasping and holding her chest, Savannah stepped backward.

My weapon, she thought. *It's in the closet.*

But the closet was six feet away and he was never going to let her get that far.

Besides, she was already shot, several times.

As the strength left her legs, she crumpled to the ground and lay there on her side.

Chad stood over her, looking down at her.

"You're gonna die! You're gonna die for what you did to us . . . to me!" he shouted at her.

As though from far away, she heard and saw the next two blasts. She was dimly aware that one had hit her leg and another her abdomen.

I'm dying, she thought. *He's killing me right here in my own house.*

She looked down at the front of her night-gown—Granny Reid's nightgown—and saw that it had several black holes in it and the entire front was stained red with blood.

"You ruined it," she said. She could hear the liquid sound in her chest as she tried to speak. She knew that meant she'd been hit in the lung. She knew it was very bad. But she mostly felt indignant that he had ruined her grandmother's lovely nightdress.

She tried to think of some way she could fight back.

But there was no fighting back. She couldn't move.

She looked up at him and watched as he leaned down and placed the barrel of the gun against her forehead. The weapon filled her vision. She tried to swat it away, but her arms weren't working.

"Okay," he said. "Now you're gonna die."

In an instant, she decided that she didn't want his face to be the last thing she saw. So she closed her eyes . . . and prayed that Grandpa Reid and the angels were waiting on the other side to take her heaven.

Chapter 26

She heard the explosion. She smelled more smoke. And waited, expecting to enter some sort of restful darkness or heaven's bright lights.

Instead, she heard an enormous thud. She felt it in the wooden floor she was lying on.

Footsteps pounded across her porch, through the open doorway, and into her foyer.

She opened her eyes... and was staring into the dead eyes of Chad Avery.

He was lying on his side on the floor next to her, facing her. And even though she could hear the sick, burbling, death rattle in his throat, she knew he wasn't truly breathing.

Chad was no longer among the living.

She wasn't completely sure if she was either.

Then she became aware of hands on her, touching her. Big hands. Gentle hands.

"Savannah! Oh God, baby! Van! No! No! No!"

She felt something being laid over her. It smelled of leather and cinnamon and Old Spice. It was Dirk's old bomber jacket, still warm from his body.

"Dirk," she murmured.

"I'm here, honey. I've got you. I've got you."

She heard him punch three buttons on his phone. Then he said her address and told them, "Officer down! Officer down! Ambulance! Code Three! Get it here *now*!"

But I'm not an officer anymore, she thought, as the world spun around her. *Doesn't Dirk know I'm not a cop anymore?*

"Savannah," she heard him saying, "I'll be right back honey. Right back. You stay awake for me, okay? Stay awake."

She fought to keep her eyes open until he returned a moment later and shoved some things under her legs to elevate them. She could feel their texture against her calves, and she realized they were the cushions from her sofa.

"There, baby," he said. "You lay really still for me and try to stay awake. Stay with me, honey. Please, stay with me."

He moved the jacket aside just a bit to look at her wounds. Then he pulled his tee-shirt off, wadded it into a ball, and pressed it tightly beneath her left breast.

It hurt terribly, but she didn't complain. Deep inside, beneath the pain and beyond the weakness, she realized he was fighting for her life.

"I need . . ." she whispered to him.

"What, honey?" He leaned his head down to her as he pressed his shirt against her wound. "What do you need?"

"You. You wanted me to. . . . I need you. . . ."

*   *   *

Savannah floated in and out of consciousness in the ambulance on the way to the hospital. At one point, when she woke, she saw a paramedic standing over her, working on her, wearing a white face mask.

She thought he was her attacker. Weakly she flailed at him and tried to yell, "No! Get away from . . ."

But her arms were useless and her voice only a whisper.

"It's okay, Van," she heard Dirk say. "No one's going to hurt you. You're safe now. Rest. Just rest."

His deep, calm voice reached inside her and touched her fear. Dirk was there. He wouldn't let anyone hurt her now.

"It's over," he said. "The worst has already happened, and you're okay." He smoothed her hair back from her forehead. She could feel his hand trembling. "You *are* okay, aren't you, sweetheart? Please . . . tell me you're all right."

"I'm okay," she whispered.

She saw the look of relief on his face and considered that her reward for lying. And she was lying. Because she couldn't feel her arms or legs anymore. And a coldness like she had never experienced before was growing from the core of her body.

Her wounds burned and ached terribly, but that wasn't what frightened her. It was the coldness deep inside that was draining the life from her. And it was spreading by the moment.

No, she thought. *I'm not okay. Not okay.*

*   *   *

When the ambulance arrived at the emergency room entrance, two paramedics rushed to unload her and the gurney she was lying on. But Dirk took over for one. "Let me," Savannah heard him say. "I have to do something."

As they wheeled her through the large doors and into the hospital, she was finding it harder and harder to stay awake, to concentrate on what was happening around her.

Everything looked hazy and everyone seemed so far away.

She couldn't seem to think clearly.

She looked up at Dirk's bare, blood-smeared chest. "Oh, no, you're shot," she whispered, trying to reach up to touch him.

He clasped her hand. "No, honey. I'm not shot."

She closed her eyes, tried to squeeze his hand, and couldn't. "I'm glad," she said. "I'm glad you're not hit."

She heard one of the paramedics say, "Her vitals are dropping."

And Dirk say, "Multiple GSWs."

"How many?" a female asked.

"Five," Dirk said, his voice choking.

Five, Savannah thought. *Five gunshot wounds! Boy, somebody's hurt bad. Lord, help them,* she prayed silently. *Please help that person with the five gunshots.*

"It feels like we've been in this room for ten hours at least," Dirk mumbled as he toyed with his foam coffee cup that had been empty for ages.

He was sitting on a hard plastic chair in the waiting room. And in the chairs around him sat Ryan and John, and a sobbing Tammy.

Dirk was wearing a tee-shirt. When Ryan and John had arrived, Ryan had removed the under-shirt from beneath his dress shirt and given it to Dirk.

John reached over and gently eased the cup from his hand. "I'll go get us some fresh ones," he said.

Ryan glanced at his watch. "I know what you mean, but it's only been three. The doctor said the surgeries would take hours. They've got a lot of work to do on her."

"Were they sure they'd have to remove her spleen?" Tammy asked, crying into a handful of tis-sues. "She needs her spleen. It does important things in your body."

"They said it's torn and bleeding really badly. If they can't fix it, it has to come out." Dirk wiped a weary hand across his face. "It's the bullet in her lung that they're the most worried about. They don't think the one in the belly tore any of her in-testines. Oh, God."

"That bastard really did a number on her," Ryan said. "I can't help but say it: I'm glad you took care of him. No trial necessary."

They all three turned to look at Tammy, who started crying even harder.

John reached over and wrapped his arm around her shoulders, hugging her close. "I'm sorry, love. We forget that he meant something to you . . . and this is a double tragedy for you."

"No," Tammy said, her eyes blazing. "He's no loss. I'm glad he's dead, too. I don't want Savannah to have to go through a trial, looking at him there in court, remembering what he did to her."

They sat silently for a moment, then Tammy whispered, "If she makes it, that is."

"She'll make it," Ryan said.

Dirk twisted his hands that were still smeared with her blood. "The doctor said he gives her a fifty-fifty chance . . . at best." He shook his head. "God, when he said those words, it felt like the earth had just opened up and swallowed me whole."

Ryan reached over and gave him a quick, vigorous back rub. "Hey, that's our superwoman you're talking about there. The doctor doesn't realize who he's dealing with."

"Yes," John added, "I'd lay much better odds for our girl than that. We're not talking about just any ordinary female."

"She is strong," Tammy said. "And healthy . . . especially considering all the crap she eats."

"She's very tough," Ryan agreed. "Strong willed and determined. That counts for a lot at times like this."

Dirk looked at them with tortured eyes. "You guys didn't see her. I did. He shot the hell out of her. She's a mess."

Dirk started to cry. Tammy continued to cry. And a moment later, they were all four crying.

And that was the way the doctor found them when he walked into the waiting room.

Chapter 27

When Savannah awoke in the recovery room, she thought she had rheumatic fever again.

In her pre-Granny Reid days, when she had been five-years-old, she'd suffered a particularly bad bout of it, and she would never forget what it felt like to lie in bed, every inch of her body aching, weak, afraid, and alone.

She remembered what it was like to have her body failing, under a terrible attack, and losing the battle.

But, even though the pain was far, far worse than it was all those years ago, and in spite of the feeling of her life energy ebbing . . . it wasn't quite so bad this time.

She wasn't alone. Someone was holding her hand.

"Hey, Sleeping Beauty's awake!" Dirk said as he jumped to his feet and bent over her bed.

He kissed her on the forehead. "How are you feeling?"

She gave him a weak smile. "Like . . . alligator's . . . chew toy."

"Does it hurt pretty bad?"

"Yeah. Bad." She looked around the room, trying to orient herself. "Am I sick?"

"No, honey. You were hurt."

"How?" Every word caused an awful pain in her chest.

"You were shot."

"Shot?" She looked down at her body. She saw bandages around her wrist. She could feel bandaging above her breast and below it, more on her abdomen, and still more around her thigh.

She groaned. "Oh . . . five GSWs . . . me." She looked up at Dirk. "Who shot me?"

"Tammy's ex-boyfriend. Remember?"

She nodded slightly. "Yes." The nightmarish events began to flood back into her mind. She recalled seeing Chad's dead eyes staring at her. "You . . . kill him?"

"Yes, I did. I pulled into your driveway and saw your front door open. You were on the floor, and he was pointing his gun at . . . well . . . Yeah. I killed him."

She squeezed his hand. "Thank you."

She glanced down at the hospital gown and the bandages. Sharp, searing pain radiated from so many places deep inside her. She had never felt so weak, so cold, so vulnerable . . . not even when she'd had rheumatic fever.

"I'm . . . torn up," she whispered.

"You look beautiful to me." He reached over and stroked her cheek with his forefinger. "I never saw anything as lovely in my life as you opening your eyes just now."

"No," she said. "Inside. Really . . . torn up."

"You're going to be okay, Savannah. Do you hear me?" He leaned over until his face was inches from hers. His eyes filled her vision. "You're strong, and you're loved, and you're going to fight, and you're going to be okay."

"I don't know, Dirk. I can tell. It's bad."

"Well, I know! I just got off the phone with your granny, and she said to tell you she's getting on a plane to come see you, and she'll be praying the whole way here. And you know what a praying saint she is!"

Savannah's eyes flooded with tears. "Take care of her . . . for me. Please."

"No! I will not. You're going to take care of her yourself."

She started to shiver as the cold numbness went deeper and deeper. "My heart . . ." she murmured. "If it goes into my heart . . ."

"What, baby? If what goes into your heart?"

"The cold. Dirk, I'm so cold."

She was only vaguely aware of him lifting her and moving her to the side of the bed. And she wasn't sure what was happening when he lay down next to her and pulled her close, aligning his body with hers.

With one arm beneath her head and the other gently around her waist, he cuddled her against him, kissing the top of her hair, her forehead, her cheeks.

"Just rest, baby," he said. "I've got you, and I'm never gonna let go. You rest and heal."

As he held her, she felt a blissful warmth radiating from his body into hers. It was chasing the awful cold away.

And she felt something else . . . something powerful and life-giving. As she faded off to sleep, she realized what it was.

It was love.

When Savannah awoke, she felt a hand holding hers. But this time it wasn't Dirk's big, rough hand. It was a smaller, infinitely soft hand. And before she even opened her eyes, she knew.

"Granny," she said.

"Yes, child. I'm here."

To her left, Savannah saw the cloud of silver hair, the bright blue eyes, so like her own, and the concerned, sweet smile.

"Don't worry," she told her grandmother. "I'm all right."

"I know you are, darlin'," Granny replied in her thick, Southern drawl. "I been prayin' for three days and nights, and I knew you would be."

Savannah chuckled. "And the Good Lord wouldn't dare say no to you!"

"Well, he has a couple of times, but, thank goodness, not this go-around."

Savannah looked to her right and saw Dirk sitting in a chair, a tired, but happy smile on his face.

"You been here three days and nights, too?" she asked him.

"How can you tell?" he asked.

"Your eyes look like a road map o' Georgia, and that's a three-day whisker growth if ever I saw one."

"He wouldn't go home," Gran said. "He wouldn't even go down to the waiting room to get some sleep. He's been sitting right there in that chair the whole blamed time."

Savannah glanced at Dirk and they exchanged a little knowing look.

"Oh?" Savannah said to him. "Since Granny arrived you've been glued to the chair, huh?"

"Just sitting here with my teeth in my mouth, as y'all say," he replied.

"We've been here, too." Someone wriggled her toe through the blanket.

She looked down to the foot of her bed and saw Tammy, John, and Ryan. Ryan was the toe tweaker.

"Hi, guys," she said.

"You had us worried there, love," John said. "But you're looking so much better now."

"I feel a little better, too," Savannah told him.

She looked at Tammy, who was standing there, staring at the floor, the picture of guilt and sadness.

"You, kiddo," Savannah said. "Get over here and give me some sugar."

Shyly, Tammy skirted around the bed. Dirk moved his chair aside to make room for her.

She bent down and placed a quick peck on Savannah's cheek.

"Well, that was short and sweet," Savannah said. "I'll need another one just like it."

Tammy gave a small, grateful laugh, and did as she was told. "I'm so, so sorry, Savannah," she said. "I never thought I'd cause you to be hurt. I—"

"Hush up," Granny told her. "We'll have no more of that nonsense talk. This ain't no more your fault, Tammy, than the man in the moon. The feller who did it done paid for it, and that's the end of that."

Savannah smiled at Tammy. "Granny's ruled. Case closed."

"Besides," Dirk said, "if you've got any residual guilt, the doc says she's gonna need a lot of physical therapy on that arm and leg. You can work it off that way."

Tammy lit up. "Oh, sure! I'll have her walking, jogging, and lifting weights, and I'll blend up some special, healing drinks for her. Let me go get a pen and some paper. I'm going to start making notes, coming up with an exercise regimen, and . . ."

As she scurried from the room to get her writing materials, Savannah shot Dirk a withering look. "Healing drinks? Exercise regimen? I hate you."

"No ya don't." He stood and turned to her grandmother. "Granny, there's something I need to do, an errand I have to run. Could you watch our girl here for just a little while?"

"I ain't goin' no place." She waved him away. "Skedaddle, boy. Do whatcha gotta do."

Dirk leaned over and kissed Savannah. "I'll be back before long."

As he walked by Ryan, he said, "If you aren't too tied up for the next hour or so, could I ask you to come along with me? I'd sure appreciate it."

Ryan looked surprised, as did the others in the room. But he quickly nodded and said, "Sure. No problem. Be glad to."

As they watched Dirk and Ryan leave the room, Savannah said, "What do you reckon he needs Ryan for? It's not like he needs help with a shower and a shave."

"Mysterious," John said. "Quite mysterious, indeed."

* * *

Several hours later, Ryan and a freshly shaven and showered Dirk returned, carrying several shopping bags each.

Dirk looked around at Granny, Tammy, and John. "Could Ryan and I see all of you out in the hallway for a moment . . . please?"

"Can I come, too?" Savannah asked as she watched them leaving the room.

"Yeah, right," Dirk said. "Don't you so much as twitch. Be right back."

He left, closing the door behind him. And a few moments later, she heard a lot of giggling and chattering in the hallway.

"Probably get-well balloons," she said to herself. "Hopefully somebody thought to throw a get-well box of chocolate in there, too."

It was at least three or four minutes before he returned alone. "All right," he said, grabbing the privacy curtain and pulling it on its runner all the way around her bed. "We're just going to close you in here for a minute."

Good heavens, she thought, *never saw such a fuss over some balloons. Maybe flowers, too . . . a spring bouquet with lots of daisies.*

She heard much shuffling of feet, some tittering, whispers, a bang, and an under-the-breath curse as someone crashed into something.

Finally, there was a noisy exodus out the door.

She heard someone closing the window shade. Then they flipped off the overhead light.

"What's going on out there," she called.

Dirk pulled back the privacy curtain.

There were no balloons or daisies. But there were flowers.

Her hospital room was filled with red roses and

white candles, dozens of both, everywhere. Their beautiful perfume filled the air as the flames flickered, softly lighting the scene.

She felt like she had stepped into a moonlight rose garden.

"What is this?" she asked.

Dirk laughed nervously and walked over to her bed. "Hopefully," he said, "it's romance."

"Romance? In a hospital room?"

He shrugged and looked like a little boy offering his first valentine. "Yeah. How'd we do?"

"It's beautiful! But why?"

He dropped onto one knee beside her bed, then realized his head was too far down for him to even see her. So, he dragged a chair over, and knelt on it.

"I know I should wait," he said, "until you get out of this place, and I can take you to a beach or a nice restaurant or whatever, but . . . hell, Van, we've waited long enough."

"For what?" she asked, her heart starting to pound.

"This thing scared me, Savannah. I was thinking, what the heck, we've got our whole lives ahead of us, but you never know. Nobody knows how much time they've got. You can't waste time. It's too precious."

"Okay. But what does that have to do with . . . ?"

"I love you, Savannah," he said. "I loved you from the minute I met you. You walked into that station house with your uniform on. And I said, 'Wow! Look at the rack on that one and . . . ' Oh, sorry, that's not very romantic, but . . . well . . . anyway . . . And then you shook my hand and said something to me in that sexy, Southern drawl of yours, and looked at me with those blue eyes of yours, and I never had a chance. I was a goner."

"You were? Really? A goner?"

"Oh, totally. And all these years, I thought, maybe she'd have me if I worked on my table manners and left the toilet seat down and didn't put my feet on her coffee table, but you seemed to like living by yourself. After all those brothers and sisters, I don't blame you for that, but . . . damn . . . I'm messin' this up."

She reached over and ran her fingers slowly through his hair. "You're not messin' up anything, darlin'," she said softly. "Take a deep breath. You're doing just fine."

He paused to regroup, then continued more calmly. "Savannah, my friendship with you, it's the best thing that's ever happened to me. And I've always been afraid I might lose it if I . . . you know . . . reached for more."

She nodded. "It's so good, I was afraid to change anything. I was afraid, if it didn't work out, then we couldn't go back to being . . . us."

"Me, too. But the other night, when you were so bad, and I laid down by you . . . That was the first time in my life I ever held someone in my arms the whole night long."

"It was? But you were married before."

"Just trust me," he said. "It was a first for me. And it felt really good. It felt really right, holding you, being strong for you. For the first time I knew that someone really needed me. And it was you. I was so glad it was you."

"Oh, Dirk. It meant a lot to me, too. It meant everything to me." She said, her voice choking as her eyes filled with tears.

"Then, what I'm trying to say is"—he reached into his back pocket and pulled out a small box—"Savannah, if you'll marry me, I promise you, I'll try my very, very best to be a good husband to you, because you're the finest person I've ever known, and you deserve it."

He flipped the lid of the box open, and Savannah caught her breath when she saw an exquisite engagement ring. Its enormous princess-cut stone twinkled with a hundred rainbow prisms in the candlelight.

"I hope you like it," he said. "Ryan took me to his jeweler, and he said it's a really good stone."

"Oh, Dirk! It's absolutely gorgeous! It's . . . it's *huge*! How can you afford . . . ? I mean . . ."

He laughed. "Didn't expect cheap old Dirk to buy a diamond the size of a doorknob, huh?"

"Well . . . I . . ."

"I make a good salary," he said. "And, as you know, I never spend a nickel I don't have to. So, I've got a ton of money in the bank. Marry me, and I'll pay for a new roof on your house."

"You got a deal, buddy!" she said, slipping the ring on her finger.

"So, that's a yes?"

"It's a big yes!"

He stood, gently wrapped his arms around her, and kissed her.

It wasn't like any short, routine, doesn't-mean-anything kiss they had ever shared before.

Dirk took his time, and when he was finally finished with her, Savannah was feeling simply incredible from her head to her toes—five GSWs or not.

"Wow," she said, breathlessly. "If I'd known you

could do *that*, I'd have married you a long time ago."

He gave her a sexy smile and a throaty laugh that went straight to heart and then traveled to other, more intimate, areas. "There's a lot more where that came from, babycakes."

"Ummm . . . something to look forward to. Maybe I'll put *you* in charge of my physical therapy."

He turned to the door and yelled, "She said yes!"

Instantly, shouts of joy erupted in the hallway.

"Can we come in?" Tammy called out.

Dirk looked at Savannah. She nodded.

"They're gonna kiss us and hug us to death," he grumbled.

"Yeah, they will." She held up her hand and turned it this way and that, admiring her ring. "Open the door and go with the flow. If you fight it, it'll just make it worse."

AUTHOR'S NOTE

Dear Readers,

As you may have guessed from reading this book, I have deep feelings and strong opinions about domestic abuse. Everyone has the right to a life that is free of the fear of violence. For even one woman, man, or child to be denied that freedom is a tragedy.

Every day, abuse happens to thousands of people, regardless of their gender, age, race, financial standing, educational background, sexual orientation, religious affiliation, occupation, or social status. It occurs among people who are married, divorced, separated, dating, and sometimes even between people who have very little history together. **Abuse can happen to anyone.**

Chances are high that you know someone who is being abused. Or you may be yourself. If you are, and you have children, there is a fifty percent chance they're being abused, too.

What is abuse?

Abuse is a set of behaviors used by someone in a relationship to control the other person. Among others, these behaviors may include:

- Calling you names, putting you down
- Humiliating and embarrassing you in front of others
- Cursing and shouting at you
- Shoving, slapping, choking, or hitting you
- Saying you're a bad parent, threatening to take the children from you
- Exhibiting jealousy and suspicion
- Controlling who you see and speak to and where you go
- Insisting on making all the decisions
- Preventing you from working or going to school
- Interfering with you seeing your family and/or friends
- Destroying your property (or threatening to)
- Harming your pets (or threatening to)
- Intimidating you with guns, knives, or other weapons
- Controlling the money, making you financially dependent on them
- Acting like the abuse is no big deal, saying it was your fault, or denying it
- Forcing you to have sex or some form of sex that you don't like
- Forcing you to drop charges
- Threatening to commit suicide
- Threatening to kill you (and/or people you love)

If you recognize your situation or someone else's in the list above, please know three things:

1. **You aren't alone.**
2. **It isn't your fault.**
3. **Help is available.**

If something about your relationship scares you, and you need to talk, call the National Domestic Violence Hotline at this number:

1-800-799-SAFE (7233)

The National Domestic Violence Hotline receives more than 21,000 calls a month from people just like you, who find the strength to reach out. When you call, a compassionate, nonjudgmental advocate on the other end of the phone is there to listen. **Everything** you tell them **is completely confidential and anonymous.** (They don't even have caller ID.)

It may be one of the hardest things you've ever done, making that call. It takes enormous courage to tell someone your secret. But think of all the things you've already endured in your life. You may be a victim of abuse, but you're also a survivor! You've done a lot of hard things, and you don't have to handle this alone. If you call that number, you'll find there are people in this world who understand what you're going through, who care about you, and who want to help.

You deserve to live the life of your dreams. A life of your design and your choosing. A life free from fear.

My dear friend, this is my wish for you: May your wounded heart find healing, your heavy spirit be uplifted in joy, and your troubled mind find peace profound.

Sincerely,
Sonja Massie
(G. A. McKevett)

National Domestic Violence Hotline recommended reading:

- *Why Does He Do That?* Lundy Bancroft. Berkeley Trade, 2003
- *Saving Beauty from the Beast.* Vicki Crompton & Ellen Zelda Kessner. Little, Brown, 2003
- *In Love and In Danger.* Barrie Levy. Seal Press, 1998
- *When Violence Begins at Home: A Comprehensive Guide to Understanding and Ending Domestic Abuse.* K. J. Wilson, Ed.D. Hunter House, 1997
- *Helping Her Get Free: A Guide for Families and Friends of Abused Women.* Susan Brewster. Seal Press, 2006

After a recent brush with death, plus-sized P.I. and bride-to-be Savannah Reid has decided to stop sweating the small stuff. But when an event planner comes in to arrange her wedding, Savannah discovers that murder can ruin even the best laid plans . . .

Hailed as the wedding planner to the stars, Madeline Aberson has orchestrated some of the most exclusive soirees in Hollywood. But when Madeline becomes embroiled in a nasty divorce, her life falls apart, and rumors swirl that her parties have become total duds. Desperate for work, Madeline finds herself planning far less glamorous affairs, including none other than Savannah Reid's wedding to Dirk Coulter.

It doesn't take long for the opinionated Madeline to get on Savannah's last nerve, and when the big day finally arrives, Savannah can't wait to send Madeline packing. But when the bride finds Madeline's body face down in the pool, floating among an elegant array of rose petals, it's clear that someone has already hastened the diva's departure. For better or worse Savannah and Dirk put their wedding on hold, vowing instead to find out who killed Madeline and why . . .

Please turn the page for an exciting sneak peek of G.A. McKevett's BURIED IN BUTTERCREAM coming next month!

Chapter 1

"This ain't exactly the roarin' hot time we had planned for this evening, huh, babe?" Dirk Coulter said to the woman at his side.

Savannah Reid couldn't take her eyes off the red wall of flames that had jumped the fire line half an hour ago and was rapidly consuming the town's community center. The building where she and the guy next to her were to have exchanged wedding vows an hour ago.

"Not even close," she said, slipping her arm around Dirk's waist and leaning against him. "I had much more ambitious plans for you this evening, big boy."

He put his arm across her shoulders and pulled her closer. His voice cracked a bit when he kissed the top of her head and said, "I'm sorry I couldn't get your wedding gown out, Van."

She blinked back some tears that had nothing to do with the smoke in the air or the ash falling like dirty snow around them and the crowd assembled to watch the battle. It was all-out war between the San Carmelita Fire Department versus Mother Nature, and Big Momma was winning.

"Hey, you tried," she replied. "If you'd tried any harder, I'd be bailing out my groom-to-be on our so-called wedding night, and that'd just be the cherry on the crap sundae."

"I only hit him once."

"Yeah, and that was one time too many, you knucklehead."

Dirk flexed his hand. "A love tap . . . that's all it was."

"And if you and Jim weren't poker buddies, he'd have pressed charges then and there."

"Eh, he knows I'm a man under duress. If there's anything harder on a guy's nerves than gettin' hitched, it's having the place he's supposed to do it in get torched on his wedding day."

"Well, you be sure and mention that 'duress' business to him," she said, "'cause here he comes now. And he ain't lookin' none too friendly."

An enormous fireman was elbowing his way through the mob, composed of countless other firefighters, copious members of the media, town cops galore, and an overabundance of run-of-the-mill gawkers.

When Jim Barbera reached them, he stuck his finger in Dirk's face and said, "I don't care if you *do* have a gold detective's badge, Coulter. Don't you ever lay a hand on me again like that or I swear, I'll—"

Slipping deftly between the two men, Savannah flashed the firefighter her best Southern belle, eyelash-batting, deep-dimpled smile. "Please don't hold it against him, Jim," she said in a soft, down-homesy drawl. "Dirk was willing to risk life and limb to go into that burning building to rescue my wedding gown. And I know you'd have done the same for that pretty little wife of yours . . . what's her name . . . Lilly? She's expecting, isn't she? And this is, what, your third younger?"

"Uh-huh." Jim was trying hard not to succumb to Dixie charm. "You shouldn't have let your man go into a burning building, Savannah," he grumbled. "Not for anything. That's the number-one rule."

Savannah could feel her dander rising. The dimples got a tad less deep, the smile a bit less wide. The drawl had a bite to it when she said, "In the first place, he ain't *my man* yet, thanks to this blasted fire. And even if he was—knowing him like I do—I don't reckon I'll be doing a lot of 'letting' him do this or that. He's got a mind of his own and that's the way I like it . . . most of the time."

Fortunately, Jim got a call on his cell phone. He answered it with a predictable degree of gruffness, considering the conversation he was having, the smoke he had inhaled, and the fact that the fire behind him had totally engulfed the structure he and his company had been fighting to save.

"Yeah," he said into the phone. "Oh? Okay." He glanced around at the bystanders, then at Dirk. "Coulter's standing right here. I'll tell him."

He stuck the phone back into his pocket. "That was the chief," he said. "They're at the point of origin. It's the same guy again . . . a pentagram drawn in the dirt and a black candle in the center of it."

Immediately, Savannah turned toward the mob of spectators, and her eyes began to scan each face in the crowd, one by one. Nobody had to tell her what Jim and Dirk were thinking as they did the same. Odds were high that their arsonist with the creepy rituals was among them, watching with everyone else, enjoying the drama, the destructive fruits of his labor.

What was the point of unleashing hell on a community if you couldn't be there, firsthand, to watch the calamity?

This was his fourth fire in less than a month. They had to catch him before he burned the whole county down.

After a long, dry summer, Southern California had enough problems with wildfires without a pyromaniac getting his jollies by setting more.

"The wind shifted two hours ago," Jim said. "And they announced it on the local news."

"He had to know it was coming this way," Savannah added. "Plenty of time for him to get here."

Dirk switched from his Grumpy, Thwarted-Bridegroom Mode to his usual—Harried, Cynical Police Detective Mode.

His modes didn't vary much.

"Let's socialize," he said to Savannah, "mingle a bit."

"Yeah, you do that," Jim told them. "I'm gonna get back to work, if I've got your word, Coulter, that you won't be trying to rescue any more bridal apparel."

But Jim didn't need to finagle any promises out of Dirk. Ruined wedding plans pushed aside for the moment, Detective Sergeant Coulter and his still bride-to-be were on a mission. They had an arsonist to apprehend and a strong, personal investment in his capture.

"If I get my hands on him," Savannah said, as they headed for the crowd of onlookers, "I'm gonna mash him like a spider on a sidewalk, until he's nothing but a big, greasy spot."

"No, you've gotta save me some."

Dirk took her hand and led her over the uneven, rocky ground with a paternal tenderness that was sweet and touching.

Three months ago—when both of their lives had been changed forever—all that loving concern had meant the world to her. His constant attention and unfailing devotion had been exactly what she had needed to survive her ordeal and heal the damage that had been done to her body and spirit. She never would have made it without him.

Two months ago, his endless support and help had been comforting, even convenient, as he had scurried about, running errands for her, waiting on her hand and foot.

But now, she was getting tired of being treated like a victim. She was a survivor. And all this solicitous hovering was getting to be a bit much.

Gently, she withdrew her hand from his. "Let's split up," she said. "We'll cover more ground that way. You work this end of the crowd, and I'll take the other end. Meet you in the middle."

Instantly, disapproval registered on his face in the form of his standard-issue showdown-at-high-noon cowboy scowl. "You're gonna go by yourself?" he said.

"Yes. I am. Just like I go to the little girls' room all by myself." She gave him a smile that was sweeter than her words. After all, he wasn't deliberately being a pain in the rear end; he meant well.

So, she wouldn't smack him upside the head . . . this time.

But he wasn't going to let it go. "I don't know how happy I am about you going off by yourself so soon after—"

"Then, darlin', you can just get happy in the same bloomers that you got unhappy in," she said as she started to walk away from him.

"Be careful!"

She smiled back at him over her shoulder, and lightly scratched the tip of her nose with her middle finger.

Chuckling, he shook his head. "Well, at least don't tackle anybody. You know what the doctor said."

As she left him behind and worked her way to the opposite end of the crowd, she tried not to think about what the doctor had said.

"Ms. Reid, you're a very lucky lady. Three of those five shots could have easily been lethal, had they been an inch or two to the right or the left."

No, some memories should remain on the shelf marked, "Best Left Alone."

"The worst is over, Savannah girl," she whispered to herself, as she had so many times during the past three months. "The worst is over and done with. Move on."

She passed a group of teenaged girls wearing far less than their mommas should have let them out of the house in. She checked them off her mental list.

Most arsonists were male. And the majority of them had practical reasons for setting their fires. Revenge, insurance fraud, or to destroy the evidence of other evil-doing . . . those were the most usual reasons for blaze-setting.

But Savannah remembered, all too well, the class she had taken while still on the police force, the points the arson specialist had made when profiling what he had called the "pure arsonist." Though rare, there were individuals who derived their own strange brand of sexual gratification from setting fires, watching them burn, and reveling in the secret joy of knowing they had created the ensuing havoc.

She ran down the mental checklist: 90 percent male, usually white, age seventeen to twenty-six, possibly some form of mental illness, substance abuse, previous felony convictions.

And she decided to add one more qualifier: mud-wallowin', slop-suckin' pigs, who ruin other people's wedding days.

Of those assembled to watch the mayhem, only a few fit the description, and even less when she ruled out those young, white men who were excitedly chattering with others about the drama before them.

Instinctively, she knew she was looking for a loner.

And at the edge of the crowd, she found one.

On the opposite side of the community center's parking lot, on a small hill dotted with sagebrush, stood a solitary figure—a young, Caucasian man, dressed in baggy, dark clothes, who looked like he had just emerged from his mother's basement for a rare outing. He was farther from the fire than the rest of the spectators, but from his elevated position, he had one of the best views in town.

Gradually, Savannah worked her way through the crowd to get closer to him and have a better look.

Leaving the rest of the spectators, she casually strolled across the asphalt parking lot toward his hill, trying her best to watch him without being too obvious. Instead of making a beeline for him, she turned left and meandered in the direction of a path that appeared to lead from the lot up to where he stood.

Concerned that he would spot her, she moved slowly, trying to stay behind any tall brush that would provide cover. Fortunately, he seemed so fixated on the scene below that he was oblivious to all else.

Drawing closer, she could see that he was young, probably early twenties. He was dressed all in black, and once, when he turned her way for a moment, she caught the glint of a large, silver medallion around his neck.

Her pulse rate quickened. She was pretty sure she'd seen a star on the pendant. Maybe a pentacle?

Ducking behind a tree, she reached into her jacket pocket, pulled out her cell phone, and gave Dirk a call.

"Yeah?" he said.

"Other side of the parking lot, on the hill," she whispered. "The guy in black, watching the fire. I think it's him."

"Where? Oh, yeah. I see him."

"Where are you?" she asked.

"On the far side of the crowd. Where are—? What the hell!"

She grinned. He'd spotted her. And even from

sixty yards away, she could read his indignation in his body language. She gave him a little wave.

Instantly, he started to elbow his way through the spectators, heading in her direction.

"Don't even think about taking him yourself," he told her. "You wait for me."

Savannah's grin disappeared. "I know the drill," she said.

And she did. Having been a cop—his partner, in fact—she knew all too well about waiting for back-up. But it was one thing to wait for assistance as part of the routine. It was another to have some-one—especially a former partner—tell you to do so because he was afraid you couldn't handle a sit-uation by yourself.

"Be very careful, Ms. Reid," she could hear the doctor saying. *"I know your work involves physical al-tercations from time to time. You can't afford to—"*

"Oh, shut up," she whispered to the voice in her head.

"No," Dirk barked back. "I won't shut up! You wait for me!"

Rather than admit she'd been talking to herself, she just said, "I'm waiting, okay?" and clicked the phone off.

He'll be here lickety split anyway, she thought to herself as she watched Dirk push through the crowd like a football player within a few yards of a Hail Mary touchdown. *Even if he has to mow down women, children, and a couple of grandpas to get here.*

Poking her head out from behind the tree, she sneaked another peek at her suspect.

And saw him staring right at her.

Nailed, she thought. *Shoot f're. Now what?*

She stuck her best ain't-it-just-a-fine-day look on

her face and came out from behind the tree. "Boy, this here's a steep hill," she said, strolling up the path toward him, pretending to be out of breath. "But it looks like you got the best view from up here. Mind if I join ya?"

The look on his face told her, yes, he minded. Very much.

He also looked quite excited . . . in a way that reminded her of when she'd walked into the bathroom and caught her younger brother, Macon, with a girlie magazine.

She took one quick glance down at the front of his pants.

Yep . . . highly excited.

He also looked highly annoyed.

"Get outta here," he said. "I don't want company."

"Well, now . . . that ain't very neighborly of you," she said, continuing to close the distance between them. "I just want a good look at the fire. That's all."

"Look at it somewhere else," he shouted, getting more agitated by the moment. "Leave me alone."

Then, under his breath, she heard him mutter, "You're *ruining* it."

As she drew within ten feet of him, she could see his medallion clearly. And, yes, it was a pentacle, a large, inverted one, hanging on a thick chain, in the center of his chest.

She wanted to glance back over her shoulder and see where Dirk was now. But she didn't want to give away the fact that she had reinforcements on the way.

Besides, Dirk had to have seen her continue on

up the path. And knowing him as she did, she was certain he was now racing toward them, grubby sneakers barely touching the ground as he ran.

He was a darlin' . . . if a pain.

She stopped about six feet away from the guy and studied him carefully. Approximately five feet, six inches tall, weighing at most a hundred and thirty . . . he wasn't a very large man. She'd wrestled much bigger. And won.

Even from that distance she could smell alcohol on him. His eyes looked glassy. His speech was slightly slurred when he said, "I'm not kidding, lady. You go someplace else to watch it. I was here first."

Taking one step closer, she fixed him with eyes so cold they would have given pause to someone more astute, someone less fixated on his sexual obsession.

"Exactly what am I ruining for you?" she asked him in a deadly, even tone.

"What?"

"I heard you say I was ruining it for you. What's that? The fire? Watching it?" She nodded her head in the direction of the blaze that had now completely engulfed the building below and was casting a lurid glow across the twilit landscape.

He said nothing, but his breathing became heavier, faster as he stared at her, rage in his eyes.

She felt a fury of her own welling up as she thought of the plans she'd had for this day . . . this night.

"You go setting fires to get your rocks off," she told him. "You don't give a tinker's damn what it costs others."

He gasped, his eyes wide. "How . . . how do you know? Who are you?"

"I'm somebody who knows what a crazy twitch you are," she replied. "You set these awful fires that destroy property, kill wildlife—and even people sometimes—and all because you've got crazy urges inside you that you can't, or won't, control."

He moved toward her. She braced herself . . . and wished she'd strapped on her weapon before leaving the house earlier.

"What's it to you?" he shouted in her face. "Mind your own damned business."

He tried to move past her.

She blocked him.

"Oh, it's my business," she replied, her voice soft and deceptively calm. "It's very much my business."

"Get out of my way!" He reached out and shoved her, hard.

A moment later, he was lying on the ground at her feet, curled into a ball, holding his head and moaning . . . a small trickle of blood running down his forehead.

She heard Dirk pounding up the hill toward her. She turned and saw him, panting, face red and sweating, his Smith and Wesson in his hand.

"You can put that away," she told him, nodding toward the drawn weapon. "He's down."

"Yeah," Dirk replied, gasping for breath. "I see that."

"She hit me!" the arsonist told Dirk as he knelt beside him and examined the damage to his forehead. "She's crazy! She hit me for no reason . . . really hard . . . with her purse!"

Savannah glanced down at her hand and realized for the first time that she was, indeed, holding her pocketbook. And apparently, without thinking, she had smacked him with it.

"For no reason, huh?" Dirk said, reaching down and turning the pentacle medallion first one way, then the other.

"Yeah. No reason at all. And her purse was really hard!" complained her victim. "And heavy! I think there's a brick in it!"

Dirk shook his head. "Naw. I know what she carries in her purse. Usually just some nail polish and a few candy bars."

Savannah hefted her handbag a couple of times, testing the weight.

Yes, as a matter of fact, it *did* seem heavier than usual. It seemed a *lot* heavier.

She opened it and saw the gleam of her 9mm Beretta.

"Oh, yeah," she said. "I forgot I put that in there." She pulled out the weapon.

The guy on the ground gagged when he saw it and held up his hands in front of his face. "Don't!" he yelled. "Don't let her shoot me!" he said to Dirk. "I'm telling you, she's crazy!"

"Naw, she ain't crazy," Dirk said as he pulled a pair of handcuffs from behind his back and rolled his prisoner onto his face in the dirt. "She's just been stressed out lately. She's a bride-to-be. And you know how *they* get. It's a wonder she didn't shoot you."

"I'd forgotten I was packin' or I would've," Savannah told him, replacing her gun in her purse. "Believe you me."

Dirk snapped the cuffs on him, then yanked him to his feet. "Dude, if it weren't for you," he told him, "right now I'd be gettin' a piece o'—" He glanced at Savannah. "I mean . . . enjoying the bliss of my nuptial union."

"What?" The guy looked genuinely confused. "What's that?"

"Something you ain't never gonna know nothin' about." Dirk started down the hill, his detainee in tow.

"Unless you establish a close, meaningful relationship with your prison cellmate . . . which is a strong possibility," Savannah added, following close behind.

In the ever-deepening darkness, they had to choose their footing more carefully as they descended the path.

"Be careful, Savannah," Dirk said over his shoulder. "Watch your step through here."

For a moment, her temper flared. She made a mental note to have a serious sit-down with her groom-to-be. He was going to have to pull back on this overprotective crap, or they'd never make it through their honeymoon. She could already hear the chickie-pooh on the evening news: "Bride bludgeons groom senseless with bouquet! Film at eleven!"

She surveyed the scene below them—the exhausted firefighters, still battling in vain to save the community center, the spectators, some of whom were wondering if it would spread into their neighborhood and consume their homes. No doubt, countless animals were running for their lives, their own habitats destroyed.

She told herself that this guy's crimes had far more devastating consequences than just her postponed ceremony.

But when she thought of her beautiful wedding gown, now nothing but a pile of black ash inside that burning building, she had more than a passing fancy to plant her foot on that skinny little nerd's butt and send him tumbling down the cactus-strewn hill.

"Ruin my wedding day, would ya," she muttered. And instead, gave him a smack on the back of the head.

"Hey! What was that for?" he whined, trying to turn around to look at her while Dirk dragged him along with even less tender loving kindness than was usually offered by members of the San Carmelita Police Department.

"Oh, shut up," she said, "you dim-witted, devil-worshippin', fire-startin', pestilence. And keep movin'."